S0-BYU-861

MURDER
at
ABBEYMEAD FARM

BOOKS BY MERRYN ALLINGHAM

MURDER
at
ABBEYMEAD FARM

Merryn Allingham

bookouture

Published by Bookouture in 2023

An imprint of Storyfire Ltd.
Carmelite House
50 Victoria Embankment
London EC4Y 0DZ

www.bookouture.com

Copyright © Merryn Allingham, 2023

Merryn Allingham has asserted her right to be
identified as the author of this work.

All rights reserved. No part of this publication may be reproduced, stored in
any retrieval system, or transmitted, in any form or by any means, electronic,
mechanical, photocopying, recording or otherwise, without the prior written
permission of the publishers.

ISBN: 978-1-83790-303-0
eBook ISBN: 978-1-83790-302-3

This book is a work of fiction. Names, characters, businesses, organizations,
places and events other than those clearly in the public domain, are either the
product of the author's imagination or are used fictitiously. Any resemblance
to actual persons, living or dead, events or locales is entirely coincidental.

PROLOGUE
ABBEYMEAD, SUSSEX, APRIL 1957

Opening the cellar door, he was met by a well of blackness. His hand reached out, fumbling for the light switch, but without success. Stupid of me, he thought, there'll be no electricity, the house has been unoccupied for months. The slightest glimmer of light was visible at the far end of the cellar – it must come from a small window on the exterior wall – but the staircase itself, even with the cellar door left ajar, remained in darkness. Should he wait? He held up his wrist to the muted light coming from the passage behind and peered at his watch. He had time before the meeting and it had been a sensible suggestion to take a look around. If he did, he'd know better what he was talking about. And that was important.

Starting down the staircase, he took the steps carefully, scolding himself that he'd not thought to bring a torch. He was halfway down when his foot met thin air. For an instant, he teetered, his balance precarious. Then, losing the struggle, he plunged forwards, tumbling down the remaining stairs and landing in a huddle on the flagstones below. His head hit the cold granite with a sickening crack.

His half-opened eye caught sight of a trickle of blood staining the grey slabs beneath him and he tried to raise his head. He must get up, get help, but the pain was too much, and he fell back, defeated. Someone will come, he thought thickly, someone will help. And, closing his eyelids, he fell unconscious.

1

ONE DAY EARLIER

'Good morning, Mr Milburn.' Flora Steele greeted the short, wiry figure who'd walked through her bookshop door. 'More research? What is it today?' She glanced proudly at the orderly rows of books she had just finished dusting.

Percy Milburn had become one of her best customers, his curiosity and desire for knowledge ensuring plenty of orders – biographies, memoirs, 'how to' books, even a primer on local architecture.

'No books this morning, Miss Steele, I'm afraid. It's a favour I'm after. I've had a bunch of flyers printed and I was hoping you'd take some for your front table here.' Smiling, he handed her a sheaf of paper.

Flora took the wad of flyers and glanced at the message. 'A meeting in the village hall tomorrow? Abbeymead will be interested.'

'I hope so. Miss Ticehurst has been difficult, but at least she's given me the chance to speak. It's a real shame, though, that the leaflets are late. That's the printer's fault – he promised them last week – but I hope there'll still be a decent turnout. I need to get the village behind my plans for Birds Acre.'

'I'll make sure I mention the meeting to every customer,' she promised.

'Thank you, Miss Steele, you're a pal.'

Flora wouldn't describe herself as a pal exactly, but she liked Percy Milburn. Had liked him from the moment he'd first walked into the All's Well looking for books on Sussex. His son had been killed during the war, Flora had learned, and he'd emigrated south from his native Yorkshire after losing his wife and selling a string of woollen mills. His immediate wish had been to learn more of his adopted county.

'The hostel is going ahead then?' Flora knew only that Birds Acre Farm was to be sold and that Percy had plans for its future, plans sufficiently advanced, it seemed, to set before the village.

His face came alive. 'If I've got anything to do with it, it is! It's what Abbeymead needs. Decent accommodation for people on a budget. The Cross Keys isn't exactly cheap and the Priory Hotel is all very well if you've got money, but how many working folk can afford those rooms?'

He rubbed his chin, as though by doing so he might solve the conundrum. Percy had grown a beard last winter – *to make me look serious*, he'd confided to Flora – but had shaved it off once the weather warmed and the birds began to sing. Flora wasn't sure the beard had made much difference. She'd always taken this small, intense Yorkshireman seriously.

'I'm glad Sir Frederick Neville has agreed at last.'

'Not exactly agreed,' Percy said cautiously. 'Not whole-heartedly. We've a verbal arrangement that I'll buy Birds Acre Farm; he likes the sound of my money, but he's still dragging his feet on the hostel idea. What good is another posh hotel? I asked him. That's the maggot he's got in his head. It's ordinary people we want to encourage to Sussex, town folk who've hardly ever seen a green field. It's them I want to come. Want them to see how beautiful this county is – the Downs and the sea, and the river. And a lively town like Brighton just a few miles away.

Abbeymead will make a perfect holiday. And converting Birds Acre is the first step.'

The farm had been leased to generations of Martins by Lord Edward Templeton but, on his death several years ago, had been bought by Sir Frederick along with several others from the Templeton estate. The purchase had seemed to the village a natural progression, and it had come as a shock that Sir Frederick had decided to sell rather than search for a new tenant when, sadly, Robert Martin had died a few months previously. His wife, unable to continue farming alone, had moved to Eastbourne to live with her sister, while their only child, Thomas, who would normally have succeeded to the tenancy, had been killed during the war. Murdered, Flora reminded herself. It had been a frightening case last year, her Cornish holiday beset by a violence that had travelled through time and erupted on her doorstep. But along with Jack Carrington, her fellow sleuth and favourite crime writer, she'd unearthed the villain who'd robbed the Martins of their only child.

'I'm sure you'll manage to persuade Sir Frederick,' she said, emerging from memories of their trip. 'Faced with your determination, he's bound to capitulate!' Flora's hazel eyes held amusement.

'I try not to frighten the horses,' Percy said, pulling his mouth into a grimace, 'though I know I can be a bit pushy. Can't help myself, that's the truth. Still, the old boy and I get on OK. Both of us without wives, both lost our boys. It's a sorrow we share.'

'And golf,' she reminded him. 'You share a passion for golf.' Percy had met Sir Frederick at the Lexington, he'd told her, striking up a friendship on the second tee. They'd gone for a drink afterwards and discovered they'd both lost sons in the war, and from there it had been only a small step before Sir Frederick had confessed gloomily to needing money, and decided to sell Bird's Acre Farm to Percy.

'Golf and me are never going to be best friends.' Percy gave a chuckle. 'But I've arranged to meet Neville at the farm tomorrow afternoon, along with his land agent. I'm hopeful we can come to an agreement. I thought' – Percy's lined face broke into a smile – 'that if I could get the old beggar to look round the farm with me, room by room, I could explain just how my plans would work – communicate my vision as it were – and that would get him on side. A bit of a bully, Sir Frederick. Used to getting his own way, you know. Well, he would be. Inherited that great pile, everything on a plate from the time he was born.'

'And if it doesn't get him on side?'

'The chap's holding a large deposit of mine. Offered it as a token of good faith. He won't want to give that back – he's desperate for money. And if he tries any funny business, I'll sue him for every penny. That will sink him good and proper.'

'I hope it won't come to that.' Percy's great project had the potential to become a very nasty dispute and it worried Flora a little.

'I think I can win this one, Miss Steele,' he said with energy. 'I've convinced his agent. Palmer, that's his name. He was a bit dubious at the start, but once I got to work on him, he was all for it.'

'Then I'm sure you'll succeed with Sir Frederick as well. First things first, though. I'll find a place for these.' She fanned the leaflets in a line across the display tables.

Percy nodded, looking pleased. 'That's champion. The meeting will be important. I've had a lot of trouble from Winifred Ticehurst and her campaign, Keep Abbeymead for the villagers, or some such nonsense. After Sir Fred, I'll be gunning for the village's approval.'

'A foregone conclusion!'

They both laughed, knowing very well that it wouldn't be.

2

The loud jangle of conversation hit Jack squarely between the ears as he walked into the dimly lit village hall the following evening, Flora a few paces ahead. It seemed that most of Abbeymead had come to Percy's meeting and few seats remained empty.

'There are spaces several rows down,' he said in her ear, nudging her slim figure to the left.

She turned to speak to him, her eyes wide. 'So many people, Jack! Percy's hostel has stirred a hornets' nest.'

Jack felt a vague unease. Hornets' nests could mean trouble. 'Whoever is up for being stung, we're not getting involved,' he said firmly. 'You've the alterations at the shop to contend with and I'm about to start a new book. A few quiet months is what we need.'

'Particularly after the riotous Christmas we had,' she teased.

He pulled a face. Christmas had been anything but riotous – minced pies at the vicarage, a shared chicken lunch and, later, tea and cakes with their friends Alice and Kate. His stay at Flora's cottage had been similarly quiet, yet he'd never felt so content as the days they had spent together between Christmas and New Year, cheerfully defying village gossip. An unmarried couple sharing the same house! It had kept Abbeymead's rumour mill going for months.

Since then, they'd been far more discreet but, as he followed Flora, her red-brown waves bobbing ahead, Jack was filled with a happiness he'd rarely known. And filled with hope for the future. Marriage was a word he'd been careful not to mention, though it was never far from his mind. He smiled to himself. He was too conventional, that was the problem. Probably a reaction to the way his father had always conducted *his* life. And Flora? Her need for independence, her evident mistrust of matrimony, no doubt had its roots in childhood as well. The sins of the fathers, he thought.

'Look, there's Alice.' She waved her hand at the plump woman sitting three rows from the front and Alice Jenner waved back. 'I'll just go over and say hello.'

Flora had begun to edge her way towards her friend when a stocky figure sitting at a table on the raised platform – the chairwoman, Jack presumed – banged her mallet loudly and called the meeting to order.

Winifred Ticehurst had once been the Abbeymead schoolmistress and since then, according to Flora, become the village spokeswoman and, if you were being unkind, a general busybody. It seemed appropriate, therefore, that she was the one wielding the gavel. The woman was peering down at the crowded hall, her eyes darting between rows of chairs on either side of the narrow aisle, judging perhaps when she should speak. Jack grabbed Flora's hand and hurried her into the seat he'd spied.

An empty chair on the stage had been set aside for Percy Milburn, he assumed, since the meeting had been called for the man to present his plans for Birds Acre Farm. Privately, Jack thought he'd be lucky to get Abbeymead's approval, but perhaps he didn't need it. Percy had apparently made an offer on the farm that had been accepted. Whichever way the village voted, the hostel was likely to go ahead.

'Good evening, ladies and gentlemen,' Winifred began. Her voice was as impressive as her figure. 'As you will know, our dear friend Robert Martin passed away some months ago and his widow has understandably felt unable to continue the farm without him. In Mr and Mrs Martin, the village has lost two of its most generous and community-minded members, and I know we all wish Lily the very best for her new life in Eastbourne.'

A ripple of agreement drifted through the ranks of chairs.

'However,' Winifred continued inexorably, 'we are here tonight to learn what the future of Birds Acre Farm might be if Mr Milburn's plan should go ahead. In brief, Mr Milburn wishes to turn the farmhouse, the barns and outbuildings of what has always been the Martin farm into a hostel for holiday-makers. Hikers and so forth.' There was a definite sniff at the word 'hikers'.

'My own feeling, if I'm allowed to express it' – was she, Jack wondered? – 'is that such a plan is out of keeping with the village we cherish. However, I am but one voice.' Here, she bowed her head in a show of modesty, which didn't quite ring true. 'But Mr Milburn will be here shortly,' she rallied, 'and will lay out his plans for you to decide for yourself. In fact' – she looked pointedly at the large wood-framed clock hanging on the wall opposite – 'he should be here now.'

'I don't think Miss Ticehurst should have offered her opinion,' Flora whispered. 'She's the chairwoman.'

'Maybe not, but I reckon it's the majority view.'

'Not mine, it isn't. I think it's a brilliant idea. The farm is within walking distance of the village, yet completely rural. It will make a wonderful holiday home at half the price of the Priory. Have you ever been to Birds Acre?'

When he shook his head, she said, 'It has a truly beautiful

setting, Jack – pastureland on either side of the farmhouse, a stream running through the fields and, at the rear, there's a wood that climbs up the hill.'

'Are you sure it's not you who wants to buy?' He covered her hand with his.

'I'd love to live there,' she confessed. 'If I had the money. Think of the view from the top of that hill. The North Downs on one side and our own splendid South Downs on the other.'

'The setting is probably why people don't like the idea. Exploiting a local beauty spot isn't likely to go down well.'

'It's not exploitation,' she protested. 'Percy Milburn is a public-spirited man. He won't make money from the hostel, that's for sure. He's doing it out of love for his adopted county. And out of fellow feeling, I guess, with the kind of people he's known all his working life.'

Jack said nothing, thinking it best he remained neutral. He was fairly certain that as a relatively recent inhabitant his opinion would, in any case, be ignored. Despite having lived in Abbeymead for some time, he was still seen as a stranger by most of the village. The same went for Percy Milburn, of course. He'd moved to Abbeymead a mere five years ago and Jack knew that, in both their cases, it might as well be five minutes as five years for the people sitting around him this evening.

'Where *is* Percy?' Flora fidgeted in her seat, twisting round to face the door that had remained open at the rear of the hall. 'It's gone quarter past and the meeting should have begun at eight.'

'Miss Ticehurst is getting restless, too. Just look at her.'

The chairwoman was fiddling with the bow of her silk shirt, then taking up her pen and tapping a low tattoo on the table. In the hall, feet had begun to shuffle, and murmurs grow louder. Several villagers retrieved their coats from beneath their seats –

it was a cool evening and over the past half hour the air had grown considerably chillier.

'We should start without him,' some bold spark shouted out.

'Yes. Let's have *our* say first,' another echoed.

Jack craned his neck. It was the postmistress, Dilys Fuller, who'd spoken. Tonight, she was wearing a particularly vivid woollen dress.

'Did she actually knit that?' he whispered to Flora.

'She's bound to have.'

'But it's a dress.' Until now, Dilys had confined herself to producing a never-ending series of blindingly bright jumpers or cardigans.

'And it's orange.'

Flora shrugged. 'So? It's Dilys, remember.'

'As far as I'm concerned,' the postmistress boomed, 'we already have enough visitors. Sometimes my post office is so crowded, I can't see daylight. And there's only me to serve now Miss Unwin is back at the surgery.' All eyes turned to the red-headed girl sitting a row behind Dilys.

Jack saw Maggie's pale face flush. 'The post office does get busy,' she admitted, her voice barely audible, 'but a hostel might be a good idea.' It was a nervous addition. 'It's not always easy to find accommodation round here and Abbeymead isn't always very... very welcoming.'

The murmurs had turned to mutters, some of them angry. Maggie Unwin was hardly a favourite with the elders of Abbeymead, her disgraceful liaison last year with Dr Hanson's locum still a topic of gossip.

'What I say...' another voice intervened, its stridency issuing from an unlikely source, 'what I say, is a hostel is likely to bring the worst kind of people to the village. People who know nothing about the countryside. They leave gates open, let their dogs run wild. Who's to know what these people would get up to – causing damage, thieving from us locals. Mebbe more serious crimes.' 'Crimes' received particular emphasis. 'We'd have to lock our doors!'

'Trust Elsie,' Flora said, her mouth tightening. Elsie Flowers was one of Flora's oldest customers, avid for any type of mystery fiction, the gorier the better. 'She's intent on seeing trouble everywhere.'

'As far as Abbeymead goes, she isn't that wrong,' Jack said drily, lapsing into silence. Since meeting Flora, his life in the village seemed at times one long parade of villainy.

When people began to talk among themselves again, Winifred emerged from her seat at the table and walked to the front of the stage, a pair of sturdy brogues planted firmly on the wooden boards. She waved her arms in the direction of the audience, expecting quiet and getting it.

'Thank you for your contributions.' She smiled thinly. 'I think it might be better, however, if we delay any discussion until after Mr Milburn has given his presentation.'

'When's that goin' to be then?' a cheeky voice asked.

Winifred glared at the clock opposite, as if it were personally responsible for Percy's late arrival. 'We will wait until half past eight,' she announced magisterially, 'and if Mr Milburn has not arrived by then, I will call the meeting closed.'

A sudden hush filled the chamber, the audience suitably quelled, the only sound the loud ticking of the outsized wall clock as the hands edged their way to the half hour. When the chime finally struck, people instantly began to move, collecting hats and handbags and umbrellas. Against the general hubbub of creaking chairs and scuffling feet, Winifred once more rapped the table.

'It's clear that Mr Milburn has been delayed.'

'Or chosen not to come,' someone called out.

'He's a coward, that's what. Slunk back to Yorkshire where he belongs.'

Ignoring the interruption, Miss Ticehurst continued

unabashed, 'I hereby close this meeting. The matter, though, is too important to dismiss and the village must have its say. Details of a further meeting will be circulated later.'

There was a general murmur of assent as people made their way to the exit.

'I hope nothin' comes of it. I do really.' Alice bustled up to them, her tight, grey curls seeming to fizz with annoyance. 'I miss Lily Martin. She was a good friend to me, and I don't want to think of her home made into a dosshouse. That's what it would become.'

'Alice!' Flora protested. 'That's crazy. It's a hostel that Mr Milburn is proposing. Somewhere that visitors can stay for a modest price.'

'There's the Priory. Why do they want somewhere else to stay?' The Priory Hotel was owned and managed by Alice's niece, Sally Jenner. 'The prices aren't that bad, and how will this new place affect Sal's business? As if she's not had enough trouble already, and just when the darn place is getting back on its feet.'

'A hostel is unlikely to have any effect on the Priory,' Jack said comfortingly. 'The two establishments will attract very different visitors.'

'That's as mebbe, but it's not a fitting place,' Alice maintained. 'A farmhouse! How's that goin' to work?'

'The barns and outbuildings, too,' Flora reminded her. 'There'll be sufficient space for a small business.'

Alice snorted. 'I don't like it. I don't often agree with Elsie Flowers but this time I reckon she's hit the nail on the head. Kate won't like it either. Nor any of the shopkeepers.'

'It could mean more business for Katie's Nook,' Flora suggested. 'A tearoom is just the sort of place these visitors will like. Where is Kate this evening?'

'Out with that Tony. Where do you think? But she won't like it,' Alice repeated. 'She'll be losing a teaspoon for every

scone she sells, you'll see. And Tony won't either.' Tony
Farraday was Alice's sous-chef and Kate Mitchell's new
boyfriend.

Jack refrained from pointing out that as neither Kate nor
Tony had bothered to come to the meeting, the plans for a
hostel couldn't be that important to either of them.

'Anyways.' Alice tucked a giant handbag beneath her arm. 'I
must go. Sally's staying the night with me – a bit of a treat for
Auntie! – and she'll be wanting to know what happened. Or
didn't happen. She thought it best not to come to the meeting
herself. It will look a bit too self-interested, she said. But I
dunno. What's wrong with a bit of self-interest? Specially for
Sal, after all her troubles.'

Once Alice had disappeared through the door and into the
darkness beyond, Jack clasped Flora's hand and walked with her
out into the high street.

'It's odd that Percy Milburn didn't turn up,' he said, as they
turned right into Greenway Lane, making their way back to her
cottage. 'He's always struck me as a pretty reliable chap. I
wouldn't call him a coward, but perhaps he did get cold feet, as
someone suggested.'

Flora came to an abrupt halt, disentangling her hand and
fixing him with a severe look. 'He didn't get cold feet,' she said
with certainty. 'Percy was looking forward to sharing his plans
with the village. He was determined to persuade Abbeymead of
the benefits a hostel could bring. If he didn't arrive, it was
because he couldn't. Something must have happened, Jack.
Something we don't know about.'

3

It was three days later that Minnie Howden, Percy Milburn's housekeeper, walked through the bookshop door at the very same time in the morning as her employer had previously.

'Miss Steele, could I have a word?' The small bird-like figure hovered on the threshold.

Flora looked up from the cardboard box she was unpacking.

'Good morning, Miss Howden.' She couldn't remember ever seeing the housekeeper in the All's Well before and sensed it must spell trouble. 'Is everything all right?' she asked, without much hope the answer would be 'yes'.

'No, I'm afraid not.' The woman's voice held a slight tremble. 'That's why I'm here. I wouldn't have bothered you otherwise. I don't like to bother anyone, but I'm asking around. It's Mr Milburn, you see.' Her voice trembled more noticeably. 'Mr Percy,' she repeated. 'He's not come home.'

It was what, deep down, Flora had feared but resolutely pushed from her mind. She'd thought fleetingly of calling at the old schoolhouse to enquire of Percy, but he was a sixty-year-old man, highly competent and with enough money to ensure he could deal with most troubles, and she hadn't wanted to meddle. Hadn't, if she were truthful, wanted to know that things were not OK.

'I was wondering if you'd seen him. If you had any news,' Minnie said helplessly.

Flora gave a slow shake of her head. 'I haven't, but why don't you come and sit down?'

She led her visitor to the window seat and Minnie sank gratefully onto its cushioned surface.

'I know Mr Milburn didn't get to the village meeting.' Flora had no need to specify which meeting. They were not that frequent in Abbeymead. 'I thought he must have been held up somewhere but that later he'd arrange another date with Miss Ticehurst.'

Minnie chewed at her lip. 'I've just been to see her, but she knows nothing. In fact, she was quite unpleasant, taking me to task for Mr Milburn not turning up on Friday and wasting everyone's time.'

Poor Miss Howden. Flora reached out to take her hand. 'I'm so sorry, you must be very worried.'

'It's not like Mr Percy,' she said in a burst. 'He always lets me know if he's going away. If he'll be late for a meal, even. I've checked – all his clothes are in the wardrobe, there's nothing missing from his office. It's just not like him...' She tailed off.

Flora's mind had begun to travel along pathways she'd earlier tried to ignore and what she was thinking wasn't pleasant. She'd no wish to worry Miss Howden any more than was needful, but there was a question she had to ask.

'Have you thought of going to the police?'

'The police?' Minnie couldn't prevent a gasp.

'You say that you've asked around the village and nobody has seen Mr Milburn?'

The housekeeper nodded.

'Then he's a missing person and the police should know. They'll have the resources to find him.'

Did she really believe that? Inspector Ridley, Jack's valued contact in the Brighton police force, seemed always to be short-staffed. In the past, Alan Ridley had been a considerable help to Jack in writing his crime novels, but lately priorities had subtly changed and it had been them helping the inspector solve real-life crime.

'I don't like to do that.' Minnie's hands were clenched tightly in her lap. 'If Mr Percy turns up, what will he say if he learns the police are looking for him?'

'He'd be certain to understand why you contacted them,' Flora said rousingly. 'When did you last see Mr Milburn?'

'After lunch, on Friday. It was sandwiches, I remember. Mr Percy was dashing off to the farm to meet Sir Frederick and his agent and didn't have time for a cooked lunch.'

'How did he seem?'

Minnie put her head on one side and thought. 'Excited, I'd say. He's been working on plans for the farm a long time – his desk is cluttered with them – and, when I brought him his sandwiches, he told me he was sure that everything was falling into place at last.'

'And after he left for Birds Acre, you didn't see him again?'

'I saw him leave.' She frowned, remembering the moment. 'Waved him off from the front door. It was a lovely day, a real spring day, and he'd decided to walk. I did some ironing in the afternoon, then started on the supper. A nice steak and kidney pie it was, too,' she said mournfully. 'But Mr Percy never got to eat it.'

'Mr Milburn has been missing too long,' Flora said decisively. 'I really think you should report his disappearance as soon as possible.'

The older woman nodded dumbly, looking fixedly at the All's Well's wooden floor. Then, without saying another word, she sprang up from the window seat and walked towards the door.

Flora hurried to catch her up. 'I'm sorry I can't be more help,' she offered, thinking how limp she must sound.

Miss Howden gave a tight little smile. 'Thank you for listening. Not everyone has been so kind.' And with that, she disappeared into the high street.

Her comment gave Flora thought. Percy Milburn wasn't a favourite in the village, but she had no idea that he was disliked as much as Minnie Howden's words suggested. A certain degree of resentment seemed inevitable. Percy was a wealthy man, and wealthy from his own efforts. It seemed ironic that Abbeymead could happily accept wealth when it was inherited – Sir Frederick Neville, for example, whose lands were extensive, much of it abutting the Templetons' old estate – but a blunt Yorkshireman like Percy, with drive and energy, who'd risen to a position of power from the humblest of beginnings, was somehow an affront.

But Percy hadn't helped himself either. He was often impatient with the slow pace of the village, couldn't understand that old loyalties, old traditions, no matter how irritating and inefficient, had to be observed. His purchase of the former schoolhouse was an instance. It had proved a contentious issue from the moment the sale went through since many of the villagers had not wanted the old school closed and disliked its replacement intensely, a concrete oblong of a building on the outskirts of the village. The original Abbeymead school had been built in Victorian times for a handful of pupils who would leave at the age of twelve. Its classrooms lacked space and light and its facilities were woeful. The new building was bright and airy, the toilets sanitary and functioning, and the heating no longer a coke stove in each room. Yet, there were still complaints in the village five or six years after the old school had closed.

And Percy hadn't just bought the building. The same drive and energy that had won him a fortune had been directed at his new home. He was a retired man who couldn't retire. Percy had spent a great deal of money on converting the schoolhouse into a beautiful home, equipped with all modern conveniences, and afterwards on breathing life into a neglected garden. What did a single man want with such a big house? was the frequently muttered comment.

None of this had made him a hero to the village and, if Percy never returned, few in Abbeymead would mourn. One of those few, though, was Flora. She had enormous respect for him, for what Percy had achieved in his life, and loved that he'd committed himself so wholeheartedly to his new life in Sussex. He wouldn't willingly have missed that meeting, she was certain. The more she thought of it, the more she was convinced that he'd been deliberately prevented from attending. But what, if anything, was she going to do about it?

As soon as she closed the shop that day, she cycled to Overlay House. Since the evening at the village hall, she'd not spoken to Jack, knowing he was working on the opening chapters of his next book. It was always a fraught time and she'd learned to keep a low profile until he'd wrangled the new plot into some kind of shape. Percy's continued absence, however, was worrying her too deeply to keep away; Jack was the only person in whom she could confide. If Violet Steele had still been alive, it might have been different, but over the last year or so, Jack had helped to fill the void left by her beloved aunt. More than that, he'd become a dear friend, the first man for many years that she had learned to love and trust.

He was in the front garden, when she walked through the gate of Overlay House.

'I'm trying to decide what I should plant for summer,' he said, walking down the path towards her and enveloping her in a tight hug. 'The marguerites did well last year, so maybe I should keep to the tried and tested.'

Jack's new gardening prowess never ceased to amuse Flora – except when his vegetable patch proved superior to hers. From a man who had allowed the Overlay's large back garden to run rampant for years, and only occasionally pushed an unwilling lawnmower around the front grass, he was a creature transformed, rivalling Bill Sowerbutts from *Gardeners' Question Time* in his enthusiasm.

'Stick to the marguerites,' she advised. 'But it's not gardens I've come to talk about.'

'I didn't expect it was.' His smile was wry. 'Well then, my beautiful sleuth' – he released her from the hug and held her at arm's length – 'what is it, or rather who is it?'

'You know, don't you?'

'Percy Milburn, I'm guessing. I hear from young Charlie that the village is buzzing with the news that he still hasn't turned up.' Charlie Teague, though only thirteen years old, had constituted himself Jack's mentor for all things horticultural. 'Apparently, Percy's housekeeper has been asking around. According to Mrs Teague, she's in an agitated state.'

'She is,' Flora confirmed. 'She came to the All's Well this morning, asking if I'd seen anything of Percy. Something is seriously wrong, Jack. The last time I saw him, he was bubbling. He had a meeting at the farmhouse the next afternoon with Sir Frederick Neville and Neville's land agent, before the meeting in the village hall. Minnie Howden said how excited he was that his plans were coming to fruition. He didn't disappear voluntarily, of that, I'm sure. We don't even know if he ever got to the farmhouse.'

'This is something you want to jump into?'

'I know you're busy. I'm busy, too. Michael is starting work on the bookshop very soon. But Percy is a decent man and Miss Howden is reluctant to go to the police. Actually, a lovely man, and I owe it to him to find out what's happened.'

'We could ask Neville, I suppose. It's his property Percy was buying.'

'We could, but... we might be better talking to Colin Palmer first. He's the land agent and was supposed to be at the farm, too. I think we'd get more out of him than Neville. I've only met Sir Frederick a few times but, from what I remember, he was a pompous man. Standoffish. Could you spare an hour tomorrow morning, if I open the shop a little late?'

She made a silent apology to Violet. Her aunt had always insisted they were in the shop and ready to serve by ten minutes to nine every day, no matter that their first customer invariably walked through the door at least an hour later.

'Why not? I've spent the last three days trying and failing to work out how my villain, shrapnel in both his legs, could reach the bridge of an ocean-going liner and throw the captain over-board. Another few hours won't matter.'

'The plot will come together,' she said with confidence. 'It always does. Nine o'clock then at Palmer's office?'

Jack looked bemused. 'At Bramber Hall?' This was Frederick Neville's country seat.

'Actually no. I've seen Palmer's name plate when I've called on Alice. He has an office almost next door to her cottage. The block adjoins Mr Houseman's shop on the other side.' Jim Houseman was the village greengrocer and an old ally of Flora's. 'It's interesting he operates separately from the estate, isn't it?'

'Maybe, but he's still Neville's man,' Jack warned. 'We should keep that in mind.'

Colin Palmer was a young man who wore his duties lightly. As the sole remaining partner in a firm specialising in land agency, he had the air of being permanently on holiday. Looking at his tanned face at what was the beginning of an English spring,

Flora felt the incongruity sharply and wondered where he spent his winters. She couldn't imagine that working for Sir Frederick Neville was so lucrative he could afford frequent vacations.

'Mr Milburn?' Colin said indifferently, once they were seated opposite him. 'I've had some dealings with him, though not a great many. Sir Frederick's landholdings are extensive and, as you can imagine, as his agent I'm in touch with a large number of people.'

He sounded as pompous as his employer, Flora thought.

'We're talking about four days ago,' Jack intervened. 'A very recent meeting arranged between Mr Milburn, Sir Frederick and yourself. You can't have forgotten, surely?'

'Ah, yes. Birds Acre Farm. The middle of the afternoon, wasn't it? Spoilt my usual Friday game of golf.'

'Spoilt?' Jack queried.

'The chap never turned up. I drove out to Birds Acre and hung around for I don't know how long, but Mr Milburn didn't appear. Sir Frederick was furious, I can tell you. He's a busy man. He was expecting to get the sale done and dusted that afternoon.'

'Really? I understood Mr Milburn had... reservations... and he needed them to be agreed before he signed.'

'Oh, that,' Palmer said impatiently. 'Yes, he kept insisting the contract included a stipulation that he was free to convert the farm into a hostel, but that was never going to happen. Not if I know Sir Frederick.'

'*He* was at the farm? Sir Frederick?' Flora was quick to ask.

'Drove over himself. Must have been Richardson's day off. That's his chauffeur. Sir Frederick drove into the farmyard just when I'd decided to call it a day and get back to the office.'

'He was late?'

'If you like.'

'Well, he *was* late,' Jack said crisply. Flora had a good idea of what might be going through his mind.

'In the event, it hardly mattered. Milburn cancelled on us and without a word of apology. That's not the way to do business. Good job I insisted on a deposit.' Palmer shook his head, trying to look the professional man, Flora thought uncharitably.

'When Percy Milburn didn't arrive at the time you'd arranged, did you go looking for him?' She caught the militant glint in Jack's eyes as he posed the question.

'Naturally,' Colin said airily. 'I went into the farmhouse. We have a set of keys but, in any case, the door was open, and I imagined that Mr Milburn had gone into the house and was waiting for us there.'

Flora frowned. 'The door was open – is that usual?'

Palmer shifted in his seat. 'Not usual. It could be that someone forgot to lock it after their visit.'

'And that someone could be you?' she persisted.

'Yes,' he admitted grudgingly, 'but there's nothing in the farmhouse worth stealing. Mrs Martin has taken her furniture with her or sold whatever wouldn't fit her new home. There's little more than the bare walls left.'

'When you went in, did you look around?' This was Jack again.

'Of course. Look, what is this? I feel I'm being interrogated.'

'You are.' Flora was deadpan. 'And it's important you answer accurately. Percy Milburn has been missing for four days and you are the last person he was supposed to see.'

'Well, I didn't see him.' The agent's voice had turned sulky. 'I went into every room and there was no sign of him. I even went down to the cellar. Climbed down – with some difficulty, I might add. The staircase had rotted, the middle stairs completely disintegrated. It was a good job I had a torch with me. Those stairs are dangerous, and the cellar door should have been locked.'

'But it wasn't?'

He shook his head. 'Wide open. It's why I went down. I

thought he might have decided to look around. Then when I saw the mess the stairs were in, I wondered if he'd started down them and had an accident.'

'And had he?'

'There was no sign of Mr Milburn.' It was emphatic. 'Now, if that's all, I'm sure you'll understand I have a day's work in front of me.'

Whether they understood or not, he was up and out of his chair, ushering them out of the door in a matter of seconds.

'Well, what do you make of that?' Jack asked as he walked with Flora to the All's Well.

Her face wore a dubious expression. She hadn't liked Colin Palmer one little bit. But more importantly, she hadn't trusted him.

4

————————

'I'm quite certain that Percy had every intention of going to the farm.' Flora tucked her arm in his.

'Which means that either he was prevented from going, or he arrived at Birds Acre and something happened to him there. Either way, it doesn't give us much to go on. It's difficult to know where to start looking – if we're starting.'

Glancing at his watch, he saw she would open almost on time; their interview with Colin Palmer had lasted less than fifteen minutes.

'We are,' she said firmly. 'And the farm is the only place to begin.'

'Palmer made a point of saying that he'd looked around the whole building,' he cautioned.

Flora wrinkled her nose. 'Maybe, but how much confidence do you have in him? For my part, it's very little. Perhaps he carried out a cursory inspection of the house, as he said, but it wouldn't have been thorough, and what about the barns and outbuildings? He made no mention of them.'

Jack found himself nodding. He had only a hazy idea of the size of the Martins' farm but could imagine there must be a hundred and one places to conceal— He stopped himself. He'd been about to think 'body'. He hoped for Flora's sake that wasn't true but, as the days had gone by, it seemed increasingly unlikely that Percy would reappear, alive and well.

'Percy might have amnesia,' Flora said suddenly, as though she'd guessed the direction of his thoughts. 'What if, when he arrived at the farmhouse, he'd seen the cellar door open and decided to take a look? According to Palmer, the staircase is badly damaged, and Percy might not have seen that in the dark and fallen.'

'The agent was clear there was no one in the cellar when he inspected it.'

Flora was silent for a moment, but then rallied. 'Percy could have been knocked unconscious and, when he came round, had no memory of why he was there or even who he was.'

He stopped and looked down at Flora, a wide smile on his face. 'You are amazing! Your imagination is a whole other world.'

'It could happen,' she said stubbornly. 'Percy could have wandered off, not knowing where he was going. Even now, he could be walking round some village or other in a complete daze.'

'That's an outside chance, to say the least, so let me offer a better one. What if Mr Milburn set off for the farm, waved his housekeeper goodbye but, for some reason, decided to abandon the meeting?'

'That makes even less sense,' she objected. 'Why would he do that?'

They had reached the white-painted door of the All's Well and Flora delved into her bag for the big brass key. On the threshold, she turned to face him, her expression earnest. 'If Percy went to the farm, and I believe he did and hasn't been seen since, he must still be there. We need to take a look, Jack.'

He sighed but made no attempt to dispute her logic. He'd

known from the moment Colin Palmer had insisted there'd been no sign of Mr Milburn at Birds Acre that, sooner or later, they were bound for the farm.

'Tomorrow afternoon?' he asked. 'It's half-day closing—unless you want to be in the shop for Michael?'

'He's not coming now until next week. He has one or two jobs to finish first and I need to strip several bookcases before he takes them down.' She beamed up at him. 'Bring your old flashlight, the army one. There won't be any electricity and we'll need to explore the whole farm.'

Birds Acre farm might be only a brisk fifteen-minute walk across the fields from the village, but it was not so easily accessible by car. A gravelled track leading to the farm ran from the road that passed the Priory Hotel and, a little further on, the Lexington Golf Club. Its proximity to both venues seemed to Flora a bonus for any visitors to Percy's would-be hostel, although whether Sally Jenner would think so was doubtful. Sally had sunk every penny of her savings into buying and refurbishing the hotel and it had suffered a rocky beginning. These last few months, the Priory seemed at last to be turning a corner and Sally was unlikely to want a competitor so close, no matter how humble.

'These potholes are hellish,' Jack complained, as they bumped and creaked along a path around the large dips in the gravel track. 'It's almost impossible to avoid them.'

'It's the weather we've had. The winter snow for one thing but, even more, the torrents of rain.' Sussex had endured a particularly wet beginning to spring. 'And now the Martins aren't here, it's been left to disintegrate.'

'If Percy Milburn does manage to buy this place, he'll have his hands full.'

'He'll buy it,' she said with certainty. 'And make it work.'

Unless he's no longer able to was the treacherous thought that refused to go away.

The constant jumping and jolting were making Flora feel decidedly unwell, but just when she felt sure her stomach was ready to revolt, the small red Austin pulled into a wide swathe of cobbled courtyard. On one side, a long, red-roofed structure, open to the air, still contained a few bales of hay from Robert Martin's last harvest and, on the other, a dilapidated barn sported its own tiled roof, dipping so far in the middle that it sat only a few inches above the wooden entrance.

'The boards on that barn look rotten.' Jack nodded towards the wood-clad building. 'I can't see that ever making comfortable accommodation. But we can start there – if we can get through the door.'

Flora pursed her lips. 'I think... I think the farmhouse would be better. I know Mr Palmer swore there was nothing to see there, but I really don't trust him.'

Jack smiled. 'Me neither. The farmhouse it is!'

The building lay immediately in front of them, a mix of mellow red brick and white weatherboarding. Climbing roses clung to its front wall, their tendrils growing so abundantly they'd reached the roof, while latticed windows, small but plentiful, gave the house a smiling face.

'It's beautiful,' Jack said, leaning back in the driver's seat to gain a better view.

'So is the countryside all around. Let's take a look.'

Clambering from the car, Flora took his hand and walked with him to the rear of the building. A large expanse of grass spread into the distance, a small circular pond the only thing to disturb its flow into the wooded area beyond. To the right of where they stood, a wicket gate led to a large apple orchard, the trees not yet in blossom and, to the left, field after field of pastureland and a scattering of ancient trees. In the distance, the curve of the Downs held the land in a gentle embrace.

Jack turned to face the old walls of the farmhouse, bathed now in a sun that had appeared out of nowhere. 'It's beautiful,' he repeated. Then, 'Do you have a key?'

She shook her head.

'So, we're to break in?'

'Nothing so violent. Look.' She pointed to a first-floor window that had been left slightly ajar. 'There's a very sturdy chestnut tree right next to it. You were a soldier – it should be child's play.'

'Thanks,' he said laconically, sizing up the tree as he walked across to it. The branches looked strong and well-spaced, and he would need to climb only halfway before reaching the window. Swinging himself onto the lowest branch, it proved an easy enough climb and, in a few minutes, he had flicked back the window catch and heaved himself over the sill and into a bedroom.

Flora looked up and saw his triumphant smile. 'Maybe I'll take a look around on my own,' he teased.

'If you do, I'm following you.' She began to walk towards the tree.

'No! Don't try it. I'll meet you at the front.'

He was a long time getting there and, when he finally appeared at the open door, Flora was wearing an impatient frown. 'You were an age,' she greeted him.

'I had a quick look around the first floor. Four bedrooms and a bathroom. The agent was right. The rooms are completely bare.'

'Any clue that Percy has ever been there?'

'Absolutely nothing.'

There continued to be nothing as they searched first the sitting room, then a small square of a room that must have been Robert Martin's office – marks on the walls indicated they had once held two or three rows of shelves – and the large farm-house kitchen, its ceiling hosting the occasional spider's web and its red-tiled floor, once Lily Martin's pride and joy, now scuffed and dusty.

'Well, the Aga is still here,' Flora said brightly.

'You think Percy may be hiding in there?'

'No, I don't,' she said, giving him a gentle poke in the ribs. 'But we can still take a look.'

Jack bent to unlatch the oven door and peered inside. 'Nope. No Percy, I can confirm. And no clue to his whereabouts.'

'It looks as though Palmer was right.' Her voice sounded flat. 'There's only the cellar left. Did you bring the torch?'

'I did. But if the climb down is too steep, you must let *me* do it.'

'Why should you have all the fun?'

'For one thing, because I've the longer legs.'

Despite Palmer's insistence that the broken stairs were dangerous, the cellar door remained unlocked. 'As an agent, you'd think he'd be more careful,' Jack remarked.

'He didn't strike me as someone whose heart is in the job. I reckon it's Sir Frederick that's the draw, not the work.'

'A social climber?'

She nodded. 'Without a doubt. Do you want me to shine the torch for you?'

'I think it might be better if I took it with me. It's as black as night down there.'

Holding the flashlight high, Jack negotiated the first three steps, then dangled a leg across the wide gap left by the broken staircase, until he found a foothold. The remaining stairs presented no problem.

'It's not easy,' he warned, flashing the light upwards so that Flora could see the staircase below. 'Why don't I just take a look around? I can smell apples but there doesn't seem much to see.' He redirected the torch beam, shining it towards the far reaches of the cellar. 'A few wooden barrels, that's all. Empty, I should think.'

'I'm coming down,' she announced, unhappy at being left out. 'I want to look around, too. Hold the light steady, Jack.'

She had reached the gap in the staircase when the sound of an explosion tore through her ears and she felt something hard scrape past her, knocking her off balance, the granite flagstones rushing up to meet her. In an instant, Jack had leapt forward, managing to catch hold of her as she fell.

'What the hell! Are you hurt?'

Flora steadied herself, clinging to his arm. 'No, thanks to you. A bit bruised maybe. My legs... something cannoned into me. I've no idea what. It came from over there, I think.'

She pointed to the dark space further into the cellar.

Jack shone the torch ahead. 'There's something on the floor.' He walked over to inspect. 'It's the lid off one of those barrels!'

She gave a shaky laugh. 'They weren't empty after all.'

'How do you make that out?'

'They must contain cider. You saw the orchard. The Martins always used every one of their apples.'

'So why an exploding barrel?'

Flora gave a tiny shrug. 'The pressure release valve maybe. Gases that build up during fermentation are supposed to blow through the pressure release rubber, but if the valve has been damaged in some way, or maybe loosened... I think we should go – the other barrels might have been messed with, too.'

Jack stood looking across at the wooden casks. 'But who would have tampered with them? Is it Mrs Martin's revenge, do you think?' He was laughing.

'It could be accidental. Colin Palmer's been down here. He may have interfered with the valve. He's ignorant enough not to know the danger.'

Jack nodded. 'OK, let's get upstairs, but I'd better make sure the other barrels are reasonably secure. Wooden lids being hurled around are a danger.'

He walked across to the barrels standing against one of the roughly plastered walls, taking the torch with him, while Flora stayed at the bottom of the stairs.

She saw him pause and lift the torch high. Was that a gasp? Not from Jack, surely. Jack didn't gasp. She started towards him.

'Stay back!' he ordered. 'You don't want to see this.'

Taking no notice, she stumbled through the darkness to arrive by his side, in the process paddling through a wide spill of liquid. Jack had continued to stare down at the one open casket. He appeared fixated.

Following his gaze, it was Flora's turn to let out a gasp. A body was curled foetus-like into the barrel, a pale hand outstretched and strands of grey hair floating just below the surface of the cider.

And the body was unmistakably Percy Milburn's.

5

Flora said nothing on the way back to the village. She hadn't cried but Jack knew that once alone, the tears would fall. She had been desperately upset when she'd looked down into that barrel, and he hadn't felt much better. It was seeing a man, not exactly in his prime but healthy and full of energy, murdered in the most callous of fashions, discarded as though he were a piece of inconvenient litter.

He drove quickly and, once back in Flora's cottage, sat her down in an armchair and retreated to the kitchen to make tea. Hot, sweet tea. Since their first meeting, he seemed to have done that rather too often.

When he brought the tray into the sitting room, she was sitting bolt upright, staring at the sideboard. Staring at the photograph she loved, the one of her aunt Violet in the vegetable garden. He'd barely known Violet Steele, their only contact the occasional handwritten note she'd sent to accompany his order from the All's Well, but he wished he had. Most of all, he wished Violet were here. Her niece needed comfort in a way that Jack hadn't seen before.

Walking over to the armchair, he knelt by its side and put

his arms around her to hold her tight against him. She nestled into the hollow of his neck and he felt her trying to swallow her tears. For a long time, they remained motionless until Jack felt his knees giving way and was forced to his feet. Wordlessly, he handed her a cup.

'I'll have to telephone Inspector Ridley,' he said eventually.

Flora simply nodded and continued to sip the sweet tea.

He'd no wish for her to overhear his conversation and, walking into the hall, shut the sitting room door behind him.

'Another body?' The inspector sounded tired, his tone resigned. 'You keep finding 'em, Jack. You've got to stop.'

'I wish I could, particularly this time. It was a horrible discovery.' And in as few words as possible, he described for Ridley the scene they'd encountered in the farm's cellar.

The inspector let out a breath. Jack could imagine the tightened lips. 'That is nasty,' was all he said, however.

'Murky, too.'

'In what way?'

'Mr Milburn had agreed to buy the farm where he was killed. At least, I'm assuming he was killed at Birds Acre. But there was a dispute between him and the owner of the land as to how the farm should be developed. Percy was meeting the owner and his land agent there in the hope they could resolve the argument.'

'You think it might have been resolved with murder?'

'It's possible.'

'OK. I'll send a team there now. I hope you didn't touch anything.'

'Alan, please...'

'Who's the owner, do you know, and who's the agent?'

'A chap called Colin Palmer is the agent.'

'Oh, him.' Ridley sounded dismissive. 'I've come across him at the local Lions Club. I couldn't make out why he'd joined.'

'Social climbing?'

'Probably. It would fit. And the farm's owner?'

'The Birds Acre land is part of Sir Frederick Neville's estate.'

There was a long silence.

'Neville, you say?'

'Yes. Is that a problem?' What did Alan Ridley know that was giving him pause?

'No, no problem,' the inspector said, attempting to sound unconcerned but not succeeding. 'It's the super. He and Neville are best buddies, and any questioning could be difficult. Still' – he brightened – 'I might not need to talk to the chap.'

'But Neville was at the farm at a time when Mr Milburn was lying dead in the cellar,' Jack objected. 'According to Colin Palmer, they both turned up, but Percy didn't.'

There was another long silence.

'Would you like me to speak to Sir Frederick? Informally.' It had been a sudden inspiration, close to genius, Jack thought. 'I could let you know if I feel you need to step in.'

'It might help,' Ridley said slowly. 'You know the man, then?'

'No,' he said breezily, 'but I soon will.'

'What did the inspector say?' Flora looked up. There was a suspicion of a tear stain on each cheek.

'He seems to think I conjure bodies from the ether.'

'He blamed you for discovering Percy?'

'Not exactly, but he sounded weary, and another murder investigation is probably the last thing he needs. When I offered to help, he didn't refuse.'

He saw the hazel eyes become alert. 'Help how?'

'By talking to Sir Frederick Neville.'

She wriggled to the edge of her seat. 'Someone needs to question him, for sure.'

'Talk, not question, Flora,' he warned.

'The man was at the farm along with Palmer. He turned up late, *and* he was driving himself. Palmer remarked on the absence of his chauffeur which means it wasn't usual for Neville to take the car himself. Who's to say he didn't get there before Palmer, meet Percy, then double back and pretend he'd only just arrived? He had a motive for murder.' She swallowed hard.

'What motive, though?' Jack took a seat opposite and settled himself to think. 'Neville had agreed to sell, true, and maybe he wanted out. But he'd signed nothing. There was no legal contract. He could have refused to go ahead.'

Flora gave a small bounce, shaking her head vigorously. 'I'm not so sure. Percy wouldn't let him off the hook that easily. He'd keep him to the agreement, and if Sir Fred refused to go ahead, he'd take him to court. Percy told me that.'

'He might have threatened, but would he really have gone ahead? Taking the case to court would cost a great deal of money. Not to mention the gossip it would provoke. That could make his life in the village very uncomfortable.'

'Percy would do it.' Flora was adamant. 'He felt passionately enough about his project to spend every penny of his fortune making it come true.'

'But if there's no evidence of an agreement? If it was made verbally, with a handshake the only confirmation?'

'Knowing what an astute businessman Percy was, I reckon there's something in writing somewhere. And even if there isn't, there's always that deposit. Percy would have demanded a receipt and the money is sitting in Sir Frederick's bank right now.'

'I wonder what frame of mind Neville was in when he went to that meeting. Do you think he went prepared to compromise?'

'There isn't a compromise,' she pointed out. 'Percy would

insist on his right to build what he wanted, in this case a hostel. And a hostel and an expensive hotel couldn't be more different. Percy went to that meeting hoping to persuade, but I reckon Neville's agenda was quite different. He went to make his refusal clear.'

'So, there'd likely be a quarrel.'

'A monumental one, if what we saw was the result.'

'It would have had to get wildly out of hand for that to happen, Flora.'

'Maybe it did. Let's go and see Sir Fred.' She jumped up, straightening her skirt and casting around for her handbag.

'We can't go now.'

'Why not? There's a poor dead man a few miles away depending on us to find out who did this to him.'

Jack got up and took her hands, pushing her back into the chair. 'We'll have to make an appointment. We can't just bound up to his front door and ask to be admitted.'

'I don't see why we shouldn't. And why is Neville going to agree to an appointment? Do you know him personally, because I don't?'

'I don't, but Ridley's boss does. They're friends and we need to tread softly.'

'Really? Then we spring a surprise. Turn up out of the blue. Say we were out on a ramble and thought we'd call in to say how sorry we were to hear of the dreadful events at Birds Acre farm.'

'Out for a ramble!' Jack exploded.

'Yes, you know, you find a few lanes, put one foot in front of the other and soon you're at the front door of Bramber Hall.'

'He's never going to buy that.'

'Probably not, but what's the betting he'll be too fazed to do much about it. We may even get tea and cakes!'

· · ·

The proposal to beard Sir Frederick at home had lifted Flora's spirits, but her buoyant mood did not last long. By the time she climbed the stairs to bed that night, an ever-threatening gloom had made a stealthy advance. The reality of Percy's death was slowly sinking in. She was a turmoil of feelings – immense distress at losing a kind acquaintance but rage, too, at the unfairness of life. Percy had been the most decent of human beings and to die in such a dreadful fashion was the last thing he deserved.

Changing into pyjamas, brushing her teeth, laying out clothes for another day at the All's Well, her mind continued to worry at the problem of why, of all people, Percy had become a murder victim. He might not have had many admirers in Abbeymead, but surely even a strong dislike would not have led to his killing.

The answer had to lie with the farm or, more specifically, with its sale. The suggestion of a dispute between Sir Frederick and Percy before the land agent ever arrived had taken hold of her mind. Percy was wiry but small in stature whereas Neville, from her admittedly hazy recollection, was barrel-chested and at least a foot taller. If they'd fallen into a quarrel and been standing at the top of that faulty flight of stairs, how easy it would have been for Percy to fall during a tussle. Plummeting to the flagstones, he could have died immediately. They would know soon enough from the post-mortem – Jack was sure to wheedle the information out of Alan Ridley. He'd been the one to find the poor man, after all, and deserved to know.

Say that Percy had died from the fall – her mind continued its quest to find some order in the most disordered of days. Say he'd died and Sir Frederick had panicked. He would see a charge of murder looming, once their disagreement became known, even if it had been an accident. The fallout could be huge, whichever way an investigation went. His life might never be the same again. But if he disposed of the body and got as far away from the farm as possible... His land agent was due to arrive at any minute, but then he'd see the barrels stored against one wall and come to a decision. He'd store the body in one of them and return later to give the chap a decent burial. Opening the lid, though, he'd find not the empty space he expected but a tub full of cider. He would be sent into a frenzy. What to do? What to do? Without thinking, he'd scoop Percy off the floor and stuff him into the barrel, at the same time dislodging the pressure valve.

At this point in her conjecture, Flora felt physically sick. She mustn't go on thinking in this way. Probably nothing like that had happened, she told herself. She was allowing her imagination to grow and feed on itself. But Percy Milburn hadn't arrived in that barrel unaided, had he? Someone had done just what she'd pictured.

For most of the night she slept little and rode to the All's Well the next morning barely able to open her eyes. It was only her faithful bicycle, Betty, that made sure she arrived safely. Betty knew the way blindfold.

It was a decidedly lacklustre Flora who opened the till, tidied her desk and picked up a duster to begin the daily clean. She was saved from doing so when the doorbell jingled and Alice bustled into the shop, looking horribly bright-eyed.

'I've a few hours off this mornin'. I've left Joan – she's the new kitchen maid and much better than the last one – to prepare the veg for lunch. She'll do it well. I wanted to drop by and ask you about Friday.'

Flora looked blank. Friday was the traditional evening for her supper with Alice and Kate Mitchell, the owner of the village café, and one of Flora's closest friends.

'I'm thinking it would be best if we missed meetin' this

Friday but did a bumper meal the next week. I wanted to make sure you were all right with that.'

'Yes,' Flora stammered. At the moment, eating seemed the least important thing in the world.

'Jack's invited, too.'

'Jack?' She was even more bemused.

'It's a special week, Flora.' Alice wore a huge smile. 'We've something to celebrate. But why are you lookin' so miserable?' Her smile was fading quickly.

Flora had never felt less like celebrating. 'A man has died, Alice,' she reminded her. 'Died a horrible death.'

'Oh, that man, Milburn. Yes, I know. Nasty, but then what do you expect?'

'What do you mean?'

'Interferin' in the village like he did. Comin' from goodness knows where and puttin' everyone on end with his plans. Bringin' his factory habits with him. He's used to makin' money and it's money talkin'. I've said it before, Lily Martin would hate the idea of her home ruined in that way. No one wants a hostel in the village.'

'That is so unfair. Percy would have gained nothing. In fact, he was likely to lose money. But he wanted to do the right thing.'

Alice had grown to be a firm friend, even more so since Violet's death, but Flora had never felt more out of charity with her. Her evident lack of feeling, the utter disregard for Percy's life, had Flora compressing her lips very tightly before she said something she would regret.

'Well, we're never goin' to agree on that,' Alice said peaceably. 'And you're bound to be feelin' bad about it, what with you bein' the one to find him. You just can't keep out of trouble, it's what I always say. So' – she took a breath – 'what about missin' this Friday and making the next one a special occasion?'

'What about it?' Flora asked a trifle crossly.

'Dear, dear, you are in a pet. Well, when you come out of it, perhaps you'll let me know. I'm cookin' and I'd like to have an idea for how many.' She paused and fixed Flora with a fierce look. 'I'd have thought you'd want to wish one of your best friends congratulations.'

'I've really no idea what you're talking about, Alice.'

''Course you don't. You're more interested in a man that doesn't come from here and causes trouble. Kate, I'm talkin' about Kate. She's got engaged!'

Flora stared at her. 'To Tony?' Tony Farraday's friendship with the widowed Kate had been followed with interest by most of Abbeymead, though by Flora with much less enthusiasm.

'Well, who else?'

'It's a bit sudden, isn't it?'

Alice folded her lips. 'If Kate is happy...'

Flora nodded dumbly. 'I suppose.'

'So, are you comin' or not?'

'Yes,' she said miserably.

'And Jack?'

'And Jack.'

6

'What do you think of the engagement?' Jack asked, opening the door of the Austin for her. Flora was still in the doldrums, he could tell, and Kate's engagement seemed to be adding to her worries.

It was Sunday morning. Sunday had seemed as good a day as any to unearth their quarry. If Sir Frederick had a family – Jack didn't know, and Flora was unsure – he was most likely to be at home. Morning service followed by a large roast dinner and an hour's nap was still very much the order of the day for men in Sir Frederick's position.

'I hope it works out,' she said, her tone anything but cheerful.

'Kate is very sensible. She wouldn't have said yes unless she was sure.'

'She said yes to Bernie Mitchell. That wasn't too sensible,' she retorted. Bernie, now thankfully departed, had been the worst husband ever, according to Flora.

'I didn't know Mitchell, but Tony's a good chap. Kate will be OK with him.' When she didn't respond, he switched on the ignition. 'Ready for Bramber Hall?'

The ramble that Flora had jokingly suggested had been rejected. Bramber Hall turned out to be a good five miles away when Jack consulted his now crumpled map and there was no way he would undertake a ten-mile walk there and back in order to have the door slammed in his face. In his view, that was the most likely welcome they'd receive.

The Austin was soon at the top of Fern Hill, Jack turning right onto the road that passed the entrance to the Priory Hotel and, a mile or so later, the Lexington Golf Club. It was also the road that ran past the track leading to the farmhouse and he noticed that Flora averted her eyes as they drove by. A short while after the Birds Acre turning, he spied a signpost to the Hall directing him towards a minor road, and just a mile later he was slewing left and pulling up outside a pair of decorated wrought-iron gates. A lodge stood to one side and, at the toot of Jack's horn, the keeper emerged from his front door, stretching his limbs and giving his hair an occasional scratch. Naps were not the sole province of the aristocracy, it seemed.

Jack wound down his window. 'We've come to see Sir Frederick,' he said, with unflappable confidence. 'For tea and cakes.' He smiled to himself. Tea and cakes could surely only be a whisper away.

The lodgekeeper's frown vanished. He had seemed dubious initially, but this magical phrase appeared to unlock the door. Literally.

'Oh, ah,' he said, and swung back one of the wide gates far enough for the small saloon to pass through.

'I thought he was going to bar our way,' Flora confided as soon as they were well past.

'So did I. Thank the Lord that Sir Fred's security is non-existent.'

She settled back in her seat. 'Now all we have to do is convince the butler.'

'He's all yours,' Jack said and drove on.

Bramber Hall was approached by a long sweeping driveway that wound a leisurely path across parkland and through woods, only revealing the mansion at its very end.

'Quite some property,' he remarked, as they pulled into the turning area to the right of the house, parking the car in front of what appeared to be a line of garages.

'I heard he collects classic cars,' Flora said.

'Good to know. We'll have something in common.' With a grin, he patted the Austin's dashboard.

A spur led off the driveway, passing through what had once been a carriage porch and ending at a short flight of steps and the Hall's front entrance.

'Over to you.' Jack stood to one side at the top of the steps.

She reached up and pulled the bell. A harsh clanging was set in motion, seeming to ricochet through the entire building, but it was several minutes before there was any response. Flora was about to repeat the deafening noise when the front door slid silently open, and a black-suited man stood on the threshold.

'Yes?'

'Good afternoon,' she said cheerfully. 'My name is Flora Steele, and this is Jack Carrington.' She plucked at Jack's sleeve, as though to exhibit him. 'We've come to see Sir Frederick.'

She hadn't mentioned tea and cakes, Jack noticed, which was probably wise. The butler's expression could only be described as tortured, as though suffering from particularly bad indigestion.

'Sir Frederick is expecting you?'

'Oh yes,' she said confidently. 'Well, in a manner of speaking. Mr Carrington is a friend of Inspector Ridley and Sir Frederick is very close to the inspector's immediate superior.'

Jack wondered if this tortuous explanation would have the door slamming shut, but the butler seemed more puzzled than annoyed – perhaps he, too, had been taking a nap – and he merely gestured them into a vast hall, its double-height walls oak-panelled, with a balustraded minstrels' gallery at the far end.

'If you will wait in the library,' he said, showing them into one of the rooms that led off this lofty space, 'I will inform Sir Frederick that you are here.'

Once the butler had disappeared on his mission, Flora did a small jump. 'We're in!' Her voice was buoyant, and Jack was relieved to see she'd regained some of her usual spirit.

'No counting chickens. We can be out just as quickly.' He turned in a circle, taking in his surroundings. 'More palatial than the Priory, isn't it?'

'And much less comfortable.'

The library was a high-ceilinged, generous-sized room, with tall windows that looked out onto acres of grass, the rolling Sussex countryside a distant backdrop. Walking to the windows for a closer look, Jack spied a tennis court – a swimming pool, he imagined, would not be too far away.

Inside, an elegant marble fireplace filled most of one wall, a massive, fitted bookshelf taking up another. The books were large, leather-bound volumes and looked never to have shifted an inch since first being shelved. The third wall contained a jumbled collection of paintings – scenes depicting various historical events, as far as Jack could make out. Copies of better-known works, he reckoned, and bad ones at that. Overall, the room seemed designed for show rather than pleasure, and certainly not for comfort.

His survey was interrupted by the sound of boots on the parquet floor, a heavy tread that became heavier as it drew near. Sir Frederick Neville strode into the room, his imposing figure temporarily blocking what light filtered from the hall. A man in his sixties, broad-shouldered, a little overweight, but exuding a kind of brute strength.

'Higgins said I had visitors.' He was unsmiling, his dark brown eyes suspicious. 'Do I know you?'

Flora stepped forward. 'I think we've met, Sir Frederick. At the summer fair. It must be around four years ago.' Jack knew she'd been unsure when it was that she'd met him, and the fierceness of the man's gaze must have had her wondering if she ever had.

'Abbeymead,' she prompted faintly.

'Oh, Abbeymead.' The village name was waved away, but its mention seemed to relax their reluctant host. 'Not been there since Edward died. No reason to.' He spoke in the peculiarly upper-class way of chopping sentences to make them as brief as possible.

Jack felt her take a deep breath beside him before she embarked on the 'talk' they'd agreed together.

'Sir Frederick, we wanted to speak to you about a former tenant of yours.' Though the Martins' farm had once belonged to Lord Edward Templeton, it was an incongruity that its lands sat at the outer edges of the Neville estate. 'Robert Martin?'

'Dead, poor chap.'

'Yes, we know. Abbeymead was very sad to lose him. But his farm...'

'Interested in buying, eh?' This seemed to amuse their host, who allowed his lips to part in a semblance of a smile.

'Not in buying,' Jack interposed, 'but in the man who wanted to buy. The man who died a few days ago – Percy Milburn. I believe you knew him quite well.'

'Hardly. My agent had dealings with him. Nothing to do with that side of the estate myself. It's Palmer you need to talk to. Has an office in your village. Go and see him.'

He'd turned his back on them when Flora said sharply, 'We've been to see Mr Palmer. It's you we'd like to talk to, Sir Frederick.'

He wheeled around, his eyes sparking with anger. 'What the deuce! What's any of this got to do with you?'

'Inspector Ridley,' Jack said simply. 'I believe you are friends with his superior, Superintendent Manners.'

'What if I am?' His tone was belligerent.

'The police would like to keep the investigation into Mr Milburn's death low-key. You understand?'

Sir Frederick frowned.

'In order to do that,' Jack continued smoothly, 'Inspector Ridley would rather not send a team of officers here to ask questions.' He was deliberately exaggerating, but it had the effect he'd hoped it would.

A shudder seemed to pass through their host. 'Good grief. How appalling!'

Sir Frederick walked towards an Italian marble-topped table, then back again, until he was once more directly facing them.

'So, what have you come to talk about?'

At last, Jack thought, we're getting somewhere.

'You were due to meet Mr Milburn at the farm on the day he died, but he never turned up,' Flora said calmly.

'Wasted my time. Wasted Palmer's, too.'

'What did you think when he didn't come?'

Sir Frederick sucked in his mouth. 'Damn silly question. Thought he was late and hung around a while. Mind you, I was late, too.' He seemed to Jack to make a point of this. 'Bunting, she's my housekeeper, was in a state over some missing silver. Silver's Higgins' job, I said, but the old girl had got her bloomers in a twist. Wouldn't rest until the whole damn stock was counted.' He chuckled at the memory.

'When it was clear that Mr Milburn wasn't coming, what did you think?' Flora pursued.

'Blighter had buggered off. Got cold feet.'

'And now that you know he was lying dead in the farm's cellar all the time?'

'Don't think anything. Total mystery, m'dear.'

'There was a problem with the contract of sale, I believe,' Jack intervened.

Sir Frederick scowled. 'Milburn agreed to buy, then started putting obstacles in the way. Wanted a clause in the contract to say the farm would be converted into a hostel and there'd be no problem.'

'And you wanted one saying it would be a hotel?' He was guessing.

'As it should be.' Jack had guessed correctly. 'Wasn't having any damn hostel on my land. Every city rag, tag and bobtail swarming over the estate. Not on your life.'

'But why not?' Flora asked innocently. 'If Mr Milburn was buying the farm, surely it was his right to convert the property as he wished.'

Sir Frederick merely grunted. 'Should never have agreed to sell to the man. Met him on the golf course, d'you know, and thought he was an OK chap, but not up to snuff. Definitely not up to snuff.'

'You were hoping to resolve your differences, though?' Flora's voice was again innocent of guile. 'You agreed to meet at the farm for that reason, I imagine.'

'Chap wanted to bombard me with his plans. Had some idea he could persuade me to think differently. No chance. I wasn't about to change my mind.'

'There was no need to change your mind, Uncle.' Another voice had joined the conversation. It belonged to a young man, tall and willowy. He was clean-shaven, with a sallow complexion and hair that had seen rather too much Brylcreem.

The four of them stood looking blankly at each other until Sir Frederick spoke. 'Piers Neville,' he introduced him grumpily. 'Nephew.'

Piers was dressed for riding, it seemed, his breeches shinily new, a careless cravat knotted around his neck. But those boots, Jack thought, had never seen a horse.

'I'm sorry about Milburn,' Piers said, without sounding at all sorry, 'but it's the future that's important. We need to look forward and Birds Acre Farm will make a beautiful hotel.'

It was clear the Nevilles still intended to sell, as long, it seemed, as they had a say in what was built.

'You've found another buyer then?' Flora asked, her eyes wide.

'I'll say we have.' Piers smirked. 'And one who's offering a much better deal than that tight-fisted Yorkshireman, eh, Uncle?'

Distaste was written across Sir Frederick's face, but he made no comment.

'And this buyer is new?'

It was the same question that Jack had immediately asked himself. Had there really been time for a newcomer to arrive on the scene or was it rather that Percy Milburn had been up against a competitor all this time? And if so, who?

'Not exactly new,' Piers drawled, his hand fingering the slicked-back hair. 'It's been on the cards for yonks, but now Milburn's out of the way – sorry, now he's no longer with us – it's full steam ahead. Funny little chap doing the negotiations,' he mused. 'Sidney Lovejoy. You might have seen him around the village.'

Jack glimpsed Sir Frederick's expression. He looked like thunder. His nephew was evidently talking far too much.

'The chap may be a bit of an oddity but he's working for an important London consortium,' Piers went on, undeterred. 'All very businesslike. And, as I say, generous.'

It was then that Sir Frederick interposed, cutting off his nephew's flood of information. 'Naturally, it's sad that Mr

Milburn met such an unpleasant death but, as Piers said, we have to move on.'

'You could always find another tenant,' Flora suggested. 'I don't imagine it would be difficult.'

Their host shook his head. 'No money in farming, m'dear. Not today. And the estate eats money. Death duties, taxes. Got to look after it. Can't have what happened to Templeton's land, split up and distributed here, there and everywhere. Made a bad mistake with the Martin farm, though. Shouldn't have bought it. Never contributed to the coffers, just the opposite. It needs to do better.'

Jack paused, wondering if he dared ask what was in truth an impertinent question, then steamed ahead. 'If the land is no longer yours, how will a hotel built by someone else be of help?' Just what financial agreement had been reached, he was wondering, and with whom?

'That's easy.' Piers bounced back into the conversation. 'We get a... a commission,' he said. 'A slice of the profit.'

His uncle took a step forward, as if he would physically silence him. A rake-off, Jack amended to himself. No wonder Sir Frederick hadn't wanted a hostel. There would have been precious little profit in that.

'The hotel will be small and exclusive,' Piers boasted, ignoring his uncle's clenched fists, 'far more exclusive than the Priory. It's certain to attract the very best people.'

A young woman, encased in several layers of diaphanous material, drifted into the room at that moment and walked over to Piers, sliding a thin arm around his waist. Almond-shaped eyes looked adoringly up at him, while Sir Frederick stayed silent and scowling. No one made any attempt to introduce the newcomer.

'We'll wish you success then,' Flora said quietly.

'Don't worry. It will be fabulous, won't it, darling?' He bent his willowy form towards the woman who still clung to his arm. His girlfriend, Flora presumed.

'Prue is going to help me.' Piers bent his head to kiss the girl's cheek but missed by some inches. Straightening up, he swelled with importance. 'We're to be the management team, you know – when Prue isn't working – and together, we're sure to create a sensation!'

7

'Are you thinking what I'm thinking?' Flora asked, as they were shown out of the door by the stately Higgins.

'That Sir Frederick Neville is a prime suspect?'

She nodded. 'He has money troubles. He wants to sell to the highest bidder and the agreement he made with Percy was in his way.'

Jack took her hand as they walked to the car. 'I'm not entirely convinced. The fact remains that it was only a verbal agreement. I know all this business of shaking hands on a deal, my word is my bond et cetera, but if Neville chose to renege on the agreement, there really was nothing to stop him.'

He opened the car door for her, but she made no move to get in. 'It's not just that he'd agreed to sell. Sir Frederick accepted a deposit for the sale. There will be paperwork to prove he was paid a large sum of money and, as Percy said himself, he wouldn't want to return the cash. Perhaps he couldn't return it. The sale was definitely going ahead, until Percy insisted on a clause in the contract stating the farm was to be developed as a hostel. Neville was in deep and, until Percy died, he would have found it very difficult to slide away.'

'Why insist on that clause, do you think?' Jack walked round the car and slid into the driver's seat. 'Once Milburn had purchased the farm, he could do what he wanted with the land.'

'He couldn't have trusted Sir Frederick, or rather Sir Frederick's lawyers. He may have suspected they'd word the contract in a way that might challenge how he developed the farm.'

Jack nodded, steering the car around the turning circle and starting back along the lengthy driveway. 'I wonder if he had in mind the kind of commission scam that Piers Neville was suggesting?'

'Is it a scam?'

'I've never heard of any seller demanding money for his property after he's sold it. Or any buyer – in this case, Percy – stipulating what he can do with his purchase. I think you're right. Milburn must have had an inkling that Neville was up to something. A clause perhaps that would suddenly appear in the final contract.'

'It's a rum do.' She grinned. 'That's what Percy would have said.'

'It's also a motive for murder, if the Neville family are so cash-strapped they need to engage in dubious deals. And it is dubious. What kind of person would buy the farm knowing they had Sir Frederick holding out a hand for his share of any profit they made? What's the betting this new buyer won't be squeaky clean?'

Flora silently agreed but as they turned out of the gates of Bramber Hall and headed back to the village, something else occurred to her. 'It's not just the cash, is it? Piers Neville is expecting a job out of it. A well-paid job. That wouldn't have happened with a hostel.'

'So, both uncle and nephew have reasons for eliminating Percy. Sorry, Flora.' He must have seen her face pale at the word.

'It's OK. Like you, I'm sure the contract is the reason behind Percy's death, but I'm finding it hard to accept that anyone would do such a dreadful thing over the sale of a farmhouse and a few acres of land.'

'Where money is concerned, people are capable of anything, and that includes the Nevilles. From this afternoon's showing, either one or other of them could be involved.'

'Or they plotted it together.'

'True. So, what next? Do we continue poking around or get on with our lives and leave it to Ridley?'

'We don't have a choice and you know it. Ridley has already asked for your help and, I reckon, he'll ask again. We have to keep poking. Maybe, the Lovejoy man? We should talk to him. He's the one working for the new buyer, if in fact he is new. Lovejoy might throw more light on what was going on before Percy died. He's supposed to have been in the village for some time, though I've never seen him. Have you?' She half turned to Jack as he steered the car into Greenway Lane.

'No, and by the sound of it, he's someone we'd have noticed.'

'He must be staying at the Cross Keys – Sally hasn't mentioned a long-term guest at the Priory. He shouldn't be difficult to run to ground.'

'Before we collar him, I'll call at the pub and speak to the new landlord. I reckon he'll be happy to have someone to talk to. He's not gone down too well with the locals and they're virtually ignoring him. A little too keen on rules, I think: no wellingtons in the lounge bar, no dogs after six o'clock.'

Flora raised her eyebrows as they pulled up outside her cottage.

'Don't ask me what that's about.' Jack grimaced. 'Maybe he's trying to make his mark.'

'He can make his mark by telling you what he knows about

Lovejoy,' she said, climbing out of the car. 'Are you coming in? I've fresh scones for tea.'

'Need you ask? I'll beat you to the kitchen.'

It was late the following day that Flora received an unexpected visit. With the help of young Charlie Teague, she had stripped the contents of the two floor-length bookcases at the rear of the building and was about to pack the stack of books into cardboard boxes. They would be stored in the cellar for safety while Michael, the odd-job man, worked on fitting a new door to the back wall of the All's Well. The lack of an exit to the cobbled yard at the rear of the shop had been a frustration for years but, at last, the rural district council had agreed that Flora could make alterations to what was a very old building, in parts dating from Jacobean times.

Jack had not been enthusiastic when she'd told him. *It's an invitation,* he'd complained. *Any ne'er-do-well bent on mischief will have another way of getting into the building.* Flora had already suffered two break-ins and she could understand his concern, but surely lightning wouldn't strike a third time.

'You've done a splendid job,' she said, watching Charlie expertly tape up the four large cardboard boxes.

She was lucky to have his help. The Easter holidays had finished and today should have marked a return to school but, during the interim, the toilets had overflowed and flooded a good portion of the ground floor. The building had had to close for an entire week while the plumbers got to work, and the caretaker made good the damage.

As always, Charlie was proving an indefatigable worker. Whether he was mowing lawns, weeding flowerbeds, running errands or helping at local events, the boy threw himself into whatever activity he was being paid for. Flora used to think the lure of money was the attraction, though neither she nor Jack –

Charlie had helped Jack establish a garden at Overlay House virtually from scratch – had worked out what it was the boy was saving for. Recently, though, she'd come to realise it was far simpler. Charlie had such an abundance of energy that a small community like Abbeymead, with only the most basic of resources, could never fully satisfy.

'The boxes can't be too heavy,' she warned him. 'We've somehow to get them down that steep flight of stairs to the cellar and then once Mr Worthington has finished, bring them up again.'

'When's he startin', Miss Steele. Mr Worthington?'

'It should have been tomorrow, but the small jobs he had to finish are taking him a lot longer than he thought. He won't be here until next week now and maybe later.' She gave him a hard look. 'But you won't be helping him, young man. You'll be back at school.'

'Not if the bogs aren't mended.'

'They will be. And Michael won't want another pair of hands getting in the way.'

'I wouldn't be a nuisance,' he protested. 'I'd be a help.'

Before she had time to answer, the sound of the handbell she kept on her desk rang through the shop. Flora looked up, surprised. No one ever rang the handbell. It had been a perennial joke between Violet and herself – returning from the nether regions of the shop, they'd see people eyeing the bell suspiciously and then turning to browse the shelves until one or other of them appeared to serve.

There was another imperious ring. 'D'you want me to go, Miss Steele?'

'No, Charlie, thanks. Best you keep packing. But don't worry about getting the titles in any order. We'll have to mix heavy volumes with the lighter ones and sort them out once they're back on the shelves.'

When she reached the front of the shop, she found

Winifred Ticehurst waiting for her. The woman was about to sound the bell again when she spotted Flora coming towards her.

'Ah, there you are. Thought you must have gone to sleep.'

'Not asleep, Miss Ticehurst,' she said, carefully pleasant. 'Working at the rear of the shop.'

'You need someone at the desk. Anyone could walk in, steal half your stock before you knew it.'

'I tend to trust my fellow humans,' Flora returned sweetly.

'Never a good idea,' her visitor muttered.

'How can I help you?'

She was keen to rid the shop of a woman she hardly knew but was beginning to dislike heartily. Winifred Ticehurst had taken up the position of head teacher at the village school several years after Flora had left to attend the grammar school in Steyning.

'I hear you paid Bramber Hall a visit.' Winifred's expression was critical.

The news had evidently travelled around the village faster than Flora expected. One of the Neville servants must have talked, though surely not the butler!

'I hope you told Sir Frederick that whatever dreadful scheme he has in mind should be dropped,' the woman pronounced. 'Birds Acre needs to remain a farm, and there is no sign yet of another tenant. There needs to be.'

'I'm not in a position to tell Sir Frederick how to run his estate,' she said calmly, 'but from what I can see, another tenant looks unlikely – it appears Sir Frederick means to sell.'

The woman's face bloomed an uncomfortable red. 'The farm turned into a hostel! Quite shocking! Any plans to do so should be scotched immediately.'

'I believe it's a hotel that is being planned rather than a hostel.'

'As if that's any better. As if we've not suffered enough with our magnificent Priory brought to ruin. A gentleman's seat turned into accommodation for whichever riff-raff passes by! It was a sad day when Edward Templeton died. The rot started then.'

'You're entitled to your opinion, but I think we should tread carefully in what we say. A man has met a brutal death and most likely because of arguments over Birds Acre Farm.' It irked Flora that not one word had been said of Percy's wretched end.

Winifred gave an angry snort. 'Your aunt was never frightened of the truth. She would have had something to say about it, I'm sure. And Mr Milburn had only himself to blame for what happened. He never belonged in Abbeymead, and he should have recognised that. Instead, he thought to ride roughshod over village feeling. It was foolish of him to interfere, and foolish of you, young lady, if you choose to do the same. Violet always said you were a nosy child, but you should have grown out of it by now.'

Miss Ticehurst's stout figure wheeled around and was out of the shop door before Flora recovered from her surprise. Had she heard aright?

'I'm not sure how heavy is heavy.' It was Charlie, coming from behind one of the bookcases, angled in the wider section of the shop to create more space.

The layout of the All's Well was higgledy-piggledy, as befitted a centuries' old building, and there had been times when Aunt Violet had had to ride to the rescue, discovering a customer in one of its hidden nooks, unable to find their way back to the front door.

'Why didn't you say hello to Miss Ticehurst?' Flora asked him. 'She must have been your head teacher when you were at the village school.'

Charlie scowled. 'Yeah, she wuz. I didn't like her. None of us kids liked her.'

'Why was that?' She was curious, having felt an instant dislike herself.

'She wuz bossy. Always makin' up rules and then punishin' you if you forgot 'em.'

'Right.' Miss Ticehurst was going to have a problem making up rules for Sir Frederick Neville, she thought.

'And the teachers didn't like her either. We heard 'em talkin' in the staffroom.'

Flora thought it best to keep silent on that. Instead, she walked back to the rear of the bookshop and picked up the box that Charlie had filled.

'This will do, I think. It's just about manageable. Let's finish the others and then brave the cellar.'

8

Jack had settled to a morning's writing when the shrill of the telephone had him slam the carriage return on the Remington and, in frustration, gallop downstairs.

It was Alan Ridley on the line with the suggestion that they should meet. Jack was torn. Intent on making a substantial start on the new book – several chapters already written and a vague map in his mind of where he'd go next – he still wanted to hear the results of Percy's post-mortem and was keen to discover whatever else the inspector was willing to divulge. Juggling in his mind which was the most important, he tried to sound happy at the interruption.

'I'm in your neck of the woods this morning,' the inspector announced cheerfully. 'How about lunch at the Cross Keys?'

'You know the landlord has changed?'

'Course I do. Got to know the last one quite well! Remember?'

Jack's spirits sank a little. Lunch at the Cross Keys was once more something to be endured rather than enjoyed. On the other hand, Ridley might have news that Flora would be desperate to hear. He knew she was still deeply upset over

Percy's death and anything he could tell her that pushed the investigation forward must help. There was also the fact – Jack was visited by a sudden thought – that the mysterious Sidney Lovejoy was staying at the inn. This might be a chance to find out more from the landlord, maybe even meet Lovejoy himself or, at least, observe him from afar.

'I'll be there around twelve thirty, Alan, if that's OK.' There was a muttered assent at the end of the line.

Feeling a new optimism, Jack put down the phone and returned to his study. He had a Remington to put to bed.

Once they were settled in Ridley's favourite corner of the pub, packets of crisps and two of the dreaded pork pies sitting between them, the inspector took a sip of his beer and offered his first piece of information. It was stark.

'Percy Milburn was drowned.'

Jack felt shock run through him. 'Drowned?' he repeated.

''Fraid so. In the cider. The pathologist reckons he was still alive when he was dunked in that barrel.'

'That's horrendous.'

'At least the poor chap wouldn't have known much about it. The fall down the stairs must have knocked him out while the cider finished him off.'

'And the damage to the staircase – was that deliberate, do you think?'

Alan Ridley pushed a bag of Smith's crisps towards Jack. 'Eat up! It looks like the missing stairs were part of the plan, yes. Of course, there's always the possibility the killing was opportunistic. The staircase could have been damaged when Mrs Martin moved out. Percy Milburn decides to recce the cellar, doesn't see the damage and falls. Then our murderer pops up and takes advantage of the situation.'

Jack fished for the little blue bag of salt, the crisps preferable to the pie. 'That doesn't seem very likely,' he said mildly.

'I agree. I'm thinking the meeting was set up with the specific goal of eliminating Mr Milburn. The chap was keen to talk through his plans, I've been told, and there would have been no trouble in persuading him to go to Bird's Acre. The killer arrived some time earlier maybe, went into hiding, and watched his victim approach the cellar. Then struck.'

Jack wondered if he should mention the problem with the inspector's theory, it seemed almost too obvious. 'The murderer couldn't have known Percy would definitely go to the cellar.'

'True enough but, if he didn't, our villain probably had a few other ideas in mind. Once Milburn had been lured to the farm, the killer could await his opportunity. In the end, they didn't have to exert themselves too much. Percy walking down those steps worked brilliantly for whoever. Between you and me, I've got my eye on the land agent.'

Jack frowned. 'Colin Palmer? Why him? What would he gain from Milburn's death? If anything, he'd lose commission if the sale failed to materialise.'

The inspector wagged his finger. '"If" is the operative word. Neville could be persuaded to sell to someone else, if Milburn wasn't around. Someone with deeper pockets and therefore a larger commission for our friend, Palmer.'

Jack shook his head. 'He'd have to be pretty desperate for money to commit murder for a larger commission.'

The inspector looked fatigued. 'You'd be surprised what people will kill for. And I've heard that Sir Frederick still intends to sell so...'

It might be the time, Jack decided, to mention the Sunday visit. 'Flora and I went to Bramber Hall a couple of days ago and spoke to Sir Frederick. There *is* another buyer in the offing and one who's willing to pay a good deal more for the farm.'

'There you go then.'

'Not necessarily, Alan. The sale will benefit Frederick

Neville as well as his agent. Not to mention the nephew who seems confident he'll be running the show once this supposedly elite hotel is built. Either of them could have got rid of Percy when a larger sum of money appeared on the horizon. The old boy was proving difficult over the contract and the Neville family seem strapped for cash.'

Ridley bit into his pork pie and chewed for a while. 'Not bad,' he opined. 'Not comparable to Vaisey's – he was a great publican – but there, you can't have everything.' He fixed Jack with a furtive look. 'I'm telling you this on the quiet. We're looking into Neville's finances, but it's not the easiest task.'

'Are they that bad?' Jack was surprised the police had taken this step. Sir Frederick had been keen to mention his expenses, but Bramber Hall hadn't seemed exactly shabby.

'It's early days, but it's clear the estate is very costly to run and that young man – Piers Neville – hasn't helped. It looks like he's wasted a good deal of the family's money.'

'The two of them – uncle and nephew – have motive,' Jack agreed. '*And* opportunity. They both knew Milburn would be at the farm and it's a fact that Sir Frederick went to the meeting. He was late, but he was there and, unusually, drove himself. Why on that day did he dispense with the services of his chauffeur? Flora reckons it could be significant. If Sir Frederick drove himself to the farm in advance of the meeting, he could have doubled back and pretended he'd only just arrived. There'd be no chauffeur to contradict his version of events.'

'Miss Steele is a canny young woman, but I'd have to be very, very sure if I were to pursue that line of enquiry. It's hard enough looking into the man's finances.'

'Because Sir Frederick is who he is?'

The inspector sighed. ''Fraid so. Even in the 1950s we're still metaphorically doffing our caps.'

Jack dusted the remains of salty crisps from his hands. 'I thought the law was supposed to be impartial.'

'That's the theory.' Alan Ridley gave another long sigh and applied himself to the rest of the pie. Jack sat looking at his own plate while the pie looked back at him. He really couldn't face it.

He'd been wondering how he could quietly dispose of the wretched thing when he caught sight of a hunched figure sitting at the bar. The man wore a pair of checked trousers beneath a corduroy jacket, which was odd enough, but on his head was a black felt beret. As if he were a French onion seller, Jack thought. Wisps of thin grey hair protruded from beneath the beret, reaching almost to his shoulders. The man must be Sidney Lovejoy – few strangers drank at the Cross Keys – and no visitor Jack had ever seen had looked quite so... singular. For someone charged with conducting delicate negotiations, the man was hardly unobtrusive, his figure more likely to inflame local gossip than maintain secrecy.

Ridley finished off his pint. 'Drink up, Jack. You've not eaten a thing, and I've got to go. I'm due back in Brighton in less than an hour.'

'Sorry. In a daydream. I've just begun a new book,' he said.

'Ah, that explains it.' The creative process was a mystery to the inspector and Jack could always use it to excuse any odd behaviour.

After his companion had picked up his hat and jacket and walked to the door, Jack pushed aside the uneaten pie and walked over to the bar.

'Mr Lovejoy?' he asked, as he took his place alongside, seeming as though waiting to order a drink. Up close, the man looked even more exceptional, his head beneath the beret too big for his spindly body.

'That's me, squire. How d'you know me?' An unusually mellow voice belied the appearance.

'I imagine most of Abbeymead must know you by now,' Jack said easily.

'Gossipy little place, isn't it?' The man's small eyes, so dark they were almost black, darted around the room as he spoke.

Jack smiled. 'It is,' he agreed, 'particularly when strangers come to stay.'

'Well, they can relax now. I'm off soon, and I won't be sorry. Nice enough village, but a bit too quiet, you know.'

'If you're a city man, I guess.'

'From London, bless her. Nowhere like it.'

Jack contemplated how best to dig deeper and decided that Lovejoy was probably a man on whom subtlety would be wasted.

'Your holiday's coming to an end then?'

'Lord, love you, it's hardly been a holiday. I know where to go for a good time and, begging your pardon, Abbeymead isn't it.'

Jack nodded sagely. 'So, business?'

Sidney took off his beret and scratched his thinning pate. The straggly beard that clung to his chin seemed to have thieved what hair there had ever been.

'Got it in one. Big business, too.' He pulled a face, his expression smug.

'Really?' Jack arranged his features to look impressed. Lovejoy was not above boasting, it seemed, a flaw that could prove useful.

'I'd say so.' Sidney tapped his nose. 'Negotiations that are pretty...' He held his hands out wide to demonstrate the scope of his dealings.

'Really?' Jack repeated, deliberately widening his eyes.

'You'll see for yourself soon enough. Let's just say I'm buying somewhere near here.'

Jack managed to look perplexed. 'You're going to settle in the countryside?'

Sidney roared with laughter. 'As if. I'm not buying for me.'

He lowered his voice. 'I'm working for some very important people.'

'It sounds a serious undertaking.'

'You're right, it is. These blokes, they're in the same business – a kind of consortium – and they want a base they can share. That's understandable, I guess. And they don't mind how much they spend. Oodles of money between 'em.'

'Would I know any of the businesses?'

For the first time Sidney looked uncomfortable. 'Perhaps not,' he muttered and, when Jack didn't press him further, seemed relieved, as though realising he'd said too much to this nosy stranger.

'I heard someone in the village was doing the same – trying to buy in the countryside.' It might be the time, Jack thought, to push a little harder. 'You may have met him. Mr Milburn? He may have been after the same place even.'

Lovejoy nodded. 'I know the name. Poor chap's dead, isn't he? But he wouldn't have managed to buy, even if he hadn't copped it. Could never offer the money that Tyler can.'

They sat in mutual silence for some minutes, Lovejoy staring moodily at the shelves of bottles above the bar, probably, Jack thought, wishing he'd kept his mouth shut. The silence went on until the man suddenly broke the spell by asking, 'Can I buy you a drink, squire?'

'Thank you, but no,' Jack said hastily. He made a play of consulting his watch. 'I have to run – late already.'

Walking back to Overlay House, he turned the conversation over in his mind, trying to pinpoint what exactly he'd learnt: that Sidney Lovejoy had been employed to purchase Birds Acre Farm by people who'd no wish to be known. People about whom Lovejoy himself didn't seem entirely comfortable. Businessmen, he'd said. What kind of business, though? He'd been far less forthcoming on that. And who was this Tyler chap, a man with so much money he was indifferent to expense? Finding the answers to those questions might be the next step.

9

Turning into the high street from Greenway Lane a few days later, Flora pedalled hard. She had slept badly and, instead of flinging back the covers as soon as the alarm rang, had fallen into a troubled doze. Now she was late, and the St Saviour's clock would be striking nine before she opened the All's Well's door. Aunt Violet would have been cross.

Ever since Jack had rung to tell her what he'd learned from his meeting with Alan Ridley, dreadful images of drowning had punctuated her nights, bathing her in a terrified sweat and forcing her awake. He'd tried to soften the details of Percy's death, but really there was no softening the hideousness of the poor man's fate, and Jack had hurried on with information that he knew would distract her – his conversation with Sidney Lovejoy and the shadowy appearance of a consortium keen to buy a chunk of Sussex, but far less keen to reveal their identity. In fact, it had done nothing to make her feel better. Had these mysterious 'businessmen' been behind Percy's death?

It wasn't only Percy's dreadful end that was unsettling Flora, however. Tomorrow meant the usual Friday supper with

Kate and Alice – the three friends had, for years, taken it in turns to host a meal. But this week, it wouldn't be usual at all. For one thing, Jack was invited, and Tony Farraday, too, Flora presumed, since he was the one who'd asked Kate to be his wife. Her friend's decision had worried Flora from the moment she'd heard the news, fearing that Kate had been persuaded into an engagement far too quickly.

Over the last year, her friend had begun to lose the toxic aftermath left behind by Bernie Mitchell, her errant and wholly unsatisfactory first husband. Kate had grown ten times happier since Bernie's death, gaining huge enjoyment from running her café and generally throwing herself into village life. She had begun to take an interest in how she looked, and she looked beautiful. Glowing. Why would she risk such a wonderful renaissance by once more tying herself to a man? Even while Flora thought it, she was aware of how differently others would see the engagement. Congratulations would pour in from all sides – Kate was saying goodbye to widowhood, reprieved from the sad singledom she'd faced. That would be the general view.

Parking Betty in the cobbled courtyard behind the shop, Flora walked round to the All's Well's front door, fumbling in her handbag for the key. It didn't immediately come to hand, and she went methodically through every section of the bag, opening zips and plunging her hand into each of its pockets. In frustration, she upended the bag and tipped its contents onto the pavement. The key was not among them.

It was impossible. There was no way she could have left it behind at the cottage. Her daily routine had been honed for how many years? So many, she couldn't count. Purse, handkerchief, lipstick, keys... then a check that the bike pump was in place and that Betty's wicker basket contained everything she needed for the day.

She would have to use the spare, she decided and, retracing

her steps to the courtyard, bent to retrieve a second key from under a large stone. Her fingers felt around, then felt some more. No key. Memory flooded back – some months ago she'd entrusted the spare to Jack. After the second break-in at the shop, it had seemed safer to leave the key at Overlay House rather than under a stone, a hiding place that anyone bent on trouble might guess. Debating whether or not to return home and double check the key wasn't there, or cycle straight to Jack, she plumped for the latter, resigned to opening the bookshop very late.

At Overlay House she had to ring the doorbell twice before Jack, red-eyed and weary, stood on the threshold. His hair was doing its usual wayward flop and he looked as though he'd only just fallen out of bed, his trousers lacking a belt and his shirt undone. Flora looked the other way. Now wasn't the time.

'Didn't you sleep?' she asked, walking into the tiled hall. It felt cold and dank. Overlay wasn't at its best in a damp spring.

'Eventually, but I was awake for an age. I stayed up writing.'

Had he also been plagued with images of poor dead Percy? she wondered, and kissed him on the cheek.

'Is that all I get?' He took hold of her arm and pulled her close.

'For the moment,' she said, wriggling free. 'I've lost the All's Well's key.'

'How did you manage that?' He shook his head, running a hand through already tousled hair.

'If I knew, I wouldn't be here,' she pointed out.

'True, true.' He pulled at his hair again. 'You'd better get the locks changed. The key could be anywhere.'

'I will. Just as soon as I get the shop door open. I'm terribly late.'

'Relax.' He yawned. 'You're not likely to have customers queuing at this hour. What is the time, anyway?'

'It's nearly half past nine, and the key?' Flora could feel impatience mount. Writers had all the time in the world, it seemed, but shopkeepers didn't.

Jack took the hint and trundled into the kitchen. He opened a cabinet drawer. Then another, and another. 'I know I stowed it away here,' he said over his shoulder.

'You've lost it!' Flora bounced up to him, her expression accusing.

He held up his hand, as though to protect himself. 'Not so. It'll be here... somewhere.'

'Jack!'

'I know, I know, but I stored it in a really safe place.'

'Which you can't remember.'

'I will, I promise. Look, why don't you ride back to the shop, explain the problem to anyone waiting – if there is anyone – and, once I'm fully dressed, I'll tear this room apart for the wretched thing.'

'You'll bring it to the shop?'

'Need you ask, my favourite sleuth?'

The figure standing outside the All's Well, arms folded, was that of Elsie Flowers. As Flora steered the bike into the kerb, the church clock chimed ten.

Elsie cocked her head. 'What time d'you call this then? The shop was never late opening when Violet ran it.'

'I'm sorry, Mrs Flowers.' Politeness won over frustration. Elsie was one of Flora's best customers. 'There's been a problem with the key, but a spare one is on its way right now. Mr Carrington is bringing it.' Metaphorically, she crossed her fingers.

'I've come for that Daphne book. It's supposed to be good.'

'Daphne du Maurier?'

'Some fancy name. It's a thriller, isn't it?' The word 'thriller' trilled on her tongue.

'*The Scapegoat*? Yes. I haven't read it myself, but I do have a copy.'

'Well then...' Elsie looked expectant.

'I'll just wheel Betty round to her shelter, but Mr Carrington shouldn't be long.' She tried a smile but glanced anxiously down the road.

It was another ten minutes, however, and a good deal of foot tapping on Elsie's part before the small red Austin pulled up outside the shop.

'The cavalry has arrived!' Jack exclaimed, jumping out of the Austin. 'In the coffee jar,' he murmured to Flora. 'Good morning, Mrs Flowers.' He turned to Flora's single customer and beamed. 'Looking for a good read?'

'I was, but I should have been home ages ago.' Elsie's tone had become noticeably milder. Flora prickled. It was annoying that it had taken Jack's smile to mollify her. 'Winifred will be furious.'

'Winifred?' he queried.

'Miss Ticehurst.'

'Oh yes, you share a house, don't you?'

'The house is mine,' Elsie said, reverting to her former tartness. 'Winifred rents a room from me, that's all. I did her a favour when she lost her job – and her home besides.'

'I'm sure you did.' Flora was quick to intervene. 'But why will Miss Ticehurst be furious?'

'Because I promised to be home by ten.' Elsie spelled it out slowly, as though she were explaining to a small child. 'Winifred is running this protest movement. The one about Birds Acre? And she has a Very Important Meeting to convene.'

'Right.' The words were heavily emphasised, and Flora understood their message.

'She thinks crime novels are frivolous and I shouldn't be

buying them.' Elsie sniffed loudly. 'You should read Jane Austen, she says to me, all superior like, then you'd know what good writing looks like.' There was a small pause. 'I did try but I couldn't get on with it – not a body in sight – *and* I've caught Miss Hoity-Toity looking at my books when she didn't see me watching!'

Jack hid a smile. 'You must make sure then to keep *The Scapegoat* to yourself,' he said.

Flora took the proffered key and flung the white-painted door wide. She had taken only a few steps inside when she came to an abrupt halt, Elsie and Jack, who'd been following closely, struggling not to fall over each other in the doorway.

'Oh, my goodness.' Flora stood stock-still.

Ducking beneath Jack's arm, Elsie was soon at her side. 'Oh, my goodness,' she echoed.

When Jack finally made it into the shop, he saw immediately what had brought Flora to a sharp halt. The front table where she displayed her stock of recently published books, ones she judged would prove most popular, was awash with fragments of white. Every volume, including Elsie's intended purchase, had been decimated, their covers wrenched off and their pages torn and pulped.

Flora felt the tears prick and blinked them away. This shop was not just a means of earning her living, it was her world. From a very young age, a visceral part of her being. Everything about the place – its smell, its feel, its bookish quiet, was in her blood and an attack on the All's Well was an attack on her.

Jack was looking at her, his grey eyes dark with concern. It seemed he was about to say something but, instead, turned to Elsie, standing immobile at Flora's side.

'Why don't I find you a copy of *The Scapegoat* and deliver it personally?'

Elsie's lower lip protruded. 'Will you?'

'Of course I will, but maybe right now you should be making for home.'

At that moment, the Victorian station clock, a timepiece Aunt Violet had been thrilled to find at one of the many auctions she enjoyed, struck the quarter hour as though to underline Jack's words.

'Oh gawd,' Elsie exclaimed. 'I'm off. Make sure you keep your word, young man.'

The doorbell jingled and Flora found herself led to the seat that ran beneath the latticed window.

'Elsie will spread the word there's been another break-in at the bookshop,' she said. 'It will soon be all round the village.' She paused, swallowing hard. 'And the book she's after was published months ago, in January. I only had a single copy left. You won't find one.'

'Who says I won't? Elsie will get her book if I have to tour every shop in the district. But what are we going to do about this?' He gestured to the heap of broken novels.

'Clear it up,' she said tearfully, trying at the same time to smile. 'Start again. Find other books to display.'

'That's not what I mean, Flora, and you know it. You didn't just lose that key. It had to have been stolen by someone. How did they get hold of it?'

'I've no idea.'

'OK, but stolen by a person who meant you harm,' he went on. 'Someone who wanted to hurt you where it hurt most.'

'Someone in the village? But who?'

'We need to find out.' He was silent for several minutes, while Flora wiped her eyes and blew her nose.

'I reckon this attack is connected to Percy Milburn's death. It can't be a coincidence that it's happened after our visit to Bramber Hall. *And* after my talk with Sidney Lovejoy.'

'That can't be right, Jack. Why would your meeting with Lovejoy have anything to do with it? I wasn't even in the pub at the time. He's never met me. In all probability, he doesn't know I exist.'

'Except... I could have aroused his suspicions. Lovejoy can't be the oddity he looks, if he's been entrusted by a group of businessmen, if that's what they are, to negotiate for the farm. He'll be sharp-witted. Maybe ruthless. It's likely my pose as a country bumpkin didn't deceive him, at least in retrospect, and he's regretted telling me as much as he did. It wouldn't take much for him to discover my relationship with you and decide to give me a warning.'

She wrinkled her nose. 'Too convoluted. I can see Lovejoy might regret talking to you, but if he considers you a danger, why go for me?'

'An easier target? I'm no doubt next on his list but, this time, it's a gentler warning than he'd have dished out to me, but one I'd still take to heart – if it's my girlfriend being attacked.'

'How gentle is attempting to destroy my livelihood?' she demanded, her fight returning.

'At least, you're in one piece, even if the books aren't.' He took her hand and squeezed it tightly. 'I'm not minimising the damage, Flora. I know how bad this must feel for you.'

'It's shaken me,' she admitted. 'To think that someone would destroy books...' It was an act of savagery she found impossible to contemplate. 'And I'm fearful, too. We've barely started this investigation and already I'm being threatened.'

'Fearful is not good.' He ran his fingers along the window seat cushion while she stared ahead.

Minutes passed before he asked, 'Would you like me to move into the cottage for a while?'

Flora hesitated. Part of her felt warm and secure at the thought, but another part – the part she listened to most often – told her she'd be making too much of a commitment.

'Think of the talk, Jack,' she said lightly, getting up to begin on the thankless task of clearing the mess. 'We'd never live it down.'

'I take it that's a no,' he said drily. 'I'd best be off then. I'll leave you to wield the dustpan and brush.'

At the door, he turned. 'Make sure you get Michael to change the lock.' His expression was serious. 'And make it today!'

10

Alice's cottage was, if anything, smaller than Flora's, sandwiched between a narrow flint and brick house, and a small, incongruously modern, office block. Alice's immediate neighbours had received a direct hit during the war, a stray missile finding its way from a German bomber on its return from a raid on London. Instead of rebuilding the cottage, the owner had opted to sell the land for office space and it now housed an architect's practice on the ground floor and above, Colin Palmer and his land agency.

Jack had been unsure whether to accept Alice's invitation, knowing what a tight circle the three women formed. Friday evening was their time to eat together, to exchange news and discuss whatever local gossip was making the rounds. Attending one of their suppers felt uncomfortably like gate-crashing. But Flora had insisted he come, if only to keep her from saying something she shouldn't.

He'd telephoned her the evening they'd discovered the ruined books. At first, he'd thought of calling at her cottage that night but, having donned jacket and fedora, thought better of it. Sometimes Flora was best left to her own company, working her way through whatever was upsetting her. He wasn't going to minimise the damage she'd suffered. The loss of books could be written off, but it was the invasive nature of the attack that he knew would hurt most. The sense of being violated.

The fact that the entire village was discussing the incident only made it worse. He realised how true that was when the first words from Charlie, who'd come by after school to begin their spring planting, had been, 'Cor, Mr C, have you heard about the bookshop? Loadsa books torn to bits. Poor Miss Steele.'

'Yes, poor Miss Steele.' He'd put a hand on the boy's shoulder in a gesture of solidarity. 'It's going to be difficult for her. Maybe, when you collect Betty for deliveries this week, you'd best not mention it.'

Charlie nodded, his face serious. 'She loves that shop, don't she?'

'She does,' Jack had agreed. 'Now, what do we plant first?'

Forcing himself from his reverie, he lifted a hand to knock at the cottage door, only to have it swing back and reveal Alice waiting for him.

'Come on in. Flora's already here,' she said. 'In the sitting room. I've set the table there – the kitchen's far too small.'

The room in which Alice had chosen to host the engagement party already felt crowded, barely large enough to contain the four people standing awkwardly amid a jumble of furniture, most of which, he'd learned from Flora, had belonged to Alice's parents. Kate was by the window, Tony hovering behind, and Sally Jenner, Alice's niece, was setting the table – he hadn't known she'd been invited.

Walking straight over to the happy couple, he held out his hand. 'Congratulations to you both. It's very good news.'

He wasn't sure if it was and Flora definitely didn't think so, but it was the conventional thing to say, and Jack was hoping the evening would go smoothly. Making his way over to Flora warming her hands by the fire, he gave her a surreptitious hug. 'I had to say something,' he murmured.

Before Flora could respond, their hostess bustled in, carrying a large white platter. 'Sit yourselves down,' she urged. 'I thought we'd start with these.'

Sally leaned over to peer at the dish her aunt had placed in the centre of the table. 'What are they?' she asked, shaking her head in puzzlement. 'They look good,' she added, quick to see Alice's pursed lips.

'They're tartlets,' their cook announced. 'Coronation chicken. Everyone knows the recipe, but I've gone one better and used it to fill small pastry cases.'

Jack was glad they were small. He'd eaten enough Coronation chicken to last him a lifetime – all that curry and chilli and tomato purée – but in Alice's hands, it proved a wholly different dish.

'Delicious,' he said, taking his first bite.

'Tony, love, can you open the wine? A special wine.' Her cheeks were pink with pleasure. 'Liebfraumilch,' she pronounced, struggling to read the bottle's label.

It was now 'Tony, love,' Jack noted. Tony, as Alice's sous chef at the Priory Hotel, was usually referred to as 'that Tony' when he wasn't performing as his chief required.

Taking another tartlet, Jack asked what he hoped was an innocuous question. 'How's the hotel faring this spring, Sally?'

'At the moment, we're doing well, but...' Her spiky blond curls got another shake.

'But?'

'I can't say I'm not worried for the future. This business with the Martins' old farm. There are so many stories doing the rounds. First, it was going to be a hostel, then it became a super posh hotel. Now I've heard it may be a nursing home. If it does turn out to be another hotel, we'll be hit badly.'

'You shouldn't worry about that.' Alice levered herself to her feet and collected their empty plates. 'It's all talk. It will never happen. We'll still be cooking for the five thousand, come Christmas, eh, Tony?'

'I hope you're right, Auntie.'

Jack said nothing and saw that Flora had her eyes fixed intently on the linen tablecloth. At this stage, it wouldn't be helpful to share what they'd learned at Bramber Hall, the Nevilles' clear intention to build the hotel Sally feared. The girl owned the Priory together with Dominic Lister and, for both of them, it had been a rocky start. Dominic hadn't been invited this evening, but that hadn't surprised Jack. These days, the man's relationship with Sally was strictly business.

'So...' Looking across at Kate, Sally changed the conversation, a determined smile on her face. 'Have you fixed a date yet?'

'Not yet, no,' Kate replied quietly.

Even to Jack's inexperienced ear, she sounded a little uncertain. Was Flora right? he wondered. Had Kate agreed to marry too quickly?

'For now, we're enjoying the engagement, aren't we?' she asked, turning to Tony seated beside her.

He smiled back and Jack relaxed. They had a sporting chance, he thought, recalling his own ill-fated liaison. He couldn't remember Helen ever saying she was enjoying the engagement. It had been a wedding she'd wanted, and as soon as possible. But when the date arrived, it turned out that it wasn't what she wanted after all, not once the plans for an elaborate English ceremony were in place. Or rather, she may still have wanted the wedding, but not him.

'Myself, I always think a summer weddin' is best.' Alice walked back into the sitting room carrying a sizzling joint of ham, decorated with pineapple rings.

'Oh, come on! What do you know about weddings, Auntie?' Sally asked. Alice's already pink cheeks reddened further.

'More'n you, young lady. I've been on this earth fifty-five years and seen what's what. If you want to do something useful, rather than make silly comments, you can fetch the veg from the kitchen.'

Alice's tone was unusually sharp, and Jack sensed Flora's discomfort. She'd said very little this evening and he could see she remained deeply unhappy. Percy's death and the attack on her beloved bookshop had been difficult to cope with. But it was also the awkwardness of celebrating an engagement she felt was wrong. He wasn't surprised when she jumped up to say, 'I'll go,' and made for the kitchen.

'You're right, Alice,' Tony agreed, attempting to smooth the waters. 'Summer is a lovely season to marry. Trouble is, it's also very busy. I'm not sure we'd have the time to put on the wedding breakfast we'd want.'

Alice gave a little shrug and followed Flora into the kitchen from where Jack heard a low muttering. Evidently, she was sharing her grievance but, when the two of them returned, Flora bearing a heavy tray, their hostess appeared mollified.

'Alice has done us proud,' Flora announced, unloading a dish of duchess potatoes and a huge bowl of pea, mint and spinach salad.

'This is so good of you.' Kate's gentle voice set the tone and Alice, good-natured as always, said a final goodbye to any irritation she still harboured. 'You deserve it, my love. It's not every day we have an engagement in Abbeymead.' She looked meaningfully at Flora.

'I met a strange-looking fellow in the village this week,' Jack said quickly. 'A Sidney Lovejoy. He's staying at the Cross Keys. Anyone know him?'

It was worth asking. One of the people around this table might have more to tell than the meagre amount he'd so far discovered.

'I saw him at that meeting.' Alice carved slices of ham from the joint and began filling their plates. 'You couldn't miss him. Odd-looking chap like you say, Jack.'

'Percy's meeting?' The mention of Percy Milburn had energised Flora.

'The one that Winifred Ticehurst called.' Alice's greying head bobbed vigorously. 'I don't go to the village hall that much, but I was keen that evenin'. Lily Martin would have wanted me there. It's her home that's being fought over, after all.'

She plumped herself down and sat staring hard at the table. 'I didn't speak to the man, but I did hear about him. From the new landlord at the Cross Keys,' she said unexpectedly. '*His* name's Timpson. That kitchen maid of mine has a sister who wants to work at the pub, and Mr Timpson asked me about the family. Wanted to get an idea about the girl before she turned up for an interview.'

'And Lovejoy?' Flora asked.

'Generous, Timpson said. A good tipper, apparently, so all the waiters want to serve him. I didn't think solicitors were that well off. That's what he is, according to Timpson. He says he's been no trouble. Except...' She paused. 'He got very agitated about a phone call he missed. Started rantin' and ravin', which the landlord found a bit strange. Up to then he'd been as quiet as a mouse, and then suddenly he's creatin' hullabaloo.'

'It must have been an important call that he missed,' Flora remarked, glancing in Jack's direction.

'Who'd know? After that, he insisted on usin' the telephone in the landlord's office. He'd make calls out, Roger Timpson said, but no one called him. Not after that missed call. Timpson thinks he's negotiatin' some kind of deal.'

'He wants to buy the Martins' farm, now Mr Milburn isn't around,' Jack threw in, wondering if it would produce a spark. He had no idea how long Lovejoy's offer had been on the table, but it was safer to pretend the bid had been made after Percy's death. A competing offer suggested conflict and a motive for murder – it was what he and Flora needed to probe, but no one else.

'Sir Frederick still wants to sell?' Tony asked.

'It seems so.'

'They'll go ahead with the hotel, you'll see.' Sally's voice had a bitter edge to it.

'Maybe not.' Jack tried to lessen the blow. 'Piers Neville seems particularly keen on the idea, but I'm not sure his uncle will go for it.'

He *had* sensed a reluctance on the older man's part, even while Sir Frederick had talked of how much the estate cost to run. Unless the man was certain a hotel would be a money spinner, Jack didn't think he would agree.

'If Piers Neville has anything to do with a hotel, it will be a disaster.' Tony chuckled.

'You know him?' Flora's gaze was once more alert.

'Anybody who's been in catering knows him. Leastways, in the south of England. He's a bit of a joke.'

'Really? He seemed very sure of himself,' she said. Agreed, Jack echoed silently.

'He's younger than me.' Tony gave a small grin. 'But he's run through any number of businesses already – a café, a tearoom, a cocktail bar. There may be more but they're the ones I know of, and they've all failed.'

'Is he still running a business?'

To Jack, this seemed crucial. The man should surely have been made a bankrupt by now, which meant he'd be unable to obtain credit and be unlikely to manage a luxury hotel.

'There's a rumour,' Tony said carefully, 'perhaps more than a rumour, that he's had his debts paid off each time.'

'You think Sir Frederick bailed him out?' Flora fidgeted in her seat, a sign Jack knew that she thought this significant. Alan Ridley had said as much, he remembered, in the pub.

'I guess.' Tony put down his knife and fork. 'But you have to wonder how many more times he'll get away with it. If he has anything to do with a hotel, it'll be a mess.'

'And Sir Frederick will have another failure on his hands,' she finished.

'Let's hope so.' This was from Sally.

'It's common knowledge his uncle is always havin' to rescue him.' Alice spooned a last portion of duchess potatoes onto her plate. 'The boy got himself into trouble several years back – apart from bein' hopeless at business – and we all reckoned it was Sir Frederick who got him out of it.'

'What kind of trouble?'

'Some fight he got into,' Alice said vaguely. 'It's not as if his uncle even likes the boy or makes any bones about it. Mind you, from what I recall, he didn't much like Piers' father either and he was his own brother.'

Flora pushed away her plate. 'That was scrumptious, Alice. Where is Piers' father? I know Sir Frederick's son died in the war, but his brother? He should be the heir, shouldn't he?'

'He died, too.' Alice said matter-of-factly. 'So many of 'em, poor young men. Rupert Neville joined the RAF as soon as he could and paid the price. Shot down in the Battle of Britain. But you had to admire him. He went his own way, refused to be his brother's pensioner.'

'Neville has suffered a great deal of loss in his life,' Jack remarked, wondering how much that might influence present decisions.

'Well...' Alice's tone was judicious. 'He wasn't close to his brother, but losin' his son was a different matter. Stayed holed up in that big house for months. I s'pose you couldn't blame him. No son, no wife. She disappeared after the boy died. That must have been the final straw.'

'Gosh!' Flora exclaimed. 'He's led a far more dramatic life than I had any idea of. What happened to his wife?'

'No one knows for sure, but...' She lowered her voice.

'Rumour?' Flora prompted.

'Most folks think she's in a nursin' home somewhere. Had a breakdown after her son died but nobody knows what happened after that. She could be dead. There's some who suggested her husband might be responsible for her disappearin'.' Alice raised her eyebrows high. 'He wouldn't be the easiest person to live with, I reckon.'

'As Piers will no doubt find out, if he's hitched his wagon to this new project,' Jack murmured.

'He might make Sir Frederick testy, but the boy's his heir and he's had to accept it.'

Flora began to stack the empty plates, despite Alice's frantic waving at her to stop. 'If what Tony says is true and Piers has already lost a good deal of money, most of it his uncle's, I can't see why he'd be allowed to get anywhere near the Birds Acre scheme.'

'I don't think we should talk any more about the Nevilles,' Sally said firmly. 'We're here to toast our newly engaged couple and wish them well.'

'Hear, hear.' Alice lifted her glass in salute, followed by raised hands around the table.

'Good luck,' they chorused.

'Who knows?' Alice said slyly. 'We might soon be toastin' another couple.'

Jack saw a terrified expression flit across Flora's face. Then she was on her feet and had whisked the plates from the table and into the kitchen, returning minutes later with Alice's pièce de résistance, a Queen of Puddings.

On the walk back to Flora's cottage, Jack was careful to say nothing of weddings or even engagements. Flora had recovered her composure but that flash of fear he'd seen was very real and, while it might feel hurtful, it was also a warning.

'I think I might take a trip to London,' he said casually. 'Sidney Lovejoy is a mystery and I want to know more. According to Alice's account, he's a solicitor or a former solicitor. That means he'll have left a professional trail somewhere. It would be useful to trace it, if I can.'

'Must you go? Remember what happened the last time you took a trip to London to delve into someone's background?'

'This time when I cross the road I'll look right and left and right again,' he promised laughingly. Being mown down in broad daylight hadn't been the best experience but he was fairly sure it couldn't happen again. Could it?

11

It was lunchtime the next day and Flora was already looking forward to the evening – an early supper and several hours of reading by the fire. April was still cold enough to put a match to the logs she'd stacked in the fireplace and enjoy the smell of apple wood. Enjoy, too, the latest Ian Fleming to arrive at the All's Well, *From Russia with Love*. She couldn't approve of his hero, but the books were wonderfully exciting.

Locking the bookshop door at twelve thirty precisely, she walked across the road to Mr Preece.

'Got some nice chops for you,' the butcher greeted her, bending below the counter and producing a bundle wrapped in white paper.

'Lovely bit of lamb,' he said, passing her the package. After a rocky beginning, Mr Preece had become a good friend, always ready to offer Flora a string of fresh sausages, a tasty small joint, or the largest chops he could find.

Whisking her supper into her basket, she thanked him and said a swift goodbye. Only one more stop – the baker's – before she could cycle home. She was tired, she realised, though not quite sure why, and the thought of a quiet afternoon at the cottage was increasingly precious.

A small queue had formed at the bakery and, as Flora took her place, she almost cannoned into the figure of a young woman. A figure that seemed vaguely familiar.

Struggling to place the pale face smiling shyly at her, she was about to confess ignorance when the girl said, 'Miss Steele? You don't remember me? Prue Norland. We met at Bramber Hall but weren't formally introduced.'

'Of course. I'm sorry. I knew I must have met you but couldn't for the moment think where. I didn't realise you lived in Abbeymead.'

'I don't, in fact. I'm in Brighton, but I've been staying at the Hall and thought I'd shop for lunch before I left the village. It's not proving as easy as I thought.' She pushed back a thick fringe that came almost down to her eyebrows. 'I need bread and there doesn't seem much choice.' She gestured towards the empty shelves behind the counter.

Flora always ordered ahead for the batch loaf she had at the weekend. It was a sensible precaution since bread sold out very early on a Saturday.

'Ah well.' The girl sighed. 'I'll have to make do with a wholemeal, though Piers won't like it. Still,' she said, brightening, 'I've a chunk of cheddar and some lovely tomatoes from Mr Houseman, and a small jar of pickle, which should go down well.'

'You're taking it all back to Brighton?'

'That's right. I promised Piers I'd bring lunch with me. He's got a flat in Chadwick Road, over the newsagents there, and I'm staying with him for a while.'

'Are you going to buy something or not?' a gruff voice behind them asked. 'Some of us are busy and need to get on.'

The queue had dispersed as they'd been talking and, when

Flora turned, she saw it was Winifred Ticehurst standing immediately behind them.

'Sorry, Miss Ticehurst,' she said calmly and made for the counter, followed by a subdued Prue.

'I'll have that one, please.' Prue pointed to one of the few unsold loaves and delved into her purse for some coins. 'You're not with your friend today?' she asked Flora, as she handed them over.

'You mean Jack?'

'That's him. He looked nice.'

'He is. No, this weekend he's chained to his desk. He's off to London on Monday – a research trip – and needs to make up the time.'

'I heard he was a writer.' Prue tucked the offending wholemeal into her basket. 'Is that what he's researching?' She sounded slightly in awe.

'Not this time,' Flora said laughingly. 'He's busy with something entirely different – solving a little puzzle we have.' It was best to say no more, and she'd probably said too much already.

A hardly concealed mutter and an irritated shuffling of feet from behind had them move quickly towards the exit. It was at the doorway that Flora had a sudden thought.

'How about a cup of tea?' she asked. Conversations over tea were often fruitful. 'The afternoon bus to Brighton doesn't leave until two and Katie's Nook is just along the road.'

Prue beamed, her ivory complexion gaining a little colour. 'I'd like that.'

Kate Mitchell was clearing the café's one free table when they arrived. 'Perfect timing,' Flora exclaimed. 'Katie, this is Prue Norland. She's a visitor trying out our Abbeymead shops.'

'It's nice to meet you, Prue. Make sure you come back often!'

Katie could always be depended on to say the right thing.

She must be bursting with curiosity, wondering how Flora had come to know this girl, but was too courteous to ask.

The mention of a return to Abbeymead had Prue look uncertain and Flora wondered if she was thinking of Piers Neville. Just what was their relationship? Once they had a pot of tea and a plate of iced fancies on the table, she prodded gently.

'Do you work with Piers?'

'Oh no!' The girl gave a loud giggle and once more swept her fringe back from her face, revealing those beautiful almond-shaped eyes. 'Sorry for that,' she apologised, 'but I'm an actress and the thought of Piers performing on stage is too comic for words.'

'An actress? That sounds exciting.'

'Most of the time, it isn't,' Prue confessed. 'I have to take all kinds of jobs to make a living, but when I get a part that I love and I'm on stage being that character, it makes me so happy.' Her languid figure had come alive as she spoke.

'You met Piers at one of your shows?' Flora hazarded.

'That's right. I had a small part in *Grab Me a Gondola* at the Lyric. Do you know it? Piers was in the audience and after-wards he came backstage and waited for me. I had no idea who he was. Imagine how I felt when he told me his uncle was *Sir* Frederick Neville.'

'Shocked, I should think. And seeing Bramber Hall for the first time... it's a very large house, and beautiful.'

'I was only there one night,' she said wistfully. 'The day you visited. Piers doesn't much like staying at the Hall. He prefers the flat.'

'I expect he likes his independence,' Flora suggested, hoping it might prove a temptation to talk.

Prue bit her lip. 'Yes, that's probably it. But Piers... he's a complex person, you know. A lovely man, don't get me wrong but...'

'Difficult?'

'Yes,' she said gratefully. 'He can be. At the moment, he's very tense. He so wants to get his new project off the ground. The farm,' she explained. 'But you know about Birds Acre, of course. Personally, I wish it had never been built, there's been so much unpleasantness over it.'

'How's that?' Flora looked interested. She was interested.

'Piers doesn't get on with his uncle too well,' her companion said carefully, 'but he was sure that he and Sir Frederick had an arrangement. His uncle was to sell the farm to someone who would build a wonderful hotel.'

'Which Piers would manage.'

'Exactly. But now, Sir Frederick seems to be wavering. The man he's been negotiating with, Sidney somebody or other, has suggested there might be more money on offer if Sir Frederick dropped the idea of a hotel.'

'Really? How strange.' It seemed decidedly odd to Flora. What would be the point of buying the farm and keeping it as it was, unless the unknown buyer was thinking of turning farmer? And wasn't a future hotel to provide a stream of income for the Neville estate?

'I know.' Prue's expression was tragic. 'And Piers is so... so driven. He's desperate for this hotel to be built and says if his uncle won't honour their agreement, he'll buy the farm and build it himself. Then he'd be the owner and not just the manager.'

'That would take a lot of money,' Flora said cautiously.

The girl's mouth closed tight, and she sat in silence for some minutes, stirring her tea mechanically, until she burst out, 'It's money that Piers doesn't have.' In a quieter voice, she added, 'He doesn't have a great record. I can tell you that, Miss Steele, I know you won't repeat it.'

'I won't, but call me Flora.'

Prue gave a faint smile at the invitation. 'Piers has had a

string of failures, that's the problem. None of them his fault, I'm sure, but it means it's almost impossible for him to borrow money to fund the project he's set his heart on.'

'That is a problem,' Flora agreed.

There was another silence, before the girl said, 'I think he may do something foolish.'

Flora raised her eyebrows. 'Such as?'

When Prue spoke, it was with difficulty, her voice barely above a murmur. 'He says he has something on his uncle. Something, if it were made public, that would be very bad for Sir Frederick.'

'You're saying that he knows something detrimental to Sir Frederick and will use it to get what he wants?'

The girl nodded, looking down at the table.

'That's blackmail, Prue.'

'Yes... I know... but I hope he won't.' There was true misery in her voice. 'The trouble is that he's so wound up, he could do something stupid. Go for broke, if you know what I mean.'

Had Piers done something else that was stupid? was Flora's immediate thought. Gone for broke already, by killing Percy Milburn and eliminating his main competitor for the farm?

'It makes me feel quite sick with worry.' Prue put her cup down with a sharp clack.

'I'm sure it must. Can't you persuade him that it would be foolhardy? He would be committing a criminal act, as well as being morally repugnant.'

The young woman gave a sad shake of her head. 'Piers isn't someone you can persuade, I've discovered. Not when he wants something badly. I feel sorry for him, Flora. He's not a bad man and that's why I've tried to help him. I know he doesn't seem it, but he's desperately insecure and this hotel idea – I think it's all to do with showing his stepfather he can be as successful.'

'And his stepfather is?'

'Trevor Duchamp. You might have heard of Duchamps? It's

an advertising agency his stepfather started after he left the RAF. The airlines are his main customers, I think, and he's become very wealthy. Piers hates him.'

'That's a strong word. Why would he hate? Has Mr Duchamp done him harm?'

'For Piers he has. He took his mother away!'

Flora took some time to respond and, while she was thinking what best to say, Katie arrived at their table, ready to clear the crockery. She was halfway through loading her tray with teapot and empty cups when, suddenly, she started back, teaspoons rattling in their saucers.

'What's the matter?' Flora asked. There'd been a look of panic on Kate's face.

'That man,' she said. 'Right up against the glass and staring in here. I saw him as I looked up – it gave me a fearful shock.'

Flora turned her head to look through the café window. Straining to see, she glimpsed a stocky figure walking rapidly along the high street and very soon disappearing from view.

'I only saw the back of him,' she said, turning to Kate. 'I suppose it was no one you recognised?'

'I've never seen him before,' Kate asserted, 'but sorry I squawked. He appeared so suddenly that he scared me. Stupid really. He was probably just checking if there was a table free.'

'Probably,' Flora agreed, while thinking quite differently. An unknown man on the prowl in a small village was yet another cause for disquiet.

12

Jack decided to take the train to London rather than trust the Austin to make the fifty or so miles without breaking down. He loved his car with a passion but had to admit its limitations. Lately, there'd been an occasional knocking coming from deep within the engine and, though the mechanic at Glittins had been unable to find any fault, it made Jack uneasy.

On the train, he debated where he should go first and plumped for Holborn, a part of London associated with the legal profession since medieval times. He'd head for Chancery Lane and the main library of the Law Society, which he knew held annual directories recording the name of every solicitor the year after he, and it was most likely a 'he', had been admitted to the roll. Consulting the law lists should, at least, tell him whether or not Sidney Lovejoy was what he said he was.

From Victoria station, he took the number eleven bus, enjoying a leisurely trip along Whitehall, across Trafalgar Square and past the Royal Courts of Justice. An expansive iron-work arch sporting the Law Society's magnificent crest was his first sight of one hundred and thirteen Chancery Lane – it was not a modest building. Walking beneath and up the steps to the main entrance, he passed between two enormous pillars, which, in turn, supported an equally enormous pediment. It was an edifice that would have found itself happy in ancient Greece.

Once inside, he made for the upper floor, climbing the mile of red-carpeted staircase with ease. The library, when he reached it, appeared almost as grand as the façade. Another set of pillars, slimmer this time and painted red with gold finials, straddled the chamber, with reading desks of English oak filling the central space. Bookshelves crowded every inch of the four walls. Jack knew from his days in journalism that the library's collection of law books was immense, some of them dating as far back as the sixteenth century. Feet above him, a wooden gallery ran around the perimeter of the room, giving access to row after row of leather-bound volumes: directories, ledgers, a host of documents of which he had no idea. He stood back and took stock. The sight was certainly dazzling, but he would need help.

A stray librarian was making for the gallery and, moving swiftly, Jack intercepted him to ask for directions.

'Sorry to interrupt,' he began, 'but I wonder... could you point me to the law lists? I'm looking for volumes that would cover 1929 to '39.'

Lovejoy, he reckoned, was around fifty and this was a rough estimate of when he might have started practising. Jack didn't think the man would have qualified earlier and 1939, with war declared, would have made it difficult for him to finish his studies any later.

'I can.' The man responded with a smile. 'Are you looking for someone with a practice in London or in the country?'

Jack didn't hesitate. Lovejoy's conversation had made it clear where his affections lay. 'In London,' he said immediately.

Asking for directions was one thing but searching through the weighty tomes he'd had pointed out was quite another. He trawled through every list for the years he'd opted for, then continued to search the years immediately before and following.

But not one mention of Lovejoy did he find. Had the man adopted an assumed name in Abbeymead? They'd had recent experience of that in the village. If so, tracing him would be a hopeless task.

Reshelving the last volume, Jack went in search of his friendly librarian and found him at his desk.

The man glanced up as he approached. 'Did you find what you were looking for?'

'Unfortunately, not. Tell me, if a solicitor doesn't appear in a list, what might be the reason?'

'He could have retired, or died,' the man said. Neither seemed likely.

'Or he could have been struck off,' he added.

That was far more possible. Either that or Lovejoy had never been a solicitor in the first place.

So far, so stuck, he muttered to himself, walking down the steps and into Chancery Lane again. He knew this area well; it was a stone's throw from Fleet Street where he'd spent more hours than he liked to remember. Fleet Street. The *Daily Mercury*. He'd go there! Ross Sadler might be at work today and, if he were, he'd be happy to help an old colleague.

Ten minutes later, Jack was standing outside the Georgian exterior of the *Mercury*. Along with every other newspaper that inhabited the street, the building could not have looked more different from the one he'd just left. Four storeys of dirty red brick, myriad dusty windows, a half-hidden entrance, and all the time the incessant noise of cars and buses and taxi cabs chugging by.

Having been recognised by the porter on the desk, an old friend of his, Jack was free to walk unaccompanied into the newsroom. There was noise here, too, though very different. A hubbub that he'd once found exhilarating.

Standing in the doorway, he was transported back in time. Reporters rushed in and out, phones shrilled, and the percussive rattle of typewriters provided a constant rhythmic background. In a secluded alcove, a small army of scissor-wielding librarians ploughed through every national newspaper, cutting out articles, however large or small, and filing them away in brown paper envelopes to join all the previous stories on the topic. There had been files on every subject under the sun, Jack remembered.

Memories flooded back. Forgotten feelings surfaced. The frantic race to meet impending deadlines, the stress of 'phoning in' an article, a copytaker typing your words into the office mainframe as you dictated down the line and leaving you with the fervent hope that he'd heard you aright. Jack had soon learned it was safer to deliver longer features by hand.

Learned, too, that it was good practice to work in the office whenever you could, not only for its immense sociability but for the professional rewards it could offer. You might bump into a clutch of editors and, ten to one, another story would land in your lap. Or a colleague would march you to the pub and there you'd meet people, who'd tell you stuff over a drink they'd never tell you over the phone. It was a truism of journalism, happening not only in the pubs off Fleet Street, but in the bars of Milan or Sydney or New York. For a crime reporter, it was gold dust.

He found Ross Sadler halfway down the newsroom, head bent, his hands flying across the keyboard.

Sensing a figure at his desk, Ross looked up, then leapt to his feet. 'If it isn't Carrington in person! It's good to see you, Jack.'

'And to see you, too. I won't keep you long, Ross, I promise. I know how busy you must be.'

'Nonsense. This is a long-running investigation.' He waved a hand at the typewriter. 'At the moment, I feel I've been living and breathing the case for my entire life. I'm more than glad of an interruption. But here, take a seat.' He dragged a spare chair up to his desk. 'So... I bet you didn't travel up from

Sussex just to see my pretty face. Can't leave crime alone, is that it?'

'It seems so.' Jack gave a wry grimace. 'These days, I'm either writing it or living it.'

'Can't be bad. Who's our villain today?'

'I'm unsure if he is a villain – for now, at least. Ever heard of a Sidney Lovejoy when you've attended court? He says he's a solicitor, but he's not listed as practising.'

'Lovejoy?' He frowned. 'It's not a common name and it's ringing some kind of bell. He's no longer a solicitor, you say?'

'It seems so. Or he never was one. I've checked with the Law Society and there's no record of him.'

'Why the interest?' Ross leaned back in his chair and flicked a pen through his fingers.

One of the new biros, Jack noticed. 'He's being employed in a negotiation to buy property in Sussex.'

'Employed by whom?'

'That's the point. Questionable people, I suspect.'

'Lovejoy, Lovejoy... yes, you're right! They would be dodgy. He got kicked out, I believe. I remember now. It was the Chilworth case – there was a fake document granting probate and forged signatures on conveyancing forms. That was Lovejoy.'

'Do you know what happened to him after he was struck off?'

'Not much. I saw him in a pub in Chancery Lane once. Drunk as a lord.'

'He must have had money to drink like that.'

'Who knows? He looked like he was on his beam ends.'

Jack thought for a while. These days, Lovejoy might be eccentric in his appearance, but he certainly didn't look to be in extreme poverty. Had someone rescued him?

'What about a man called Tyler? Does he ring bells?'

His friend stared at him. 'I'd say so. Dennis Tyler. The

name should ring a few with you. Don't you recall? About ten years ago, just after we'd stopped playing soldiers. Though...' He paused. 'You might not have returned by then. It could have been just before you were demobbed.'

'Tell me.'

'There was a brawl in a south London pub, two rival gangs, one of them led by Tyler. A turf war that erupted in an all-out fight with several men badly injured and one cold in the morgue. Someone had been carrying a knife and used it.'

'And that was Tyler?' Jack's changeable grey eyes grew dark. This was becoming uncomfortably serious.

'It was the general assumption, but no one was ever charged. The defence swore that Tyler wasn't even in the pub that night and his mates told the same story. In the end, the police had insufficient evidence to charge him. Two of Tyler's mob were jailed for grievous bodily harm, but they'd be out of prison by now.'

'Where was Tyler supposed to be when this brawl was taking place?'

'The defence produced a couple of witnesses to swear that at the crucial time they saw Tyler drinking in a club miles away.'

'These witnesses? Were they credible?'

'Upstanding citizens. Neither had a criminal record and the police had no way of getting them to admit they were lying.'

Jack leaned forward. 'But you reckon they were. They were paid?'

'Almost certainly. And...' Ross paused again, running a hand through his sandy hair. 'An interesting fact? Unusually, it was Tyler's solicitor who defended him and not a barrister... Lovejoy. It was Sidney Lovejoy.'

Jack pushed back his chair, getting up to look out of the window and then pacing up and down for several minutes. 'Let me get this right,' he said at last. 'You're suggesting that Lovejoy magicked up the two witnesses, bought their testimony, and saved Tyler from a murder charge?'

'That's about it.'

He took a seat again, his expression brooding. 'It's safe to assume then that Tyler owed him some recompense.'

'I'd say so.'

'Then how did Lovejoy end in such a mess?'

'Because of an entirely different case. Like I say, the Chilworth business. That time, he was found out, and a bent solicitor is useful only as long as he remains a solicitor. Once Lovejoy was struck off, he lost his value.'

'Yet right now he's prancing around Abbeymead, merry as a cricket. He's been staying at the Cross Keys for nearly a month. It's not a particularly expensive hostelry but it's not cheap either.'

'It will be on somebody else's money. Tyler's money? He won't be funded out of loyalty, though – Lovejoy will be a bought man. He'll be acting under some kind of duress. Tyler will want something from him, for sure. In this case, from what you say, it's a chunk of Sussex.'

'And maybe he's prepared to murder for it,' Jack said softly. 'Or get his minion to murder. But why? That's what I don't understand. This brawl... it was ten years ago. Do you reckon he could be a reformed character? It sounds crazy, but apparently Tyler is heading a consortium of so-called businessmen to buy a farm just outside my village.'

Ross laughed. 'He's about to turn farmer?'

'Not farming. The intention is to build an upmarket hotel.'

'Perhaps he means to run it as a charity for old lags,' his friend said, still laughing.

'Or it could be legitimate.' Why he was clinging to this hope, Jack didn't know.

Sadler was shaking his head. 'If Tyler is involved, it won't be. Whatever you've got your nose into, Jack, my advice is to pull back. The man runs with a dangerous mob.'

'But does he still?'

'If you find out, let me know. But be careful.'

The suggestion that a London gang might be behind the new offer on Birds Acre was unwelcome, if not frightening. What would a man who'd led a gang ten years ago want with a parcel of Sussex countryside? Why would he want to build a hotel? They were questions Jack had no answer for. What was clear was that Sidney Lovejoy had long been an unscrupulous solicitor and would be an ideal choice to negotiate with Sir Frederick Neville, a man with little understanding of the sphere in which Tyler and his associates operated. Tyler, meanwhile, could remain hidden in the shadows.

Jack needed to get back to Sussex as soon as possible and tell Flora what he'd discovered. He couldn't risk her jumping in, pursuing one of her mad spurts of imagination, and tangling with the kind of men who were behind Lovejoy. He'd take a taxi from Worthing station, he decided, and blow the expense. He could get the cabbie to drop him at Flora's cottage. The sooner he could warn her, the better.

13

It was dusk when Flora heard a knock on the front door. These last few days, she'd felt apprehensive – ever since Prue Norland had confessed her fear that Piers was prepared to blackmail in order to get what he wanted. The thought that he'd already done much worse loomed large in Flora's mind. The image of Percy, helpless and drowning, was a constant, and the need to find his murderer more urgent than ever. Apprehensive, too, when she recalled the unknown man who had stared at them through the window of the Nook. He'd seemed threatening enough to make Kate, normally a model of calm, utter a scream. Who was this man and what did he want with the café? Did he have any connection to what had happened to Percy or what was unfolding over Birds Acre Farm?

A second knock had Flora straighten her shoulders and go to the door but opening it a bare inch.

'It's me, Flora. Who were you expecting?'

Jack! And sounding amused. Annoyed with herself at appearing so timid, Flora tugged the door fully open. 'I didn't expect you tonight,' she defended herself.

'OK, but why the peering round the door?'

'I didn't peer. I was being cautious.'

'It must be the first time in your life!'

Refusing his invitation to spar, she led the way into the kitchen. 'I'll make tea – as long as you behave.'

'How could I not?' Jack stripped off his jacket and found an empty chair for his beloved fedora. 'Tea? I could do with something stronger. It's been a punishing day.'

'Tea is all I have,' she said firmly, 'but I can make it super strong. Will that do?'

By the time they were settled in the sitting room and had drunk their second cup, Flora had recounted her conversation with Prue Norland and mentioned the apparition at the café.

Jack took another custard cream from the tray. 'I'm sorry, I'm going to eat you out of biscuits. I've just realised how hungry I am.'

'What do you think then?' she asked impatiently.

'I can see why you're nervous.'

'I'm not nervous,' she pushed back. 'Well, maybe a little. The thing is... I don't understand anything about this case. There seem to be more crimes and more suspects every day. Now I've Piers Neville to worry about. He says he knows something bad about Sir Frederick. Could he have been at Birds Acre that afternoon and seen something he shouldn't?'

'Like his uncle murdering Percy Milburn?'

'Exactly. Or maybe the two are in cahoots and he helped Sir Frederick do it, but now his uncle won't agree to what he wants, Piers has turned against him.'

'The blackmail could be a bluff, a threat to pull the house down on both their heads. If Piers *was* at the farm that afternoon, he could be the killer and Sir Frederick the one who is covering for him,' Jack said through a mouthful of biscuit.

Flora shifted in her seat. 'That's what I mean. It's a complete mess, there are too many questions. But whichever way we look at it, the Nevilles are a problem.' She put her empty cup down. 'Is it only money that's driving Sir Frederick to sell? Is Piers working with his uncle or against him? Then there's Sidney Lovejoy. Was he at the farm, too? He could easily have walked from the village and left no trace that he'd ever been there. If he knew that Sir Frederick was looking for a way out of the agreement he'd made with Percy, Lovejoy could clear a path by getting rid of the poor man.'

'I can't see Lovejoy as a killer,' Jack argued. 'A liar, a defrauder, yes, but not a killer.'

'Why not? If for some reason he was desperate for the sale to go through... if the purchase was crucial for his client.' She sat back in her chair again. 'And who is his client?'

'Now that's where I can be useful.' Jack leant back himself, relaxing into one of Flora's fireside chairs. Really, he should buy one of these – it would look good with the armchair he'd bought last autumn. Perhaps two, if the current novel was successful. Flora was always complaining about his lumpy sofa – fireside chairs would be beyond reproach.

'I've a good idea now who Lovejoy is representing. You won't like it – it could make you more nervous.'

Ten minutes later, after hearing Jack's account of what he'd learned at the Law Society and, afterwards, from Ross Sadler, there was no doubt about it. Flora was feeling a good deal more nervous.

'A London gangster?' she said. 'In Abbeymead. *He* could have been at the farm. *He* could have killed Percy.'

'As a way of helping negotiations along?'

'Anything is possible. But what would a man like that want with Birds Acre?'

'It's a question I've been asking myself all the way from London. It's such a bizarre proposition that I wonder if I've called it right. Lovejoy mentioned Tyler but maybe the name was to throw me off the scent. Maybe he's working for someone else entirely.'

Flora pounced. 'The man at the café window. I bet that was Tyler!'

'Possibly, though why he'd be interested in the Nook...'

'It's "why" all the way, isn't it? Why, for instance, were my books destroyed? Did it have anything to do with this man? There are too many oddities, Jack. Too many arbitrary events. Usually by this stage, one or two strands are beginning to make sense, but not this time. It seems as though anything might happen at any time. It's making me feel unsafe.'

Jack leaned across and took her hand. 'It's not like you to be so anxious.' When she said nothing, he squeezed her hand more tightly. 'The situation isn't great, I agree. Why don't I...?' He paused, trying she realised to come up with the right words. 'Why don't I stay tonight?'

For once, she didn't hesitate. Jack was a protective shield, a loving shield, and a great deal more. 'Yes, I'd like that,' she said and, jumping up, landed a kiss on his lips.

Jack was in the bathroom the next morning, ruefully surveying the stubble that he'd have to live with until he was back at Overlay House, when he was startled by a yell. Not a loud one, it was true, but a yell, nevertheless.

Flora! He rushed downstairs, wiping his hands on a towel as he went. She was standing at the sitting room window, looking out at her front garden.

'What's the matter? What on earth's happened?'

She said nothing but simply pointed. He saw the hazel eyes he loved fill with tears and looked where she'd pointed. His gaze turned into an appalled stare. A tree, her favourite rowan, had been hacked to pieces, the entire middle section naked of branches or foliage. Timber lay strewn across the square of grass and what was left of its trunk disfigured by slashes from an axe.

He put his arms around her, cradling her for several minutes before she broke free.

'Aunt Violet planted that tree when we first arrived,' she said shakily. 'She loved it. I loved it. It was so beautiful.'

It was useless to tell her they could plant another. The tree was precious for reasons that had nothing to do with horticulture. He couldn't replace what was irreplaceable.

She turned a stricken face to him. 'Who is doing this to me? First the books I love, now the tree.'

Jack had no answer. All he could do was literally pick up the pieces. When he left her this morning, he'd walk to the Teagues' house, he decided, and leave a message for Charlie, asking the boy to help him after school, tomorrow or the next day. Together, they could clear the worst of the mess, which was cluttering a large part of the front garden. His young mentor might even have advice on whether there was any way they could encourage the rowan to shoot afresh. In the end, Jack feared, it might be better to be cruel than kind and have the entire tree cut down.

It was clear now that Flora had become a target, but whether it was connected to their investigation of Percy Milburn's murder, as he'd originally thought, he couldn't be sure. After the carnage at the bookshop, he remembered saying the perpetrator had gone for what might seem the easier prey – Flora – but that he expected to be next on their list. It appeared he'd been wrong. They hadn't been watching him after all. They'd been watching Flora and now they'd punished her.

For what, though? It made no sense. There had to be something else at work here, something that bore no connection to the murder. He could just about swallow the idea that the killer had stolen Flora's key to the All's Well and destroyed her books as a warning to them both of continuing with the Milburn investigation. But could he really believe this same person had crept into her front garden in the dead of night and taken an axe to a tree she loved? That was the point. She loved it and someone knew that and had set out to create maximum hurt. Had Flora upset one of the villagers? It was possible. Her candour, the way she spoke her mind, was something he loved about her. But not everyone did and perhaps her frank speaking had caused anger that Flora hadn't recognised, and this was the result.

After a subdued breakfast, Jack telephoned Alan Ridley, hoping to find him in his office at the Brighton police station. He was lucky. The inspector was plodding through a morning of paper-work and was only too glad to listen to Jack's news. He was particularly interested in Tyler.

'It makes sense,' he said thoughtfully.

'I'm glad you think so,' Jack retorted a trifle acidly. 'To me, it's making no sense whatever.'

'Ah, that's because you haven't the information to hand that I have. A while back, I heard from Scotland Yard. They've had success in breaking up several of the London gangs and the ruffians apparently are on the move. We were warned to look out for them, guard our own patch, as it were.'

'What guarding did you do?' Jack was still ruffled.

'None,' the inspector said cheerfully. 'There have been no crimes I can pin on them. And this Tyler – you say he's keen to buy a local farm – he could be going straight, I suppose. It's ten years since he's been in any trouble, or any trouble we know about.'

'Is it likely?'

'Innocent before proved guilty, Jack. But no, it's not likely. He's definitely dodgy. I had a call from Constable Tring yester-day. Some argy-bargy at the Cross Keys. The landlord – Timp-son, that was his name – telephoned Tring in a real state. Some bloke had come into the pub asking for Sidney Lovejoy. He wanted to know the chap's room number, but Timpson refused to pass it on. He offered instead to take a note for Lovejoy. When that wasn't good enough, there was a nasty fracas.'

'Tyler?' Jack said immediately. Tyler had been searching for Lovejoy. Flora had been right – he'd been the man staring into the café.

'Got it in one. Tyler disappeared as soon as the constable walked through the door. Slipped away like a greased eel. But not before Tring got a look at him. I must say the officer exceeded my expectations – when he got back to his office, he found the mug shots Scotland Yard had sent down, and there he was: Dennis Tyler. Tring phoned me immediately.'

'Does Timpson want to pursue the matter?'

Jack could almost hear the inspector shake his head. 'Doesn't want any more trouble, he says, but with Tyler around, there'll be plenty, I've no doubt. It fits, though, doesn't it? Lovejoy has been employed to buy the farm for Tyler and his boss comes down to Abbeymead to check on progress or, more probably, to put pressure on the man.'

'I imagine I know what form that might take.'

'I imagine Lovejoy does, too, and he'll be making himself scarce. Leave it with me, Jack. We're on Tyler's trail and if he puts a foot wrong, we'll be there.'

'There's also the matter of Piers Neville,' he reminded Ridley. 'Threatening blackmail.'

'I wouldn't put too much store on that. These young men... erratic, too easily swayed. He can't get what he wants immediately, so he lashes out. It's surely in his interest to keep in with his uncle. The boy's his heir. Young Neville will inherit the entire estate and what's a hotel to that?'

Jack replaced the receiver with an inner sigh. He didn't share Alan Ridley's confidence that Tyler would pose no problem or that Piers Neville was merely a spoilt young man. He hadn't mentioned Flora's woes, knowing instinctively that the inspector would brush the incidents to one side, viewing them as inconsequential, a sad vendetta by a villager Flora had upset. Ridley wouldn't brush it off so easily, Jack thought, if he could see how badly it was affecting her.

It was distraction she needed, he decided, and set his mind to find one, eventually coming up with the promised visit to Piers Neville. He was hopeful it would be worth the journey. At home, the man might let his guard down and talk freely. Enough, at least, for them to judge how valid Ridley's conclusion might be.

'We could drive over to Brighton tomorrow afternoon,' he said. 'If you're free. You said the girl mentioned that Piers was living in Chadwick Road.'

'Above a newsagent, she said.'

'That shouldn't be too difficult to find. If Piers isn't at Bramber Hall, he'll be at home in Brighton.'

'We can give it a go, I suppose.'

Flora sounded listless, quite unlike the girl he'd come to love. She had now been the victim of two spiteful attacks – emotionally hurtful rather than physically so – but perhaps all the sharper for that. And there was still Percy's funeral to face. A breakthrough in the case was what they needed.

14

They were forced to catch the bus to Brighton, the Austin deciding at the last minute that Wednesday afternoon was a good time to develop a fault with its brakes. Running hand-in-hand to the high street, they reached the bus stop outside the bakery just as the conductor was about to ring his bell.

Hastily, Flora clambered aboard and, in her rush, tripped over a large shopping bag that had spilled into the aisle. Its owner glared at her.

'Sorry, Miss Ticehurst,' she said, fumbling for her purse while trying to get her breath back.

'You should try wearing a watch,' the older woman snapped, her lips pursed in disapproval. 'You'd not need to throw yourself on the bus then.'

Flora would like to have snapped back but Jack's hand was beneath her elbow, steering her to the only two vacant seats. Surely the afternoon bus to Brighton wasn't always this crowded? The trip hadn't begun well.

Luckily, the journey itself was uneventful. As they trundled across the Hove boundary, Jack leaned across and gave her arm a nudge. 'We should get off at the next stop. My street map shows Chadwick Road close by.'

Flora made sure she avoided the Ticehurst basket as she left the bus. For the entire journey she'd been aware of the woman's sour presence and was relieved to leave it behind.

Chadwick Road, when they found it, was pleasant enough, running along the north side of a small park, the houses terraced and interspersed with several small shops. The sole newsagent lay at its very end.

Jack pointed to a door to one side of the shop, its dark blue paintwork blistered and its doorbell looking unused.

'Shall we try?' he asked. 'It might work.'

'The place doesn't look too inviting, does it?' She glanced up at the twin windows above, their glass dirty and their sills flaking badly. A curtain in one of the rooms appeared to have collapsed halfway along the rail and fallen drunkenly to the floor.

'It may be better inside.'

Flora smiled to herself. Jack was rarely such an optimist.

There was a surprisingly quick response to their ring, a buzzer sounding somewhere above. The door swung back, revealing a narrow hall, which looked to be in no better condition than the rest of the building, anaglypta wallpaper peeling from broken coving.

She led the way up a flight of bare, wooden stairs to a small landing. Two flats, it seemed, occupied this first floor, with neither door having a name tag. She was debating which to try when one of them was flung open and Piers Neville stood on the threshold.

'I saw you outside,' he said, addressing Flora. 'Prue mentioned she'd had tea with you. She's not here.'

'What a shame! I was looking forward to seeing her again.' She took her cue from him. 'I so much enjoyed our chat. And, as I was coming to Brighton, I thought I'd drop in and say hello.'

'She's gone to Worthing,' Piers grumbled, leading the way into what functioned as a combined sitting room and kitchen. 'An audition for a summer show.' The slurred sibilants had Flora glance back at Jack. Neville wasn't exactly drunk but he'd been drinking, it was clear.

'Fancy a beer? Got a jug from the pub down the road. Cheaper that way.'

'Not for me,' Jack assured him. The question had been directed at him. She was presumed not to be thirsty, Flora thought.

'We won't stay long.' She hoped her smile might disarm. 'Just rest our feet before we walk to the shops.' Piers could have no idea they'd come only a few steps from the bus stop, but it was still a silly excuse. Luckily, he was wholly uninterested. What interested him was Birds Acre Farm.

'Any more news about the farm?' he asked, before they'd even sat down. 'You seemed to know a lot about the sale when you came to the Hall.'

'Not that we've heard, but should there be any news?' Her tone was guileless. 'I understood that Sir Frederick was selling to Mr Lovejoy now. The sale was going ahead, and the farm would be converted into a hotel.'

Piers banged his glass down on the stained walnut table so hard it should have broken. 'That was the idea,' he muttered. 'That was the agreement. But I don't trust Lovejoy and I don't trust my uncle. He's a snake.'

'That's pretty strong,' Jack said.

Piers shrugged and picked up his glass again. 'It's how I feel. I hate my family. The whole damn lot of 'em. Do you hate yours?' he asked conversationally.

'Not hate, no. I don't always feel comfortable with them.'

'Hah! A mealy-mouthed way of putting it, I'd say, but you probably haven't got a mother like mine.' He leaned forward and Flora caught a strong whiff of beer. 'The saving grace is that she doesn't come here. I don't have to see her or the little brats she's brought into the world. Or the man who calls himself a stepfather.'

'He's Trevor Duchamp, isn't he?' Flora put in. 'I've seen him mentioned in the papers. There was one enormous magazine spread that featured him.' She hoped that might stir the pot.

'Mentioned for his rubbishy agency, you mean. Advertising, my God! What would my father think? But Duchamp makes money and that's all my mother is interested in.'

'Your father was a pilot in the last war, I was told.'

'He was a wonderful man.' The slur had increased. 'Killed in the Battle of Britain defending this great country of ours.' His mouth twisted. 'My father paid the ultimate price and what did his widow do...'

'You must have been very young,' Flora said quietly, conscious of his obvious pain. Against her better judgement, she'd begun to feel sympathy for this fragile, impotent young man.

'I was ten when Dad was shot down over Kent and left with nothing but a gravestone.'

'Memories perhaps,' she suggested tactfully.

'You can't live on memories.' His tone was harsh. 'As I've found out. It's the future I have to plan for.'

'A future that includes being Sir Frederick's heir,' she reminded him. 'It can't be that disappointing.'

Neville snorted. 'If my uncle could, he'd move heaven and earth to disinherit me.'

'But that isn't possible, is it?'

He shrugged again, slipping further down the rancid-looking sofa so that he ended almost horizontal. 'I wouldn't put anything past him. He's in cahoots with a man I'd not trust in a million years. Lovejoy will double-cross him for sure.'

'Your uncle must be aware of the kind of man he's dealing with,' Jack said.

Flora knew he didn't believe that. They'd both agreed that Sir Frederick would be no match for Lovejoy, but she could see that Jack was leading the young man on to talk. Hopefully they'd learn something of whatever deal had been cooked up.

'You think?' Neville thrust out his lower lip. 'I don't. My uncle won't care what he signs up to. All he's interested in is money. He'll do anything for it.'

Would Piers do anything for it? she wondered.

'No, my uncle will be hoodwinked,' the boy continued confidently. 'There won't be a hotel for me to manage. Once his signature is on the contract, whatever agreement he thinks he's made will be ditched.'

'If it's not to be a hotel, what will it be?'

That was the question they'd continued to mull over last night. Just why did a villain, a former villain at least, want to buy a slightly shabby farm in the middle of the Sussex country-side? Could it really have anything to do with the police harassment of London criminals, as Inspector Ridley had suggested?

'No idea,' Piers answered, 'but whatever it is, it won't bring in the cash my uncle wants. If there's money to be made, it will be flowing into other pockets. You see' – he leaned forward and for a moment the slurred speech was crystal clear – 'I've tried to tell him, persuade him to raise the money to build the hotel himself. He owns the land already, for God's sake! How difficult can it be? But he won't.' Piers slumped down even further. 'He's too short-sighted. Too miserly. Not me, though.'

Suddenly, he leapt up from his prone position, swaying slightly on his feet. 'I'm raising the capital myself. Forget being the manager. I'll be the *owner*.'

He'd come closer to Flora and the beery fumes had her fighting not to recoil.

'It will be a great deal of money to raise.' Jack had stood up, too, and moved between them.

'It is, old sport, but I'll do it, you'll see,' he swaggered. 'No more waiting around for someone else to decide my life.'

If Tony Farraday were right and Sir Frederick had bailed out his nephew on numerous occasions but was now refusing to do so, the supposed hotel must represent Piers' last chance to make good. His boastfulness was plainly a need to believe in himself more than ever.

'Will you be able to match Lovejoy's offer?' Jack asked. 'It's bound to be considerable.'

'Uncle will sell to me, whatever the offer,' he said smoothly.

'You're very sure.'

Jack was deliberately needling him, she could see, encouraging Piers to divulge whatever threat he intended to use. If only they could wring from him what that was. A revelation that his uncle was a murderer?

'Couldn't be more certain. Let's just say I know something he'd rather I didn't.'

'It sounds intriguing,' she said lightly, 'and, after all, you've only one bid to contend with now – Mr Lovejoy's.'

Piers looked blank.

'Percy Milburn?' she said. 'He was a bidder, wasn't he? Until his unfortunate death.'

'Unfortunate!' He gave a crack of laughter that set Flora's teeth on edge.

'We heard that Mr Milburn threatened to sue Sir Frederick if he reneged on their agreement,' Jack intervened. 'Was your uncle concerned?'

Piers seemed to chew over the question. 'He was angry,' he said. 'Milburn insisted he wouldn't buy unless he could build a hostel. It was the last thing my uncle wanted on his doorstep, not making any money, bringing all kinds of undesirables onto the estate. Uncle wanted out, particularly when a better offer appeared. He'd only agreed verbally that he'd sell.'

'And shaken hands? Mr Milburn could have had a case,'

Jack pursued. 'How would Sir Frederick have responded to legal action?'

'That's easy enough. He wouldn't pay. He wouldn't have been able to. Lucky for good old Unc the chap left the world when he did.'

Flora got to her feet, turning away in distaste.

'We'd best be off.' Jack swiftly joined her. 'We've a fair amount of shopping to do.'

'I'm sorry to have missed Prue,' she managed to say, turning at the door. Piers had stayed slumped on the sofa, his eyes now glassy, and made no response.

They walked down the stairs in silence. In the street, Flora took a deep breath. 'Despicable,' she said.

'Despicable,' he agreed, 'but informative, if we're opting for Sir Frederick as our villain, and that looks likely. There are two people, still alive, that we know for sure were at the farm that afternoon, and Sir Fred is one of them. Piers knowing something so bad that it will force his uncle to sell the farm to him, no matter what the market price, could prove the clincher.'

In the sea breeze, Flora's long waves escaped their Alice band, and impatiently she pushed the flying strands from her face. 'Maybe, but I can't see Sir Frederick destroying my tree or trashing my books. Nor Colin Palmer, for that matter.'

'Neither can I,' he said regretfully. 'I've changed my mind. It has to be someone else that's involved and for a whole different reason. The attacks can't be connected to Percy's murder – rather, they're a complication.'

'A complication for me,' she said morosely. 'And as for Piers knowing something, he might, I suppose. Or he might know nothing. He's a sham.'

'He is but, in this case, I don't think he's shamming about getting what he wants – the hotel he's desperate for. If he saw his uncle near the farm the afternoon that Percy was murdered *before* Frederick Neville claims to have turned up in his car,

Piers can implicate him, whether his uncle is guilty or not. And to protect himself from any taint, I reckon Sir Frederick would agree with whatever Piers wants. Think of the family name!'

'On the other hand, his nephew could be trying to cover his own tracks. He had as much interest as his uncle in getting rid of Percy. It's only now that Sir Frederick appears to have gone back on his promise that their interests have diverged.'

'We may be only a little further on, but the trip has been worth it.' Jack didn't sound too despondent, she thought, as arm in arm, they walked back to the bus stop. She tried to feel as cheerful.

'Piers wants a hotel,' he mused. 'Sir Frederick wants money and an income stream. But what does this man Tyler want? It's his rival bid that appears to have been the trigger for events.'

'Lovejoy is the one person who'll know – he's the one working for Tyler. We should ask him directly.'

'Lovejoy it is then – if we can find him!'

15

It was unlikely that Sidney Lovejoy would attend Percy's funeral but, in her heart, Flora nursed a small hope that she might glimpse him hovering on the periphery. It seemed the man was lying low but getting him to talk had become essential. If she could corner him at the church this morning, it might help her get through what was certain to be a distressing event. Yesterday's trip to Brighton had proved a valuable distraction, the encounter with Piers Neville laying bare the depth of his disillusion and the clear anger he felt towards his uncle. Today, though, as she dressed in the dark green woollen frock – her funeral frock – the image of the drowned man had returned to haunt, a constant and invasive presence.

Jack was waiting for her at her garden gate, his sombre clothes a challenge to the bright spring sunshine. She picked two daffodils as she walked down the path, harbingers of better times, and gave one to him to wear as a buttonhole.

Hand-in-hand, they strolled towards the high street, saying little but, on such a day, their shared silence felt a comfort. A single bell was tolling very slowly, long gaps between each strike, as they walked through the lych gate and into the church where a sprinkling of people were already seated. The most devout parishioners, Flora noticed. But there was no Alice. No Kate or Tony. Flora's heart ached. Had she been the only one in Abbeymead who had truly liked Percy Milburn?

They had only just slipped into a pew when the funeral began, a modest affair presided over by Reverend Hopkirk. The vicar appeared fully recovered from the chest infection plaguing him all winter and, Flora presumed, fully recovered from the death of a curate who had proved horribly false. The service was brief and businesslike, as Percy would have wanted, and within half an hour they were walking out of St Saviour's into blinding sunshine. The weather was putting on a show for Percy, even if no one else was.

To Flora's surprise, she spotted Winifred Ticehurst just ahead, talking animatedly to the vicar and trapping him against one of the lichen-covered gravestones that lined the red brick path. Flora hadn't seen her when she'd glanced around the church, though she must have been part of the congregation. She wondered where the woman could have secreted herself amid such a small gathering.

'The Ticehurst woman,' Jack said in her ear.

'Interesting, isn't it? Should we—' she began, but at that moment, Winifred finished talking to a weary-looking Hopkirk and walked directly towards Flora, moving with a surprising turn of speed.

'Good morning to you both.' A crack in the woman's face suggested an attempted smile. Ignoring Jack, she bent her gaze on Flora. 'I hadn't expected to see you here, Miss Steele. I would have thought you had a bookshop to run.'

Flora flared with annoyance and only just kept her temper.

'Good morning, Miss Ticehurst,' she returned in a voice edged with splinters. 'I happen to have liked Mr Milburn a great deal. The least I could do was attend his funeral. But you... I wouldn't have expected *you* to be here.'

In stately fashion, Winifred drew herself to her full height. 'I felt it particularly important that I pay my respects today. Mr Milburn and I may have had our differences, but he did not deserve to die in such an appalling fashion. There is to be another meeting tomorrow evening to discuss the future of Birds Acre Farm. I trust you will both be there.' She fixed them with a hard stare. 'It's up to all of us to pull together. *My* conscience is clear. I've done all I can to ensure the village recognises the farm's importance.'

Winifred had been tireless in visiting every household in Abbeymead, Flora had learned, painting a horrifying picture of the Martins' farm sold to strangers and yet another hotel, with all its noisy comings and goings, opened little more than a mile from the village. Wasn't it enough, she'd demanded of those she'd visited, that the Templetons' beautiful old mansion had already been turned into such an establishment?

There seemed little more to say and Flora was about to respond to Jack's tug on her arm when Minnie Howden walked up to the small group. Clutching a battered leather handbag, she looked shyly around the gathering.

'Thank you all so much for coming,' she said. 'I was afraid that poor Mr Milburn would be sent on his way alone, except for me of course.'

Flora reached out for the housekeeper's hand, succeeding only in becoming entangled with the handbag. 'You must know you could count on me, Miss Howden.'

'Oh, yes, I know, dear Miss Steele,' she said helplessly, 'but the village...'

'The village thinks as it should,' Winifred said repressively.

Minnie blinked, seeming unsure what to make of the remark, but then hurried on, 'I'm afraid there won't be refreshments. Mr Milburn was very specific in his will about the funeral arrangements. No wake, he stipulated, and I've tried to follow his wishes as best I can.'

'That will come as a relief to most of us,' Flora told her. 'Funeral wakes are never comfortable gatherings.'

'Thank you.' The elderly woman smiled tremulously.

'Talking of the will, I understand you've had good fortune, Miss Howden.' Winifred attempted to put warmth into her voice.

About to join Jack who had walked on a little, the words held Flora captive. She turned and saw Jack turn, too. A second smile had blossomed on the woman's face. One, Jack later said, that you could have cut with a knife.

'Yes,' Minnie said hesitantly. 'Mr Milburn has been very kind.'

'More than kind, I'd say. It's not every housekeeper who gets to inherit such a large property, or any property for that matter.'

'No. He's been very kind,' she said again, even more helplessly.

Jack walked back, joining the group once more. Flora gave him a swift glance and together they formed a protective half circle around Minnie.

'You won't want to live there alone, I imagine.' Winifred's voice boomed out, causing several stragglers making their way along the path to stop and look.

'I really haven't thought what is best to do. Life has been a trifle... difficult.' She twisted the handbag's leather handles into what had begun to look like pieces of string. 'I may go to my brother. He's a widower now and could use my help.'

'And move away from Abbeymead? Surely not.'

'Well—' she began.

'Can I suggest an altogether better solution?' her inquisitor interrupted.

Before Miss Howden could say yes or no, Winifred trampled any resistance. 'Turn what was, after all, for many years the schoolhouse, into something worthwhile. A library and a museum! It could function as a gallery, too, for local artists. Yes, a splendid idea.' Winifred warmed to her theme. 'It could be the centre for local arts. And you could stay in the adjoining cottage,' she added generously.

'I suppose I could.' Minnie sounded doubtful. There was a pause before she dared to say, 'I believe, though, that it might be easier for me to sell and move to a smaller property.'

It would certainly be more comfortable, Flora thought. And, with the money Percy's beautiful house would raise, give Minnie Howden a worry-free old age.

'Nonsense!' Winifred cut short the perceived backsliding. 'Why would you wish to do that? You've lived in the village all your life and worked in the schoolhouse for many years. You'll be attached to it. You would feel a tremendous shock in severing your connection.'

She advanced on Minnie, who stepped back a pace. 'I know how attached one can get,' she said in a gentler voice. 'I spent more hours in that same building than I care to remember. Having to leave was wretched.'

Flora risked a sidelong glance at Jack who gave a slight nod. It was extraordinary, they were both thinking, that Winifred had been lured into revealing such personal feelings.

'It's a lovely idea,' Minnie said placatingly, 'a really lovely idea, but it would be such a huge undertaking to run. I feel too... too old to take on such a commitment. And if I didn't, who would run it for me? How would I ever find enough money to maintain the building properly?'

'No need to worry about who would run it,' Winifred said briskly. 'I'd be more than happy to help. And, as for maintenance, we could fund raise. Tap the local council, run a charity fair, ask local businesses for their support in exchange for some modest advertising. Very modest.'

'I'm not sure, Miss Ticehurst.'

There was pleading in Minnie's voice. It was plain she

yearned for a quiet cottage, tucked away, perhaps, in one of Abbeymead's many twittens, or close to her brother in the adjoining county.

'Think about it, Miss Howden. No need to decide today. But soon, mind!' she warned. 'There's no time to lose.'

When Minnie continued to look confused and a little lost, Winifred was prompted to heighten her persuasion. 'Imagine, Miss Howden,' she said with a flourish, 'how important a figure you would cut in village history! Yes, really. It's not too much to say that you would become a heroine and your name remembered for years to come.'

Another tight smile, then giving Minnie's hand an awkward pat, she walked away.

Minnie Howden as Abbeymead's heroine? Flora doubted it. Far more likely that Winifred was laying the ground for her own coronation.

'Did you notice how thunderous that woman looked when Milburn's will was mentioned?' Taking Flora's arm, Jack walked through the lych gate and into the high street.

'I did. Poor Miss Howden. You can bet on it that Winifred won't stop badgering her.'

'And Minnie Howden will succumb. Eventually.'

'I hope not. Her best plan is what she dared to suggest. Sell the schoolhouse for a grand sum and buy a small place in the village or a home near her brother if she prefers.'

'It's a pity she ever mentioned the will. If she'd simply put the place up for sale, she'd be one step ahead. The die would be cast, and Winifred would have to accept defeat before she'd even begun her campaign.'

'Winifred Ticehurst isn't the kind of person who accepts defeat.' Flora sounded concerned and he squeezed her hand.

'You can't get too involved. You've your own demons to fight.'

'We can look out for Minnie, though, can't we?'

'We can do that,' he agreed, wondering as he said it how difficult looking out for Minnie would prove. 'First, though, Sidney Lovejoy.'

'Yes, Lovejoy – I'm not sure why, but I'd hoped Percy's funeral might have tempted him to break cover.' With her free hand, she tugged frustratedly at her knot of chestnut hair, caught today in a black ribbon.

'We might have a problem finding him. So far Lovejoy has failed in his mission, and he must know the man who pulls his strings is looking for him. I reckon he'll stay elusive until he's sure he can produce what the boss wants.'

'With Sir Frederick wavering over the sale as he seems to be, how likely is that?'

'I don't know but I do know we need to get to him before Dennis Tyler does.'

16

'Are you going to the meetin' tonight?' Alice asked, when Flora met her at Katie's Nook the following morning. She'd called at the café for an iced bun to have with her eleven o'clock cup of tea and found Alice in earnest conversation with Kate.

'I thought I would, and persuade Jack to come as well.' It was unlikely they'd learn anything useful this evening, but meetings could be unpredictable, and information disclosed unintentionally.

'I don't like all this trouble,' Alice grumbled. 'It's set the village at odds. Why can't Sir Frederick find another tenant? A new one would stop all this argumentation. Still' – she brightened – 'there is some good news. Actually, very good news. Katie and I have been talkin'.'

Flora wrinkled her forehead. 'What about?'

'The weddin', of course.'

Her forehead found a few more wrinkles. 'I thought you were happy just being engaged,' she said, turning to Kate.

'I am. I love it.' Kate's pale blue eyes took on a dreamy expression. 'But I've decided – being married will be even better. It will be wonderful!'

'Will it?' Flora wondered if selective memory was at work. Kate's marriage to Bernie Mitchell had been anything but wonderful.

'Kate is thinkin' of having a September weddin'.' Alice's stare was cross, Flora receiving its full force.

'The weather should still be good,' Kate said gently, 'and the Priory won't be so busy. Alice says it will be fine for Tony to take a week off. A honeymoon,' she finished, cheeks shining. 'What do you think, Flora?'

'I think it's entirely up to you, Kate,' she said, womanfully suppressing her true feelings. She leant over and kissed her friend on the cheek, gaining a nod of approval from Alice.

'Here.' The cook's plump figure bustled around the counter. 'You've forgotten your bun – and I'll see you this evenin'.'

Flora had had to twist Jack's arm to attend another meeting chaired by Winifred Ticehurst. Only the fact that it might uncover new information had persuaded him to come this evening. They sat together in the centre of the hall, a vantage point from where they could take stock of both audience and stage. Attendance tonight was definitely patchier than at the previous meeting. Whether the villagers were growing tired of the continued uncertainty or, learning of Percy Milburn's death, they'd decided Birds Acre Farm was best left alone, Flora had no idea. But it served her purpose well. Fewer people meant a clearer view of proceedings.

Winifred was in her high-backed chair, centre stage, when they took their seats.

'She's brought her favourite gavel. Have you noticed?' Jack whispered.

'Ssh. She's about to start.'

The meeting was due to open at seven o'clock and, as the

hall clock sounded a sonorous seven chimes, Winifred wielded her wooden mallet. As she did so, Alice appeared at the end of Flora's row and with a lot of 'excuse me's' and shuffling of feet and handbags, she made her way to the seat Flora had saved. Winifred glared down at her from the stage.

'Ladies and gentlemen,' she boomed, 'can we *please* make a start?' Alice, red-faced, began to offer an incoherent apology but was immediately silenced by the gavel. 'As President of the Society for the Protection of Abbeymead,' Winifred continued her boom, 'I welcome you all to this meeting.'

'President of what?' Jack asked and was once again shushed.

'You will be aware,' their chairwoman continued, 'that there has been an inordinate amount of trouble over what for generations has been the Martin family farm.' She paused, evidently relishing the expectant faces turned towards her.

'This shouldn't be,' she announced. There were several nods from the audience. 'The village should not be threatened in this fashion. We all know of developments in the countryside that have brought with them bad consequences. This proposal is no different. It will bring mayhem to Abbeymead. It already has.' She paused for effect. 'It has brought death.'

'A murder,' someone piped up.

Winifred ignored the interruption. 'The village has no need for further accommodation,' she went on loftily, 'but it does have need of productive farms.'

Again, there were several nods.

'To me, the answer is simple. And, I hope, to you, too. Don't sell! Keep Birds Acre as a working farm. Find a new tenant to husband the land.'

There were several faint 'hear, hears' and, seemingly encouraged, Winifred arrowed straight to the nub of the meeting. 'I am suggesting that we, as a village, make our voice heard. The farm is too close to Abbeymead for us not to have an opinion. And our opinion should be conveyed to Sir Frederick Neville in the clearest possible terms.'

Pausing, she took a draught of water. 'What I am proposing' – she raised her hands as though imploring them to celebrate the proposition – 'is that we launch a petition against the sale of the farm and its land. Collect as many signatures as we can and present them at Bramber Hall within the next few weeks.'

'Who's goin' to do this blessed petition?' The voice was annoyed. 'I got more n'enough to cope with as it is.'

'I shall be the one to write it, of course,' Miss Ticehurst said frigidly. 'But you' – she glared down at the foolhardy interrupter – 'will sign it.

'*And*, ladies and gentlemen' – again the raised arms – 'you will be part of a remarkable movement. It is not just your signature we need but that of everyone you know. Talk to your family, talk to your neighbours, talk to your fellow shoppers. Impress on them the seriousness of the situation, emphasise the urgency, then send them forth with their pen.'

'Where's this dratted thing goin' to be so we can sign it?' Alice whispered loudly.

A hand floated in the air. 'Yes?' Winifred said impatiently.

'Where will the petition be held?' another intrepid questioner asked.

'I was coming to that,' she rebuked him. 'I have considered the subject thoroughly and feel, and I hope you agree, that we should have several copies of the document circulating at the same time. One can be left here in the village hall, another perhaps at the doctor's surgery, and maybe our good shopkeepers who are here today will consent to holding a copy at their place of business.'

'Do you have a date for handing the petition to Sir Frederick?'

It was Mrs Teague, Charlie's mother, who'd spoken, Flora noted with surprise. She'd always thought of her as a woman content to keep house and raise her son, with little interest in the wider village community. It proved, if proof were needed, that the fate of the farm had become a crucial issue to just about everyone in Abbeymead.

'I do have a date.' Winifred smiled approvingly. 'I am suggesting we allow up to two weeks. Sufficient time to collect everyone's signature but not too long that people forget. Urgency is what we need to engender. A sense of urgency,' she repeated.

'May I ask,' a mellow voice emerged from the back of the room, 'why you, in particular, feel such concern?'

There was a general craning of necks.

'Why do you wish to stop a development that will benefit your community?' the voice continued.

'Who is speaking? Make yourself known please.' Winifred peered angrily over the heads of the audience. 'You're a stranger here,' she accused, having finally located the figure standing by the double doors that led into the hall. A man wearing a black felt beret. 'Why should you have anything to say in the matter?'

A low mutter spread through the room – in agreement, Flora judged.

The interloper was not to be silenced, however. 'A stranger can often see more clearly what a community needs,' he said. 'For Abbeymead, it's accommodation. Superior accommodation that will encourage wealthy visitors to come and spend their money in the village. No discourtesy to the Cross Keys, an estimable hostelry as I can testify, but I am suggesting a very different experience. A hotel close to the village where the very best in society can enjoy each other's company amid an amazing landscape. A hotel that will become a must in their social calendar.'

Lovejoy, for it was he, seemed carried away by his own rhetoric. And had conveniently forgotten, Flora thought, that the Priory Hotel offered just such an experience.

'Piffle,' Winifred snapped.

'You think so, Miss Ticehurst. It is Miss Ticehurst? Let me ask you this: why are you so determined to prevent your fellow villagers benefiting from their beautiful surroundings? The hotel I'm proposing will bring a new prosperity to Abbeymead. To put it crudely, more money than has ever flowed into the village before.'

There were more low mutters, this time, it seemed, less sure of an opinion.

Winifred was about to raise her gavel, clearly hoping to silence Lovejoy, when a scuffle broke out at the rear of the hall and her antagonist's peroration was cut short. The audience once more twisted their heads in a ninety-degree circle, hardly comfortable, but this was entertainment they hadn't expected.

The corduroy jacket and black beret were vanishing through the door at that very moment, and a solid chunk of a man was chasing after them.

'Well, my goodness!' Alice stretched her neck back into shape. 'These meetings are gettin' to be proper lively!'

Winifred remained standing, a lone figure on the stage, her form stiff with what had to be suppressed anger. Her authority had been challenged.

'Ladies and gentlemen,' she declaimed, 'I hope you will forgive that unfortunate interruption. It has done nothing to change the situation. We are still threatened with the imposition of a business that will change our village for ever. I will ensure that the petitions are in place within the next two days. Please make sure that you and everyone you know signs.' Gathering her tweed skirt protectively around her knees, she sank back into the high-backed chair.

'Miss Ticehurst has exhausted herself,' Jack observed. 'She didn't like those questions, did she?'

'No,' Flora said thoughtfully, 'and Lovejoy didn't hang around to ask more.'

Alice stood up and dusted down her coat. 'Who was that man chasin' after him? I've never seen him before.'

'Nor me.' Flora looked across at Jack, giving him a warning smile. They both had a very clear idea who Lovejoy's pursuer had been.

Jack smiled back at her. 'Nor me,' he said.

17

'Can I tempt you to supper?' Jack asked, as they walked down the high street towards the turning to Greenway Lane. 'I've smoked salmon in my larder.'

'Where did that come from? No, don't tell me – Arthur. Another gift! Does he think you've been backsliding?'

Arthur Bellaby was Jack's London agent and the source of occasional treats – fresh coffee, a new wine, even caviar last Christmas. Jack was never sure whether the parcels that arrived on his doorstep were simple goodwill on Arthur's part or a barely disguised plot to encourage him to work harder.

'I've barely left my treadmill for weeks,' he protested. 'More likely it's because Arthur went to Scotland for Easter and came home with too much salmon.'

'Possibly.' She tucked her hand in his arm. 'How's the new book going? You've not mentioned it.'

'I think... it will be OK. I have changed direction, though. The Bodkin Adams case has given me a whole new line of thought.'

'The murder trial of the century?' Flora was recalling recent newspaper headlines.

'That's the one. A doctor who treats a patient to relieve his suffering and shortens his life isn't guilty of murder if he proves the death is unintentional.'

'Your villain is a doctor?'

'He is now. A ship's doctor. Adams' acquittal has given me a great idea. My villain can stand trial, be found not guilty, and then go on to murder again.'

'Will Arthur be happy with that? He might think it too close to real life.'

'Murder *is* real life.' He gave her a quick hug. 'Now, are you coming back to Overlay?'

'Who could resist smoked salmon? I've only eaten it once in my life – when Sir Edward celebrated his fiftieth birthday. Aunt Violet and I were invited to the Priory along with several others, for a birthday tea. It was magnificent.' She sighed. 'I'm glad the Priory is lived in again, glad that it's Sally running the hotel, but sometimes I wish the Templetons were still lords of the manor, Violet was alive, I was young—'

'I can't believe you were ever young!' he exclaimed. 'Twenty-seven last month! Have you remembered your spare set of teeth? Smoked salmon needs some chewing.'

Laughingly, she pushed him away and in the dark he missed his footing, almost tumbling into the ditch.

'Sorry,' she said, grabbing hold of his hand. 'But seriously, life did once seem a lot... a lot more hopeful.'

'Think what happened to that hope. Six long years of war. Six years of queuing for food, feeling hungry, patching clothes, wondering if you'd be the next unlucky one.'

'I know, and six years of brutal soldiering for you, expecting to be that unlucky one. But still...'

'What's brought on this nostalgia?'

'I suppose it's everything changing. First the Priory being sold and turned into a hotel, now generations of Martins no more, and their farm being fought over.'

'It's not exactly everything.'

'Then there's Kate and Tony getting married.'

'Ah!'

This was what was what behind Flora's longing for the past. He might have guessed. She liked Tony, he knew, but she'd always been cautious of her friend's new liaison and even more so of any possible marriage.

'Don't say "Ah" in that meaningful way. It's another big change to get used to.'

It was better, he decided, to say nothing more. Delving into his pocket for his door key, he remembered a question he should have asked her.

'Did you get the lock on the All's Well changed?'

'I did. Michael fitted a shiny new one in between all his other jobs, but I need him to do the same for the cottage. The kitchen door has begun to stick whenever I try to lock it.'

'You've left the door unlocked?'

'I've had to, but no one goes round to the back of the cottage. There was a time, Jack, when nobody locked any of their doors in Abbeymead.'

Another burst of nostalgia. He surreptitiously crossed his fingers that nobody would find their way to Flora's back door.

'What is it to be?' he asked when they'd let themselves in and drifted towards the kitchen. 'Salmon sandwiches? A salmon salad?'

'You eat far too many sandwiches.'

'But not ham this time.'

'No,' she conceded, 'but it will still be sandwiches. And it's too cold for a salad. How about scrambled eggs? Or I could make salmon potato cakes.'

'Scrambled egg sounds good but—'

'I know, you only do poached. Why don't you get a fire going – it's even colder here than home – and I'll scramble the eggs.'

'There's a fresh loaf in the bread bin. OK, I'm going,' he said, as she waved him away. 'The fire will be roaring by the time you arrive.'

It was hardly roaring, even with a mound of firewood and half a scuttle of coal, but at least it would take the chill off the air, and he was hopeful that by the time they'd eaten, the sitting room would be bearable.

'So, what did you make of the meeting?' she asked when he returned to the kitchen.

'It was interesting.'

'Is that all?' She'd slipped two rounds of bread beneath the grill and broken half a dozen eggs into a bowl. They had been his breakfast eggs for the week, he thought mournfully, but he forgave her.

'Winifred Ticehurst was riding her hobby horse hard and it seemed as though most of the audience agreed with her.' He pulled out a chair to sit down, resting his elbows on the kitchen table. 'I imagine she's likely to get the signatures she wants. As for Lovejoy's appearance – that was an oddity, wasn't it? It's clear he's been in hiding. Tyler has been searching but hasn't found him, either at the Cross Keys, or at the Nook when he peered in at you, or anywhere else in the village. Then Lovejoy turns up at a public meeting and defends the sale of the farm as though nothing has changed.'

'It is odd. Lovejoy must have known he was taking a risk in coming to the meeting. Tyler was likely to be hanging around on the off chance of spotting him.'

'And why try to persuade the village when he hasn't managed to persuade Sir Frederick yet? The offer from Tyler and his associates was well in excess of Percy's, yet Neville is still wavering over taking it.'

'Sir Fred may be wary of public opinion. Or perhaps he's asked for even more money and is waiting it out.' She took a mouthful. 'This salmon is delicious, Jack. You need to keep writing those books.'

'Asking for more might be a bad strategy when you're dealing with a man like Tyler.'

'Almost certainly, but what does Lovejoy do? He's in a difficult position. He's the go-between, in trouble from both sides. The only difference is that Sir Frederick isn't likely to kneecap him.'

'Where *did* you get that expression?'

'It's not only crime writers who know about the seedier side of life,' she said, her mouth full.

He rested his knife and fork. 'It still doesn't make sense for Lovejoy to turn up this evening. If he's scared that he's failed to clinch the sale and thinks he's likely to suffer kneecapping or whatever grotesque injury Tyler has in mind, then why reveal himself? Why not hightail it back to London and make for a hideaway?'

'Because Tyler would find him wherever he went? Maybe his appearance at the meeting was a last stand at trying to swing the argument his way. If the village gets behind the plan, Sir Frederick is far more likely to agree. His estates border Abbeymead and there's a close relationship between the two manors. If Sir Frederick is convinced that he's not about to suffer a peasants' revolt, he could stop vacillating, sign the contract, and Lovejoy is off the hook.'

'It's a thought. It might have worked that way if Lovejoy had been allowed to continue his persuasion. Unfortunately for him, his nemesis wasn't prepared to wait.'

Flora took a last mouthful of salmon. 'How long do you think Tyler's been in Abbeymead?'

'Not long, I would think, or it wouldn't only have been Kate who noticed him. But he could have been in Sussex a fair time. Ridley spoke of the Metropolitan Police breaking up several of the London gangs some weeks ago. Tyler might have arrived then.'

'So, he could have been here when Percy was killed?'

'I wondered that. The two offers must have been on the table at the same time. Without knowing, Percy was competing against him and would need to be silenced. Who better to do it?'

'If so, the farm must have been incredibly busy that afternoon,' she said pensively.

There was a long silence while they thought back to those fatal few hours until Flora broke it by saying, 'Shall I make tea?'

He jumped up. 'I'll make it. *And* wash up. You go into the sitting room. It should be warm enough by now.'

He put the kettle on to boil and filled a bowl with hot water while Flora lingered in the doorway. She was still thinking it through, he could see.

'If Tyler *was* at the farm, it doesn't have to follow that he killed Percy.'

'If he was, he's the most likely.'

'He could have seen Sir Frederick kill Percy,' she said, leaning against the door jamb. 'Or Piers, for that matter. And he wouldn't have cared who'd done it. It saved him a job. On the other hand, if he saw one of them do it, he could use that as leverage.'

'All we can say is that it could have been one of them. Ouch!' He'd plunged the plates into water that was too hot.

'And don't forget Colin Palmer!'

Jack grinned. The land agent had been the inspector's first suspect. 'I couldn't see him as a villain when Alan mentioned him, and I still can't. I wonder if Ridley has changed his mind.'

'Why not contact him? Find out if there's more to know. Are you sure about the tea?'

'Absolutely. Shoo.'

When he brought the tray through to the sitting room, she'd taken the lumpy sofa, her feet cradling the fender.

'Warm enough?'

He deposited the tray on what the landlord had called a coffee table but what for Jack was no more than a large stool. He should ask for a reduction in the rent, he thought. He seemed now to have bought most of the furniture in the house – except, of course, the dreaded sofa. It had been Overlay's secluded location that had persuaded him initially to overlook the rubbishy furnishings deemed sufficient by the landlord.

'My legs and feet are roasting, but my ears need fur muffs.'

'That's about it,' he said cheerfully. 'Summer is on the way and one day, we'll know the delights of central heating, but I wouldn't be rash enough to say when.' Stirring the pot, he asked casually, 'Has Kate decided on a date yet?'

'Sometime in September.' Flora's voice was decidedly dull.

'It's a pleasant month.'

'Was that when you were to marry Helen?'

Had she asked that to hurt? he wondered. 'Not September. July,' he replied evenly, as he poured the tea.

'I'm sorry.' She pulled him down to sit beside her. 'I shouldn't have asked you that.'

He stroked the long strands of red-brown hair. She was upset and crotchety, he knew. 'It's fine. My former fiancée no longer has the power to disturb me.'

'It's because I'm worried, Jack. I think Kate is rushing into trouble.'

'She could be rushing into happiness. Not all marriages are a disaster.'

'Kate's first marriage was. Your mother and father are divorced. My own parents – I don't know if they were happy or not. I've a horrible feeling they were badly at odds.'

Her parents' marriage bothered her hugely and he understood. She had lost them as a small child and there was so much she didn't know about them, not even where they were buried. She'd been told Highgate Cemetery and insisted it was so, furious with him when he'd gone looking for their graves and not found them. Furious when Richard, the man who'd let her down so wretchedly at the worst time of her life, had written last year to say he'd seen her parents' names in a French village churchyard.

'You don't know, that's the point.' He reached for his cup. 'You were too young when your parents died to know anything. Not that anyone ever truly knows what a marriage is like, except the two people in it. And, even with a wrong choice, there's sometimes a second chance. My mother, for instance, seems happy living in France with her Italian count. Here, Kate is being offered happiness with a decent man who loves her. She'll have chosen wisely.'

'She didn't choose wisely when she married Mitchell,' Flora said stubbornly. 'He'd been in prison for theft, but she still went ahead and married him. The truth was, she was dazzled.'

'Sometimes, Flora, it's good to be dazzled. You should give it a chance one day. Fling your bonnet, as they say... perhaps we both should.'

He waited for a response and, when it came, it wasn't what he hoped for.

'Finish your tea,' she said. 'It's getting cold.'

18

Jack hadn't gone down on his knees and offered a ring, but it was clear to Flora that he'd had marriage in mind. *Their* marriage. She might have known that Kate's wedding, along with Alice's unsubtle hints, would lead eventually to the big question. It wasn't a question she wanted to answer. Preferably ever. She was contented with her life as it was. Kate *had* said she was happy simply being engaged but had been persuaded, dragooned, Flora didn't know which, to walk up the aisle a second time. That wasn't going to happen to her. For Jack's sake, it would be far better if he dropped the idea. She would make a terrible wife.

It was late when he'd walked her back to the cottage, but he hadn't suggested staying and Flora had been glad – she'd wanted to be alone. The rest of the evening had passed without mishap, it was true, but ever since that veiled suggestion, it was plain they'd both been on edge.

She was still feeling flustered when she wheeled Betty from her shelter the next morning to ride to the All's Well. Closing the garden gate behind her, she saw Alice's stout figure labouring along the lane.

'What is it?' she asked, as her friend puffed herself to a stop. Alice wouldn't have come so far out of her way before a long day in the Priory kitchen, unless it was important. 'Something's happened?'

'I'll say it has.' Alice breathed heavily. 'My, I can't run like I used to.'

It was difficult to imagine a time when Alice could run.

'Cross country champion, I was,' she announced, taking Flora aback. She really shouldn't be so quick with her assumptions. 'Nearly got into the county team, but that was a few years ago.' The older woman's breath was still coming in small spurts. 'I'm goin' to have to sit down, my love.'

'Come into the house for a while.'

It was frustrating. Flora had set her alarm earlier than usual, intending to tackle the monthly accounts before she welcomed her first customer, but Alice's heaving chest and a complexion alternating between pale and bright red was a warning.

Offering her arm in support, she trundled Betty on one side and Alice on the other.

'My goodness, did you take an axe to the tree?' Her friend had glimpsed the massacre on the lawn. Jack and Charlie had cleared as much of the debris as possible, but there was no disguising the parlous condition of what was left. 'That rowan was some lovely. What made you do that?'

'It had a disease,' Flora invented hastily. 'But I've got someone dealing with it.'

Once they were through the front door, she settled Alice in the sitting room and brought her a glass of water. 'I could make tea,' she offered, hoping she wouldn't need to.

'I'd love a cuppa, my love, but I can't. I haven't the time. Nor you, for that matter.'

Flora was relieved. 'When you can breathe again, tell me—'

'It's about that man. You'd have heard it elsewhere, I guess, though maybe not soon enough. You've been to the meetin's, and you're worried about the farm, I know. And upset over that Milburn chap. I thought to myself, Flora needs to know the news straight away.'

'What man, Alice? What news?'

'Sidney Lovejoy.'

'Yes?'

'He's been attacked.'

'When? Where?'

'Must have been late last night. The postie found him first thing. He was on his way to collect the mail and there the chap was – spread out in a ditch, just past Larkspur Cottage.'

Dennis Tyler! It had to be. He'd chased after Lovejoy last night and, by the time she and Jack reached the street, both men had disappeared. Tyler had chased his prey and caught him. Then dished out his punishment.

'How badly is he hurt?' she asked, not relishing the grim details.

'He's not dead. Not yet. The story I got was that he's been taken to hospital. To St Luke's.'

That worried Flora. If Tyler discovered he hadn't finished the job, might he get to his victim in hospital? She had no particular liking for Lovejoy, but what he knew – about his employer and the deal he was trying to pull off – might be key to discovering Percy's murderer.

Alice patted wiry grey curls into place after her rush down the lane. 'Somethin' bad's goin' on in the village again, you mark my words, and you need to watch out.' She wagged a finger at Flora. 'That man who went after Lovejoy at the meetin' – he looked a bit of a brute. And you know what you're like, diggin' into things that don't concern you.'

'By now, the brute is probably a long way from Abbeymead,' she said airily, 'but I'll be careful, I promise.'

Alice huffed a little but levered herself up on the arms of the chair and Flora was quick to help her to her feet. 'How about a lift to the high street on my handlebars?' She couldn't prevent a grin.

'No, thank you, cheeky girl! But you're right. I need to get movin'. I've several hundred canapés to prepare for some lunchtime shenanigan and they're not goin' to make themselves. And that shop of yours isn't goin' to open on its own either.'

At least, Flora noted with relief, her friend's complexion had returned to a more normal hue. 'All true, but thank you for coming,' she said, walking to the door. 'It's always good to know—'

'What's happened to your photograph?' Alice interrupted. She was pointing to the sideboard. 'The one of Violet. It was always there.'

Flora looked and her stomach churned. The photograph *was* always there. It had been there yesterday morning when she'd left for work – she'd knocked it slightly, bending to open one of the sideboard cupboards and put it straight – and it should still be there today.

It was her favourite photograph, taken the summer before her aunt fell ill. Wearing a faded pair of dungarees, a battered sunhat and a broad smile, Violet stood clutching a lettuce in one hand and a beetroot in the other.

'I liked that photograph,' Alice said, looking across at her.

Flora couldn't speak. She wanted to cry but somehow managed to hold back the tears. Someone had taken it, deliberately, hurtfully. Maybe even smashed the frame and torn to pieces the photograph she cherished. But her friend mustn't know the misery she felt – the books, the tree, and now a precious keepsake of the woman she'd loved so dearly. If Alice knew, the calculated malice would send her into a spiral of hand-wringing and worry.

'I was dusting yesterday,' Flora lied. 'I must have mislaid it. Put the photo down somewhere else.'

It cost her nearly all her strength to smile and say the words.

And even more to leave with Alice. It would have been too pointed to have stayed in the cottage, though every fibre was beseeching her to make a search – beneath the chairs, under the beds, through every cupboard – anywhere a malignant house-breaker might have abandoned the photograph. It wasn't a housebreaker, though, was it? She remembered Jack's question about the All's Well's lock and how she'd complacently assured him that no one ever walked around to the back of her cottage. Well, now they had. And done it before. It was how they had stolen the key to the All's Well.

Leaving Alice in the high street to walk on to the Priory, she wheeled Betty into the rear courtyard of the All's Well. She could cry now if she wanted, but the tears wouldn't come. She felt sick and empty, one thought anchored in her brain. Someone in this village hated her so much they would take from her everything she held dear. Who could be filled with such spite? And what had she done to deserve it?

Opening the bookshop door, Flora half expected to face further disaster, but all was as she'd left it yesterday. She hung the pink swing jacket, her favourite for this time of the year, on the row of pegs Violet had installed in what she always insisted was a kitchenette and sat down at her desk. She should work but she couldn't. Instead, she rearranged her desktop.

She was tidying it for the fourth time when Elsie Flowers walked through the doorway. 'You're here then,' was her customer's greeting. 'I called earlier but you were shut.'

'I'm sorry, Mrs Flowers.'

'It's the second time you've been late opening. Not lost your key this time?'

'A problem at home, I'm afraid.' That would have to suffice.

'Don't you worry, my ducks. Today I've all the time in the world. Winifred is off campaigning again and won't be back to bother me for hours.' Elsie dumped a laden shopping bag onto the front display table.

'Does she bother you?' Flora was genuinely interested. Customers were always a good distraction.

'Let's say we can rub each other up the wrong way.' Elsie pulled a face. 'Two old dears together. Not that Winifred would ever agree to being old. Or dear. But it works – most of the time.'

'And when it doesn't?'

'Then we argue like billy-o. To be honest, she's a worry to me sometimes. I try to stop her but the woman's that committed to this society she's set up. The Protection of Abbeymead or whatever... it makes her too pushy for most people.' Elsie shook her head wisely. 'It means she makes enemies.'

'Has she made any in particular?'

'That Mr Lovejoy for a start. But he's come to a bad end, so I hear. Mrs Waterford at Larkspur told me. He was found in a ditch right outside her cottage. Did you know?'

When Flora nodded, Elsie continued happily, 'The Martins' old place – it stirs passions.' The word was delivered with intensity. 'Who'd have thought it? Just a common or garden farm.'

Flora had to remind herself that Elsie Flowers was a dedicated reader of crime, and any chance to infuse drama into a mundane life was seized upon.

'People get too involved,' her customer was saying, 'and do stupid things.'

'You think someone might do something stupid to Winifred?'

'Mebbe. There's times she asks for trouble.'

She gave an exaggerated shrug, the shoulder pads of her wool coat rising as though with a mind of their own. Elsie was still mending and making do. There was nothing wrong with 1940s fashion in her view; she still remembered exactly how many points that coat had cost – nearly half a year's clothing ration.

'I'll take a look around, now you're open. I need a book for tomorrow – Sunday can be that boring – and that young man of yours still hasn't found my Daphne book.' Her look was accusatory but Flora was too upset to mind, or mind the assumption that Jack and she were inseparable.

While Elsie browsed the shelves, Flora forced herself to begin the small everyday tasks that made up her regular routine. Starting on the month's accounts was out of the question – her heart was too heavy and her mind too fractured – but a zigzag in and out of the angled bookshelves with a feather duster, a stop to stroke her favourite volumes and a few minutes to breathe in the shop's cherished woodiness, helped to steady her.

In a quarter of an hour, Elsie was at the front desk again, waving an especially gruesome cover, the entire jacket splashed red. Flora laid the duster aside and went to serve her.

She was about to resume her work, having seen Elsie to the door, when the telephone rang. It was Jack at the other end of the line. Lying in bed last night, she'd spent at least an hour contemplating how best to behave when they next met, deciding eventually that she would pretend nothing untoward had happened between them, that she hadn't pushed away a suggestion of marriage, even a vague one.

But that was then and, forgetting her wariness, Flora was filled with a rush of feeling, hearing his voice down the line. He would understand about the photograph when she told him, understand the sickness in her heart.

'Have you heard?' he asked. He'd no need to specify what.

'Yes. Alice came by this morning and told me.' She tried to match his businesslike tone. 'How badly is he hurt, do you know?'

'Alan Ridley just phoned. He's been to St Luke's. That's where they took Lovejoy. It seems as though the chap escaped reasonably lightly – a broken finger, severe bruising, a black eye, and a cut on his head.'

It didn't seem so light to Flora, and she was quick to express her main concern. 'Lovejoy needs guarding at the hospital or Tyler could find his way there and attack him all over again. Then we'll never discover what the man knows.'

'The inspector doesn't consider a guard necessary.' Jack's voice was expressionless.

'Really?' she spluttered. 'Are his men even looking for Dennis Tyler?'

'Lovejoy has identified his attacker and it wasn't Tyler.'

She stood, the receiver in her hand, staring at the bookshelf opposite.

'Not Tyler? But then who?'

'Hold on to your hat, Flora. It was Piers Neville.'

19

Later that afternoon, Jack rang the inspector back – Alan
Ridley's earlier call had been brief – and invited him for a drink
at the Cross Keys the following day. It was the one sure way he
had of enticing the inspector to come to Abbeymead. Ridley
swore the beer at the Cross Keys was superior to anything he
could get in Brighton.

He was already in the pub on Sunday evening when Jack
arrived, having bagged the corner table he seemed wedded to. It
was still early, yet already swirls of smoke hit Jack as he walked
to the table, sending a longing singing through him. He'd
stopped smoking, he told himself severely, and he would stay
stopped. He tried to think of something else and there was
plenty to think of. With Lovejoy in hospital and Tyler seemingly on the loose, he was keen to know how the police were
responding.

'Got you a pint, Jack,' the inspector greeted him. 'And a
couple of bags of crisps. I best not eat too much. My mother
cooks me supper on a Sunday, a nice roast. And I need to leave
a clean plate.'

For a moment, Jack was startled. Alan Ridley had a mother,

and one who cooked him roast dinners. It felt slightly surreal, but really it shouldn't. The man couldn't always be a police inspector.

'Thanks for the beer,' he said, slipping into the seat opposite.

'Always good to catch up. I imagine you want to talk about Lovejoy?' The inspector had got straight to the point; there was to be no small talk this evening and that suited Jack.

'Lovejoy,' he agreed, 'and Piers Neville. And Dennis Tyler. I'm wondering, we're both wondering,' he corrected himself, making sure he included Flora in his question, 'what might be happening?'

'The answer to that is nothing much. We've got Neville under lock and key, though he won't be staying long. He's guilty of grievous bodily harm, he'd be convicted in any court, but Lovejoy won't prefer charges and that makes the Crown Prosecutor extremely wary of going ahead.'

Several reasons for Lovejoy's reticence passed through Jack's mind, the most obvious being that any court case might bring to light things the man would rather stay hidden.

'Do you know why Lovejoy has refused?'

Ridley shook his head. 'At the moment, he isn't up to talking much, but I reckon it's to do with that damn farm. If Lovejoy wants to clinch a deal for whoever's employing him – and I take your point that it's probably Tyler – then being responsible for Sir Frederick's nephew going to prison isn't too helpful.'

'Why is Neville still in custody if Lovejoy won't prosecute?'

'For questioning in the Milburn case. I want to find out just what happened that afternoon at Birds Acre. Sir Frederick was there, we know, and his land agent, but was Piers Neville?'

'You must have asked him.'

The inspector gave a wintry smile. 'On several occasions, Jack. Grilled him, I would say is more accurate. He maintains he wasn't at the farm.'

'We believe he was. We think he has information about that afternoon that he's using to blackmail his uncle. Mind,' he admitted, 'it's only speculation at the moment.'

'It's all speculation, that's the problem.' The inspector moodily broke open his bag of crisps. 'Tyler's another speculation. In my book, he's in the frame for murdering Percy Milburn. It was a particularly brutal killing that has Tyler's hallmark. He decides he wants to buy Birds Acre – why is an open question though I don't reckon it's to grow corn – and Percy Milburn is in the way. Milburn's offer has been verbally accepted and he's getting ready to put it in writing. If Tyler was to buy the farm, his rival had to be removed. I can prove the man was in the area at the time, but what I can't prove is that he was ever at the farm.'

'Where is he now, do you think? The last time I saw him, he was rushing from the village hall in pursuit of Lovejoy. He must have heard his so-called solicitor has been attacked.'

Ridley nodded. 'Bound to have. He's gone to ground, I reckon, but where...? We got nothing out of Lovejoy. Tried pumping him, but it was next to useless. He's refused even to confirm he's working for Tyler. Once the chap's off the sick list, we'll question him again, but I don't hold out much hope. He's sure to keep his mouth shut. Too scared – Piers Neville may have got there first, but Tyler was after him, and still will be.'

Jack scrunched his empty crisp bag into a tight ball and flicked it across the table.

'Did Piers Neville say why he went for Lovejoy?'

'Says he didn't like the way the man wore his beret. In other words, he's not talking either. Another Mr Silence is our Piers. No one's speaking and Tyler's missing. Not exactly a great place for the team to find itself in.'

'It's possible that someone in the village might spot Tyler,' Jack said cheerfully, hoping to boost the inspector's gloomy mood. 'He drew attention to himself by going after Lovejoy at a public meeting. That was stupid.'

'I said he was brutal, not clever. Employing a bent solicitor who looks a bit of an oddity wasn't too clever either. Lovejoy was bound to be noticed in a place like Abbeymead. Certain to draw comment. Then there's this Miss Ticehurst raising hell over the farm and rousing opposition in the village. That's the last thing you'd want if you're trying to do a secret deal.' He took a draught of his beer. 'I've had some complaints about Miss Ticehurst.'

Jack looked questioningly at him.

'A bit too keen on the campaigning, it seems. But she's small fry. It's Tyler I want to nail.'

'If you don't find him before Lovejoy is out of hospital...'

'Could be carnage. There's a score to settle somewhere. Lovejoy has a history. From what we've dug up, he's been involved in stuff that's barely legal and some of it definitely not. This isn't the first time he's worked for Tyler either. He'd have got a handsome pay-off for that, but maybe afterwards lost work, ran out of money and went back to Tyler for help.'

Jack nodded. 'If he's borrowed money, it would be after he was struck off.'

'So, Tyler gives him enough to survive, and tells him his job is to acquire Birds Acre on the quiet. That's a bit of a joke now. The business has gone pear-shaped and Lovejoy is in trouble. When he can, he'll probably hightail it back to London. Take his chances there and hope that by then we've got Tyler banged up in a cell.'

'What's the likelihood of that?'

'At the moment, not great. We'll bring him in for questioning once we nab him, but he's a toughie. He won't break.' Ridley sighed. 'Our best hope is to chip away at the weakest link in this saga.'

'Sir Frederick Neville?'

'That's a crime writer talking! Yes, Sir Frederick. The man seems desperate to sell his farm for the most money he can get. And not just that. He wants to make sure he has regular income from it. At least, that's the picture I'm getting.'

'It's my impression, too, though I'm surprised he's in such financial difficulty. The family's landholdings are considerable, and Neville must derive a large income from them.'

Ridley shook his head and took a long sip of beer. 'These large estates bleed their owners dry.'

Jack pondered, wondering how much of a weak link Sir Frederick might prove. 'Even if he is strapped for cash, that doesn't necessarily make him vulnerable to questioning.'

'No, but his nephew in a police cell might. As does the fact that Piers Neville faces a possible prison sentence. And the fact that he's suspected of planning to blackmail his uncle...'

'Stop!' Jack held up his hand, laughing. 'OK. Sir Frederick has a few questions to answer.'

'And I'm hoping you'll be the one to ask them.'

'You want me to go to Bramber Hall again?'

The inspector nodded. 'You, and Miss Steele. We need her clever little mind.' He wore a pleased smile. 'See, this time I got it right. I didn't mention she was your girl.'

'I'm not at all sure she is,' Jack said disconsolately, picking up his glass and finishing his beer.

When Jack walked into the bookshop early the next morning and suggested they make a visit to Bramber Hall on Wednesday afternoon, Flora was doubtful. How much more would they learn by talking to Sir Frederick again? The inspector seemed convinced that if they continued to chip away at the man, a clue to Percy's death would magically appear. It didn't seem likely to Flora, though it was more listlessness than doubt that made her unenthusiastic. This last week or so, she'd lacked the energy to do anything more than open the All's Well each day and even that was proving an effort. She felt worn down by the spectre shadowing her life: the knowledge of a malevolence that was aimed squarely at her. A knowledge that she couldn't lose.

Flora had been in tight situations before; she'd occasionally risked her life – it was a price paid for the sleuthing she so enjoyed. But they had been physical threats and somehow so much easier to deal with. She'd been threatened, she'd fought back and, so far, had emerged unscathed. Almost unscathed, she amended. But what she faced now was different. It was the sense of a brooding presence determined to hurt her. A presence close by, someone who shared her world, or how else would they have known of the photograph she cherished? Or the pain that destroying her books would inflict. Or the hurt of a beloved tree ruined. This person knew her, that was the awful thing. They knew her and hated her.

'You don't have to come,' Jack said, when she hesitated. 'If you're busy.'

She caught the slight hint of disapproval in his voice. They had never completely recovered their comfort together since the moment Jack had come close to proposing.

'I'm not sure it's worth the effort, that's all.' When he said nothing, she was stung into saying, 'But then, what is?'

'Flora!' There was a frown on his face. 'What's going on with you?'

She was about to insist that absolutely nothing was going on when the tears started. And when they started, she couldn't stop them.

Aghast, Jack was by her side in a moment, circling her with his arms. Still with his arms around her, he walked her over to the window seat and handed her a clean cotton handkerchief. After several blows and a frantic wiping of eyes, she managed to say a trifle hoarsely, 'I'm all right.'

'That you're not. What is it? You must tell me.'

She had wanted to tell him, badly, but something had held her back. A feeling that she had chosen her way and had no right to burden him with her unhappiness. But now her reserve crumbled and, between loud sniffs, she recounted her tale of the missing photograph.

Jack sat with his hands clasped together, a bleak expression on his face. 'There's a campaign being waged against you,' he said, as she trailed to an end, 'and it has to be by someone in the village. Think back, Flora – is there anyone with whom you've had a spat in recent weeks?'

'A spat! Jack, this person is targeting me through things that are... that are... My home feels violated. My shop feels violated. I feel violated.'

He gripped both her hands, holding them tight between his. 'It was a stupid question, but if it's not someone you've personally upset, then it has to be connected to the Milburn case. And I just don't see how.'

Flora wriggled her hands free, turning to face him directly. 'That's because it can't be. It simply can't. If it were, you'd be in the firing line, too. I'm tired of pointing out that you've been left untouched. And don't say it's because I'm an easier target.'

'OK, I won't, but you have to admit it leaves us precisely nowhere.' He took back his handkerchief and pushed it deep into his pocket. 'Let's hope Ridley is right and Sir Frederick proves the easy target he thinks,' he said peaceably. 'I'm to go to Bramber Hall and attempt to get him talking. Try to pierce that shell of privilege.' Jack eased himself to his feet and looked down at her, a slight frown creasing his forehead. 'Maybe, after all, it's not a good idea that you come. If by some remote chance there *is* a connection to the venom you're facing... visiting Sir Frederick for the second time might bring more retribution.'

Flora bounced up, a challenge in her eyes. 'I'm with you,' she said decidedly. 'Whoever is behind these attacks, they can do what they will. I'll not be browbeaten and, in any case, how much more of mine can they destroy?'

'You're definitely coming?'

'I'm definitely coming,' she said, clasping his hand in affirmation.

20

It was Mr Higgins who again opened the imposing doors of Bramber Hall to them. Aloof as ever, he conducted them once more to the library. The library no one ever visited, Flora thought.

This time it was some while before they heard the footsteps approach and, when Sir Frederick appeared in the doorway, he did not look pleased. Not that he had on their first visit, she reflected. But then his expression had been one of bored neutrality, now he was frowning and suspicious.

'You telephoned,' he barked out. 'Told my secretary that Inspector Ridley had asked you to call a second time.' There was no invitation to sit down.

'That's right,' Jack said easily. 'I apologise for intruding again' – there was an audible grunt from their host – 'but after recent developments, the inspector felt another chat might be beneficial.'

Inwardly, Flora smiled. A chat was unlikely. If Jack had his way it would be a grilling, and beneficial to whom?

'By recent developments, I assume you're referring to the idiot I have the misfortune to call a nephew.'

'Mr Neville is still in custody,' Jack said smoothly. 'Anything you can tell us that might help secure his release would be helpful.'

'He can stay there, as far as I'm concerned. Washed my hands of the blighter.' Sir Frederick's mouth settled into a grim line. 'Tried to do what I could for him since he was a sprog and what thanks have I ever had? Did it for his father, too, before he died, though my brother wasn't exactly my cup of tea. His mother can sort him out now – if she'll have anything to do with him. Probably not. He burnt his boats in that direction years ago.'

If there had ever been a partnership between uncle and nephew, innocent or guilty, it seemed to Flora to be out of the question now.

'Have you any idea why he would have attacked Mr Lovejoy?' she asked.

Sir Frederick looked blank. 'No idea. No idea what goes through what passes for his mind.'

'Does it seem out of character to you?' she pursued. 'Has your nephew ever done this kind of thing before?'

'Beaten someone up? He may have done, but I doubt it.'

That was a lie if Alice was right in believing Sir Frederick had rescued his nephew from a similar situation in the past.

'It's strange that he chose Sidney Lovejoy to attack.' Jack looked directly at the man, and Sir Frederick lowered his eyes, glowering at the floor. 'Lovejoy is the man negotiating the sale of the farm, isn't he?' When their host made no response, Jack continued, 'I may have it wrong, but I understood that your nephew's future is dependent on that negotiation. In which case, Lovejoy is a strange target to choose.'

Sir Frederick flicked a finger through a magazine on the table beside him. He was decidedly uncomfortable, Flora could see.

'Lovejoy was still negotiating with you when he was attacked?' Jack wasn't going to let it go.

'Yes, I suppose so,' Sir Frederick grumbled. 'Negotiating with me – and my land agent.'

It was then that Colin Palmer stepped forward. He must have slipped into the room unnoticed and been standing in the shadow of the far bookcase, unremarked but listening to every word of their conversation.

'Thought he should be here,' their host said awkwardly.

Flora stepped forward and offered her hand. 'It's good to see you again, Mr Palmer. I'm sure you'll be able to solve the mystery.'

'What mystery is that, Miss Steele?' Colin Palmer dug his hands deep into his pockets. There was a smear of Brylcreem, she noticed, on his lapel. Had he got ready in a hurry? Been called to Bramber Hall in an emergency?

'At the risk of repeating ourselves, the mystery of why Piers Neville attacked Mr Lovejoy,' she answered, a sunny smile on her face. 'As Mr Carrington mentioned, this was the man who was negotiating the sale on which Mr Neville was so keen.'

The two men looked at each other. 'My nephew and I disagreed over details,' Sir Frederick eventually admitted. 'Palmer and I were continuing the negotiation but without Piers.'

'Why would that be?' The smile had faded, replaced by a face of innocent enquiry. 'What kind of details?'

'That has absolutely nothing to do with you, or with Inspector Ridley.'

'Was it because Piers wanted the farm for himself?' Jack asked.

'If you must know, yes. The boy's a nonentity with big ideas. To shut him up, I promised the manager's job to him if the hotel was built, but that wasn't enough. Got it into his head that there'd be no hotel. No idea why, have you, Palmer?' he asked theatrically.

Palmer gave a hasty shake of his head.

'Has Piers discussed with you his plan to buy the farm?'

Sir Frederick barely suppressed a sneer. 'Absolutely no chance of that. Even if he managed to wangle a loan – and the idea is laughable – I wouldn't sell to him.'

'Because he would offer a much lower price? Or no money at all?' Flora maintained her innocent expression.

Sir Frederick stared at her.

'He threatened you, didn't he?'

At this, the man visibly started, and it was Palmer who came to his rescue.

'Nothing as sinister as a threat,' he said smoothly. 'Merely a difference of opinion.'

'Quite a difference, I think. Your nephew, Sir Frederick, discovered who Lovejoy was working for and realised that no hotel would ever be built. He knew who'd be buying Birds Acre Farm, and he didn't like it.'

It was a guess based on what Piers had already told them and Flora saw from their faces that she was right. She plunged on. 'Doesn't it bother you, Sir Frederick, that you were knowingly selling to a criminal? Doesn't it bother *you*, Mr Palmer?'

'I know nothing about a criminal,' Neville protested angrily, 'and I thank you never to repeat such a gross insinuation. My land agent has had a perfectly legal offer for the farm.' He looked towards Palmer who nodded. 'And I will accept it.'

'Despite your nephew's threat to reveal what you wish to keep hidden? I think it's known as blackmail.'

'This is utterly ludicrous.' Sir Frederick strode across the room and in a fury rang the service bell.

'Piers doesn't think so. I'm guessing he saw you at the farm the afternoon Mr Milburn was murdered.'

'Of course I was at the farm. Higgins!' he roared. 'Where is the damn man? I was at Birds Acre to meet Milburn. How many times do I have to say it? I arrived late but the man wasn't there. I'd no idea he was already dead.'

Palmer again nodded. Like one of those toy dogs she'd seen recently, Flora thought.

'Were you late because you'd been there earlier?' Jack enquired pleasantly.

'What kind of nonsense is this?'

'You drove yourself that day. That was unusual, I believe. Was it because you'd made an earlier visit to the farm that you didn't want known?'

'Your nephew saw you there and the price of his silence is the farm,' Flora rushed on, on tenterhooks that at any minute the butler would arrive and forcibly escort them to the door. 'If Piers confirms to the police exactly when he saw you, I'm sure it will prove a match for the time Mr Milburn died.'

As she had feared, Mr Higgins glided through the open doorway and bowed.

'You took your bloody time!' his master exploded. 'Get these people out of my house and make sure they're never allowed in again.'

Once outside, Flora laughed for the first time in days. 'That went well.'

'I don't think Alan will be sending us as ambassadors again.' Jack's smile was rueful.

'I hope he doesn't get into trouble with his superior,' she said, as they walked back to the Austin. 'You said Ridley's boss knows Sir Frederick well.'

'That will be Alan's problem. If he wants, he can deny all knowledge of us.'

'We're to be sacrificial lambs?'

'Something like that. But was it worth getting thrown out for?'

She stopped, her hand on the car door. 'I'm not entirely sure. We've established that Lovejoy was the go-between, but we knew that already, and that Sir Frederick knows Dennis Tyler is the purchaser but isn't bothered by the man's criminal record. Or bothered by blackmail. He intends to ride out whatever storm his nephew kicks up. The agreement with Lovejoy is too important to him.'

'He really must be desperate for money. I wonder why?'

'The inspector should be able to answer that – his team are looking into the family finances, aren't they?'

'I'm not sure they've got too far with it, but that seems a piece with everything else.'

'It was interesting that Palmer turned up,' she said, as Jack guided the car down the sweep of driveway and onto the narrow road beyond.

'My guess would be that he didn't just turn up. He was summoned to be the nodding dog.'

Flora smiled across at him, sharply aware of how much she and Jack were alike. 'Is he covering for Sir Frederick, do you think?'

'Possibly. More than likely,' he amended. 'Or maybe they planned poor Percy's death between them.'

They might have joked about their expulsion from Bramber Hall, but there was nothing humorous in what had been happening to Flora. Yesterday, she'd said little of the spiteful campaign directed against her, but Jack knew the personal attacks had upset her more than anything else she'd suffered since stumbling into a sleuthing role. The lack of an obvious motive made things worse. Despite Flora's rejection of the idea, he couldn't entirely lose the notion that a local quarrel might be at the bottom of it. Was there someone in the village seeking revenge for something she had done or said? If so, it was an exorbitant price being demanded.

But if it wasn't about revenge, petty or otherwise, it had to be connected to the murder. The campaign against her had begun the very moment they'd started to ask questions. *They* had asked questions, that was the crucial point, yet it was Flora bearing the brunt. She had been a friend of Percy's while he, Jack, had not. She was the one who'd suggested going to the farm where they'd found Milburn's body. His contacts with the police might have deterred an attack on him, maybe that was it, while Flora – she would be quick to deny it – appeared more defenceless. If he had anything to do with it, she wouldn't remain so. He'd follow his own enquiries into Percy's death but, for her safety, leave Flora out of it.

How many people had been at Birds Acre Farm that afternoon was still unclear; Sir Frederick Neville and Colin Palmer were the only certainties and it's them he should focus on. No matter how hard he tried, though, Jack couldn't see Palmer as a killer. Murdering to gain a higher commission was unlikely, but it was the man himself who didn't fit. The killing had been cold-blooded, carefully planned and with the timing crucial. The staircase had been destroyed and Percy lured to the cellar, possibly minutes before the meeting was due to begin. Did Palmer have the ability to plan so meticulously? Did he have the sheer nerve that would be required? He was smarmy, shallow and overconfident and, unless the real Palmer was hiding beneath a false front, Jack doubted it. The man would bear further investigation, but it was Sir Frederick he'd start with. He had a clear motive and possibly, Jack suspected, a brutish clever-ness that could have pulled the murder off.

The fact that Neville needed money so badly he was willing to sell to a known criminal, was an indication that he could be in far more trouble than was obvious. Money always talked and men desperate for it were liable to be dragged into a mire of corruption. That seemed to have happened to Neville.

But why was the man so hard up? And why had he chosen to sell at this time? Birds Acre had become vacant after generations of Martins had worked its fields, but the Neville family owned acres of land and a multitude of farms. Sir Frederick could have sold property at any time, so why now? Had something happened recently that meant he needed money urgently?

Trying to push the matter from his mind, at least temporarily, Jack climbed the stairs to his favourite room, and settled to write. He'd made a good start on the new book – twenty thousand words already – and was keen to keep the momentum going.

It was three hours later that the telephone rang, and Alan Ridley's voice sounded down the line.

'Just to let you know, old chap, I've had to let Piers Neville go.'

Jack lowered himself into the torn brocade of the hall chair. 'That's disappointing.'

The inspector muttered something he couldn't hear, then a little louder, 'I've still not managed to persuade Lovejoy to press charges. Says he's getting better and wants no more trouble. He'll be lucky! But it's meant that all I've been able to do is issue a severe warning to that idiot boy and escort him to the door.'

'Did you ask him again about the afternoon of the murder?'

'Course I did. Hammered him like hell. But all he'll say is that he wasn't at the farm and knows nothing about the meeting there.'

Back in his study once more, Jack fiddled with his tray of pens. It had been an annoying phone call. Piers Neville had given them nothing. No reason for attacking Lovejoy, though their guess had to be right. No admission that Piers meant to attempt blackmail – would he still carry out his threat now he was free? No information on that crucial afternoon at the farm. If he had been there and seen something incriminating, he'd lied repeatedly about it to the police. That would take some audacity but perhaps the boy had it.

Jack turned back to the Remington, his enthusiasm doused. This investigation had reached the point where it felt it was going nowhere. That always happened. There was always a moment when you began to question whether you'd be best to give up, but then something made you carry on.

This time it was Flora: the need to protect her, to keep her from further heartache. Flora would ensure he carried on.

21

Flora was disappointed that evening to hear the inspector had been forced to release Piers Neville from custody, without prising even the smallest morsel of information from the man. It was clear that Piers would never be able to raise sufficient money to buy the farm and Flora was certain she was guessing right: that he was relying on Sir Frederick to pass the property to him in exchange for his silence.

Piers must have been at the farm but what about Lovejoy? If he'd had wind of Sir Frederick's meeting with Percy Milburn, he might have thought it sensible to make an appearance, remind Sir Frederick of the advantages of his offer over Percy's. Had *he* been at the farm and seen what happened? If so... it was an intriguing thought... he might have tangled in some way with Piers' plans for blackmail and that could have been a reason for the young man's attack on him.

Even if Lovejoy had been nowhere near the farm, getting rid of the solicitor removed an obstacle for Piers as he attempted to make Birds Acre his own. By all accounts, he had hurt Lovejoy badly but hadn't killed him. Hurt him sufficiently to encourage the man to flee Abbeymead and not return? In effect, to forget the whole business of acquiring the farm. If Alice's information was correct, and it was rare for it not to be, Piers had a past conviction for violent behaviour. When he couldn't get his own way, he resorted to physical attack – strange for such a puny fellow – and getting his own way in this case was to build a hotel and luxuriate in being its owner.

Everyone in this story had some kind of relation to Piers Neville, she reflected – his uncle literally, the land agent pushing to sell to the highest bidder, Lovejoy negotiating against him, Tyler as the buyer who could ruin the young man's future. Flora doubted she'd be more successful than the inspector in persuading Piers to talk, but there might be someone more willing.

Prue Norland had seemed a decent girl and appeared genuinely worried for her boyfriend. She could be the person to talk to again. When they'd called at the Brighton flat, Piers had told them she was at an audition in Worthing for a part in an Agatha Christie play. He'd been dismissive, but Christie drew large audiences and, if Prue had been successful in winning a role, she was guaranteed work for months, not just at the Connaught Theatre – Flora had found mention of the forthcoming play listed in the latest edition of the *Worthing Echo* – but elsewhere, when the play went on tour.

Rather than return to the flat in Brighton in the hope of finding the girl at home, she chose to make a trip to Worthing. A bus ran from Abbeymead twice a day and, if she caught the early service, she could be in the town by ten o'clock. Michael had already dismantled the bookcases in preparation, but tomorrow he was due at last to cut a large hole in the All's Well's rear wall. Flora had been unsure whether or not to stay open – the noise and dust would be off-putting to customers. Now, thinking of how much she wanted to see Prue and how soon, she decided that for once the All's Well would stay closed on a Friday.

. . .

Flora's alarm failed to go off the following morning and she made the bus by a mere whisker. The driver had put the vehicle into gear and was about to drive off when the ticket collector hauled her onto the open platform.

'You cut that a bit fine, miss,' the man said.

She managed a half smile, concentrating her energies on recovering her breath. She had run at full pelt the length of Greenway Lane and half the high street and now sank exhausted into one of the many empty seats. Few passengers travelled to Worthing from Abbeymead this early in the morning.

For some while, she allowed the countryside of woods, river and fields to pass her by, her mind a restful blank. But as the roads became busier and the landscape sprouted people and dwellings, she bent her thoughts on how best to go about the day. There should be someone at the theatre, she reckoned, even though rehearsals were probably not scheduled until the afternoon. A janitor maybe, cleaners, stagehands. One of them might be able to tell her where and when she could find Prue Norland. It was at this point she realised what an enormous gamble she'd embarked on. What was to say that Prue was even in Worthing? The girl might have fluffed the audition or been offered the job and turned it down. Flora might have been better, after all, to have returned to the Brighton flat. Too late now, she thought, as the bus dropped her in South Street. From there, it was a short walk before she turned into Union Place and was standing outside the Connaught Theatre.

As she walked up to the entrance the sun, which had been hiding behind thick cloud for most of her journey, made a sudden escape, hitting the rounded curves of the art deco building and sparking its glazed white tiles with a brilliant light. A good omen, perhaps? Flora hoped so.

Inside, the foyer was a little less glittering, though scalloped wall lights and ornate ironwork banisters suggested the same artistry at work. A cleaner was pushing a mop desultorily around the floor tiles, knocking periodically into the minimalist bench seats that lined the walls.

'Good morning,' Flora said brightly. The woman behind the mop barely looked up.

'I wonder... do you know any of the actors who will be on stage tonight?' It was a feeble question but, in the circumstances, the best she could do.

The woman shook her head and bent once more to her task.

'Is there anyone I could speak to?' Flora tried, a little desperately.

'You can speak to me.' A young man wearing an open-necked shirt and creased slacks appeared from behind the hexagonal booking kiosk. He looked helpful. 'I'm the stage manager.'

'I'm trying to trace someone,' she said gratefully. 'I think she might be part of the cast in *The Spider's Web*.' She'd been reminded of the play's name by the advertising banner outside.

The young man managed to look surprised and slightly suspicious at the same time. But then, why wouldn't he? It was an odd request.

'Who are you looking for?'

'Her name is Prue Norland.'

'Oh, Prue.' He sounded relieved that he wasn't dealing with some demented fan who'd wandered in from the street on the off chance of molesting a stray actor.

'She's in the play?' Flora was relieved, too.

'She is indeed. And rehearsing right now.'

'Really? At this time of day?'

'It's a matinée afternoon. Rehearsals have to be in the morning – not always popular with certain members of the cast, but there you are.'

'I really need to speak to Prue. Have you any idea when she'll be finished?'

He scratched at the stray hairs on his chin – he seemed to be trying to grow a beard – then nodded. 'She's playing Pippa. That's the stepdaughter. She could be through with her scenes pretty soon.'

'Is there a chance you could get word to her that a friend is here?'

'I can try. Who shall I say?' Flora could still sense a whiff of scepticism.

'Flora Steele. We had tea together in Abbeymead last week.'

'If you'd like to wait in the bar, I'll see what I can do. Up the stairs and to the right.'

Flora thanked him and climbed the elaborate staircase to the first floor. Standing on the threshold, she took in the extensive space ahead: more art deco curves, she noticed, in the enormous, polished wood counter that stretched almost the entire length of the room. Tables and chairs, though, were strictly functional. She chose a table by the window and set herself to wait.

She hadn't to wait long. The sound of running feet, then Prue erupted through the door, a huge smile on her face. For a moment, Flora was disconcerted. Her friend was dressed for school: knee socks, lace-up shoes and a long plait hanging over each shoulder.

'Don't worry!' Prue burst out laughing. 'This is Pippa Hailsham-Brown, not me.'

'And Pippa is?'

'An emotionally disturbed twelve-year-old. But if you're in the mood for a murder mystery with a comic twist, I can get you a ticket.' She tripped across the room and bent to give Flora a quick hug, as though she had known her for years. 'How lovely to see you, Flora. Have you come to town to shop?'

'Something like that,' she fudged. 'When I saw the play

advertised, I thought you might be in it. You were at an audition when we called on Piers.'

'Oh, Piers.' The brightness disappeared and she looked crestfallen. 'I haven't seen him for a while. Rehearsals started immediately after the audition and I had to find a place to stay, and since then it's been busy...' She tailed off.

'I can imagine,' Flora said sympathetically. 'How was he when you saw him last?'

Prue pulled up a chair and sat down. 'I don't think he was too happy that you called at the flat,' she said cautiously. 'Not that there was anything wrong with you calling, but Piers can be... difficult... and this whole business with the farm and with his uncle has really upset him. Now, he's got himself into the most awful trouble attacking that man.'

'You heard?'

'Our neighbour in Brighton telephoned me to say the police had arrested him. It was such a shock.'

'Has he done anything like that before?' Flora believed that he had but she wondered how honest Piers had been with his girlfriend.

Prue looked down at the floor's wooden boards. 'Maybe a little.'

Something in her voice made Flora look directly at her. 'He attacked *you*?'

'Just a slap now and again. Nothing too serious. Nothing like the man in hospital suffered.'

'Oh Prue. You should never accept that a slap is OK.'

'I don't. Not any more.' Her voice wobbled slightly. 'Since I've been here, I've made friends. People in the cast, other people in Worthing. I've found somewhere nice to live while the play is on but, even when the run is over, I'm not going back. I haven't told Piers yet. Is he still in a police cell?'

'Inspector Ridley has had to let him go. Mr Lovejoy refused

to prefer charges, and there's little more the police can do if the Crown Prosecutor decides not to go ahead.'

The girl's shoulders lost their tension. 'That's such a relief. I think prison would have been disastrous for him.'

'Then he should refrain from attacking people,' Flora said curtly, unable to stop herself.

Prue shifted in her chair. 'He was so angry, you see. Angry that his uncle was still carrying on with the sale of the farm even though Sir Frederick must have known to whom he was selling. A criminal, Piers told me!'

Flora nodded. 'In that case, he should surely have attacked his uncle and not Lovejoy. Mr Lovejoy was only the negotiator.'

'I think he thought it was enough to threaten his uncle with a big revelation, whereas Mr Lovejoy was a large obstacle standing in his way. While the man was still offering to buy the farm, Piers might not get it. If this Lovejoy character could be got rid of, the sale would fall through. That's how I think he thought,' Prue finished lamely.

'He might have been right,' Flora agreed. Once out of hospital, Lovejoy would almost certainly vanish. 'But I'm sure his uncle and Colin Palmer won't let it go. They'll be looking for another buyer. Whatever threat Piers hoped to wield over Sir Frederick doesn't appear to have worked.' When the girl made no response, Flora pushed a little more. 'That threat – did you ever discover what it was about? Was it to do with Percy Milburn's death?'

'Milburn?'

'The man Sir Frederick went to meet at Birds Acre. Did Piers go there, too?'

'When was that?'

Flora pushed her fingers through long strands of hair and thought hard. 'It was a Friday. The twelfth of April.' What hope was there that Prue could remember that far back?

'The twelfth!' The girl literally squealed. 'It was my birthday!' She was beaming now. 'I'm not saying which birthday, though.'

Flora ignored the coyness and, leaning forward, her tone was urgent. 'Do you remember what you did that day?'

'We went on the Palace Pier in the morning, just for fun. Walked to the very end, then played on the slot machines, that kind of thing. Afterwards, Piers treated me to a fish and chip lunch at the Regency. That was lovely. It *was* a lovely day.' She gave a little sigh.

'So, Piers was with you that afternoon?'

'I think so.' Prue suddenly sounded uncertain. 'We went back to the flat after lunch and played a game of Monopoly. He said if I won, I could have an extra birthday present. He'd already given me a beautiful filigree brooch – Piers can be really generous.'

'And did you win?'

'I don't think we ever finished the game,' she said hazily.

'Why was that?' Flora tried to hide her excitement, but her voice betrayed her.

'I'm not sure.' She appeared surprised at the question. 'Maybe Piers had to go out. I can't remember. We'd drunk quite a lot of beer by then!'

'Does Piers own a car?'

'If you can call it a car.' Prue gave a giggle. 'It's a beaten-up old thing.'

'But it works?'

'Just about.' Her smile faltered. 'Why? Why is it important?'

Flora gave an airy shake of her head, trying hard to pretend it wasn't. 'It was just a thought. I wondered if Piers might have driven to Abbeymead that afternoon, to the farm. He seems fixated on it.'

'He could have done, I suppose,' Prue said slowly. 'Now I

think about it, I went to sleep for a while. Monopoly can be quite boring.'

'If Piers took a drive that afternoon, went to the farm and saw something bad there, do you think he might use it to threaten his uncle?'

'I thought that's what you were thinking! But I don't believe that was the threat.'

Flora waited.

'I'm not really sure why – Piers never spelt out precisely what he'd said to his uncle, except that it would be bad for Sir Frederick if it got known – but I got the impression that whatever it was happened a long time ago.' She pursed her lips. 'It's just an impression, though.'

'If it's past history, it can't be such a dangerous threat.' Flora felt deflated. She'd been on the verge, she believed, of discovering Percy's murderer. Of finding evidence that would stand up in court.

'Any threat to Sir Frederick is dangerous,' Prue said in a subdued voice.

'How do you mean?' Flora leaned forward again. Perhaps this meeting might come up trumps after all.

'I don't know Piers' uncle very well,' the girl murmured, 'but I know that he dislikes Piers and wishes him ill. He wants to be rid of him, Flora. And Sir Frederick is someone who is used to getting his own way.'

Flora frowned. 'You sound as though you're scared of Sir Frederick, but it's Piers who has proved violent.'

'His uncle frightens me far more than Piers ever has,' Prue said. 'Shall we go for a cuppa somewhere? I'm dying of thirst.'

Flora nodded. Tea might help, though she doubted it. The conversation with Prue had left her more confused than ever. She was walking through a mist that appeared impenetrable, every potential avenue ending in failure. Determined she might be, but would it be sufficient to uncover the truth?

22

Jack stretched his arms to the ceiling, then fished for the typewriter cover. The Remington had done him proud today but enough was enough. He'd earned his second coffee – Arthur was a trojan sending him the very best on a regular basis – and, in minutes, he was in the kitchen and putting the water on to boil. He'd just taken his first sip when Charlie Teague's head appeared around the back door. Jack had asked him to call this afternoon but, glancing at his watch, he was suspicious.

'You're out of school early. Not bunking, I hope,' he said, ushering in his young friend.

Charlie grinned. His face, Jack noticed, was subtly altering, the full cheeks of childhood gradually refining themselves into the facial curves of the young adult he would become. He wondered how much longer the boy would want to spend his spare time in Jack's back garden.

'We wuz let out early. Old Dobbs has got flu and there was no one to take his class.' Old Dobbs was probably only a few years older than himself, Jack realised. It made his heart sink a little.

'Are we plantin' beetroot?'

'I thought so, and carrots and French beans if you're up for it.'

Charlie fidgeted. 'Mebbe not all today. I gotta go in an hour. Gotta help Mum carry some magazines. Women's stuff,' he said scornfully.

'We can finish the planting at the weekend and it's good to help your mother. Don't look so glum.'

'We gotta go to that old people's place. It takes fer ever to get there – three buses – and it's full of old people.'

'I imagine it would be.' Jack thought for a moment, then made a decision. 'Why don't I drive you and your mum?'

Charlie's face perked up. 'Cor, that'd be good.'

'Let's knock off the beetroot before we go – we should have time.'

When Jack pulled up outside the house in Swallow Lane with Charlie in the back of the Austin and Mrs Teague learned they were to be driven to the nursing home, she couldn't say enough thank yous.

'It's a real devil to get to,' she said. 'Right out in the country. The nearest bus stop's half a mile away. I wouldn't do it if it weren't for Mrs Fellowes. I used to cook and clean for the lady when Charlie was a baby. We needed the money – Mr Teague was never exactly a good provider, if you know what I mean – and Mrs Fellowes allowed me to take Charlie to work or I'd never have been able to do it. She was such a lovely woman. Lived in a beautiful house. It was obvious she had a lot of money, but she was nice with it.'

'And you visit her regularly?' Jack heaved two large bags of magazines into the boot before helping Mrs Teague into the car.

'Not regularly. Well, I couldn't, the buses being what they are. But twice a year at least. I collect magazines for the old lady, you see. She finds reading books too hard these days with her eyesight not being what it was, but she enjoys flicking through the mags. They don't need much attention, do they?'

On Mrs Teague's directions, Jack drove out of the village in the direction of Brighton, but almost immediately took the left hand turning to Edburton and Fulking, two villages some way distant from Abbeymead. A mile or so out of Fulking, his companion tapped him on the arm and nodded towards a narrow lane they were approaching on their right.

'I'm not surprised you don't make it more than twice a year,' Jack said, driving cautiously along a thoroughfare that was no more than six feet wide in parts. He was relieved they'd met nothing coming the other way before a square wooden board appeared at the side of the road announcing that beyond the hedge was Capri Lawns.

'Capri Lawns?' he enquired.

'It's that kind of place,' Mrs Teague said comfortably. 'Posh, you know. You have to have money to get a room there.'

He could see the truth of this as they bowled up the long drive leading to the main building, a Georgian delight of red brick and rigid symmetry. The gardens on either side were immaculate. Smooth bowling green lawns interspersed with neat flowerbeds that burst with colour: pansies, peonies and delphiniums. He ticked them off one by one, feeling pride that these days he actually knew their names.

'It's clearly a moneyed place.' He gave a wry grimace. 'A nursing home, you say?'

'More convalescent, I think.'

'People won't stay too long then.'

Mrs Teague thought about it. 'I guess not, though some do, particularly if they come when they're still quite young and don't get better. But you're right about the money. Last time I came, I heard as Lady Neville was a patient.'

Jack was immediately attentive. 'Sir Frederick's wife?

That's strange. I heard she was dead.' He knew that to be a wild rumour but, as a ploy, it was worth broaching.

His companion tutted. 'No, poor thing. She's been ill all these years, apparently. She was always fragile. I remember seeing her in the village once. Looked like a little brown bird, all skin and bone even when she was fit. But then she lost her son in the war. He was her only child, and it hit her that bad. She had a breakdown. Nobody knew much but she must have needed special care and it looks like she never recovered. It's wonderful that Sir Frederick found this place. It's very good. Very peaceful.'

'I can see that.' He walked round to open the car door for her, while Charlie had climbed from the back and was opening the boot.

'I'll walk in the gardens while you're with Mrs Fellowes,' he said. 'Don't rush. Take as much time as you want.'

The weather had been gentle today and, in early evening, the light was soft and the air still warm. A stroll through the grounds suited Jack's mood and he set off along one of the many gravel pathways that led from the main drive.

The path he chose led him past a bounty of spring flowers, past a walled garden, then a fountain set amid a circle of ever-greens and, as he drew closer, towards what seemed to be a summerhouse, its outside terrace sheltered by a wisteria-entwined roof.

A woman dressed in crisp white uniform was walking away from the building and towards him. A nurse? She must have been settling one of her patients on the terrace.

'Good evening.' He stopped to greet her.

She murmured a good evening and would have continued on her way, if Jack had not raised a hand as though to stop her.

'Sorry. I know you must be busy,' he apologised. 'I've driven some friends over to visit a patient here, a Mrs Fellowes, but I was wondering – do you have any news of Lady Neville?'

'Lady Neville?' The nurse's tone was sharp. She was clearly put out.

'Yes,' Jack said smoothly, ignoring her displeasure. 'I spoke to her husband a few days ago and he was telling me of this place. He's not able to visit at the moment,' he lied adeptly, 'but if you had any news of his wife, I could pass it on.'

The woman's expression relaxed. 'Lady Neville is well. As well as can be expected,' she amended.

'That's good to know. Sir Frederick will be pleased.' He gave her a warm smile. 'It's certainly a beautiful place to live.' He turned slightly, as though taking in the grandeur of Capri Lawns for the first time. 'I imagine you must have a waiting list?'

'Not really,' she said, and Jack didn't miss the tight expression.

'The fees?' he suggested gently.

The woman pulled her mouth down. 'Exactly. And going up all the time.'

He raised his eyebrows in assumed astonishment. 'Really? From what Sir Frederick disclosed to me privately, I wouldn't have thought they could have risen much more!'

The nurse shook her head. 'It's a very costly place to run.'

'I would think so,' he said sympathetically. 'After the hard times we've all had, it's a wonder it's been able to keep going.'

'Maybe not much longer,' she said gloomily. 'There's a rumour it might go under. The staff are worried sick.'

'I can imagine. I'll hope for all of you that it doesn't happen.'

'Thanks,' she said and, with a pallid smile, walked on.

When Charlie and Mrs Teague reappeared by the side of the Austin, Jack greeted them cheerfully. 'All well with your friend?'

'She seems quite chipper,' Mrs Teague said. 'Very pleased with the magazines. She gave our Charlie a shilling to spend.'

Charlie was looking a lot more cheerful and Jack had wondered why.

Driving them back to Abbeymead, he was feeling a deal more cheerful himself. He was fairly sure now that he knew why Sir Frederick was desperate for money. Over the years, the man had paid for his wife to have the best possible life she could – in a beautiful home with constant dedicated care – and he'd want her to continue having it. The fees, according to the nurse, had risen year on year and no doubt would keep doing so. Sir Frederick had obviously managed to pay them – he might manage to meet even higher costs – but if the nursing home were to close, what did that mean for him and Lady Neville? The place would have to be sold and its future put in jeopardy. Any enforced move would disturb his wife greatly, maybe too greatly. The only way to ensure that Capri Lawns remained a nursing home was to buy it and who might be willing to do that? In Jack's estimation, the answer was plain.

23

Flora was late getting home. The afternoon bus from Worthing had been cancelled at short notice and she'd had to wait in South Street for an hour before a replacement vehicle rumbled into sight. Walking through her cottage door a little before six that evening, she was tired and still muddled in her mind, unsure of what precisely she'd learned from Prue Norland. Without waiting to take off her jacket and shoes, she picked up the telephone and called Jack. She badly needed to speak to him. Prue's words had hit home. Sir Frederick had been on their list of villains from the outset, despite Inspector Ridley's caution at upsetting his superior, but Prue's evident fear of her boyfriend's uncle had raised troubling questions, chief of which was whether they had allowed their interest in Piers Neville to distract them from their most evident suspect.

Flora was disappointed, the telephone continuing to ring unanswered. For a moment, she contemplated walking to Overlay House to check whether the Austin was absent from its usual spot in the lane, but a combination of weariness and hunger had her turn to the larder instead. There wouldn't be much choice for supper, she saw, peering hopefully from one shelf to another – the remains of an outsize cottage pie she'd cooked the previous day would have to suffice.

She hardly tasted the pie, too busy mentally walking her way through a scene that had replayed itself a dozen times since Percy's death. How could Sir Frederick have murdered Percy, driven off but then returned to meet Colin Palmer as though nothing untoward had happened? And how, when all this was going on, had Piers Neville arrived at the farm, hidden himself away, and observed his uncle killing the man who stood in the way of his accepting a better offer? Prue had been sincere, genuinely frightened of Sir Frederick. Frightened of a man who never allowed anything to get in his way.

It was as Flora was tipping the empty dishes into the sink, her mind darting back and forth over the likely scenario, that the telephone rang. It had to be Jack. At last!

'Where have you been?' she asked, barely pausing to say hello. 'There's something I need to talk to you about. Now.'

'There's something *I* need to talk to *you* about, too. That's where I've been.'

Was it possible they'd both come up with breakthroughs? Flora held tight to the idea. 'Tell me!'

'Not on the phone. I need to see you. I'd come over to the cottage now except I haven't eaten.'

'Tomorrow evening then?' Could she wait that long – Flora's patience had never been elastic.

There was a pause before he spoke again. 'I think we need to talk sooner. Why don't I pick you up from the shop at lunchtime and drive you home. We won't be overheard in the cottage!'

'That sounds good. A few hours less to wait, though I'd better get something for lunch. The larder is bare.'

'Don't worry – I'll call in at Katie's on the way. I'll be with you before one.'

'Jack.' She wanted him to stay on the line, hear his voice a little longer. 'You are OK?'

'All in one piece,' he said cheerfully. 'But my head's a mess after what I've learned.'

'Mine, too.'

'We must find a way through together – make sure you sleep well.'

Flora looked up as the shop bell clanged, putting aside the brush and pan with which she'd been clearing the debris left from Michael's handiwork. Yesterday, he'd done her proud, working hours overtime to ensure she had a back door that was safe and secure.

It was Winifred Ticehurst and, scuttling in her wake, Elsie's diminutive figure.

'Good morning, Miss Steele,' Winifred boomed, her voice making a detour around the shelves of books and landing back at Flora. 'I've come for your petition.'

'Good morning, Miss Ticehurst, but I'm afraid you'll be unlucky. I never took a copy.' After the village meeting, Flora had decided against hosting a petition at the All's Well, concerned it might provoke more trouble.

'You didn't take one!'

'You should have.' Elsie bobbed her head disapprovingly, her tight perm this morning looking more than ever like a grey helmet.

'I understood it was a free choice and up to individual businesses whether or not they displayed the petition.'

'Will it be a free choice when Birds Acre Farm becomes a den of iniquity?' Winifred asked stormily. 'Attracting the worst possible elements to our village?'

'I think that may be an overreaction. Whoever finally buys the farm, I can't imagine Sir Fredrick would allow it to degenerate into the kind of place you describe.'

In fact, Flora wasn't at all sure. Prue's words were still with her, and Sir Frederick had shown no compunction at openly encouraging a purchaser who, though he might be going straight now – which the inspector very much doubted – had a long list of violent crimes behind him.

'Overreaction!' Winifred snorted. 'I hardly think so. I had hoped for better from you, Miss Steele. I know for a fact that you have had ample opportunity to dissuade Sir Frederick, but it's evident you have refused to use it. A great shame. However, I shall be speaking to him myself in the near future – I have already made the appointment.'

Why the woman had got it into her mind that she had the power to influence Sir Frederick, Flora had no idea, but it did suggest that Winifred was keeping track of her movements. The woman seemed to know already that only three days ago she and Jack had gone on a second visit to Bramber Hall.

'That Sir Frederick, he's not a nice man,' Elsie Flowers put in.

'Why is that?' Flora asked, hoping to learn something useful.

'Always after money, for one thing. Married his poor wife for money, then put her away when she got sick.' Elsie leaned forward, breathing heavily into Flora's face. 'She may even be dead,' she offered in a sepulchral tone.

'Never mind that, Elsie,' her companion said impatiently. 'It's Sir Frederick we have to deal with. I had hoped,' she said, her voice quieter but still aggrieved, 'that once Mr Lovejoy was out of the picture, Sir Frederick would have had second thoughts.'

'Mr Lovejoy?' Flora asked innocently.

'He was the one buying the farm,' Elsie put in. 'Though not for hisself, we reckon.' So, the village had reached the right conclusion. 'He's in hospital now but he'll scarper, you'll see, once he's let out.'

'Never mind that,' Winifred repeated, a red blotch appearing on both cheeks. 'Whatever negotiations Sir Frederick has been engaged in are now dead in the water. He should abandon any further idea of selling. I shall be telling him so when I see him. I have the petitions to prove it – four hundred signatures – although not yours, Miss Steele.'

Flora tried to quell the hearty dislike she felt, but everything about the woman made her skin flare: her hectoring voice, the superior expression, even her solid tweed-covered figure planted firmly among the books Flora loved.

Inwardly, she scolded herself. She should be more understanding. Winifred Ticehurst was a woman with too much energy and too few concerns to expend it on. In her late fifties, she'd stormed into retirement after refusing to teach in the new building, one she considered a monstrosity, but had never forgiven the council for taking away the school she loved and, with it, her home. Instead, she had busied herself in finding a new role, and this was it – defending Abbeymead from anything she saw as further destroying the life she loved.

'I don't do this for fun,' Winifred said, uncannily echoing Flora's thoughts. 'I do it for the sake of the village. I could be enjoying a much easier life, living retired – in London, with my sister.'

'You wouldn't have liked the city, Win.' Elsie snapped her handbag shut, as though conscious their mission at the All's Well was at an end.

'I have no wish ever to leave Abbeymead,' she said coldly. 'And please, Elsie, refrain from calling me Win. I'll bid you goodbye, Miss Steele. I find it a sorry business that you have found yourself unable to help. Your aunt, a doughty woman, would certainly have done her bit. She would hardly be proud of your conduct, but I hope you will wish us luck. I presume that at the very least you do not wish to see the farm sold.'

'I certainly don't want to see it sold unwisely,' Flora said repressively, stung by the mention of Aunt Violet. How dare the woman use her dear aunt's name in that fashion! 'I would like, however, to see Birds Acre put to good use.'

'Then we are at one. It will be,' Winifred declared, hustling Elsie forward.

At that moment, Jack walked through the open door and, seeing the two women barring his path, swept off his fedora and made a small bow. 'Ladies,' he said grandly. Then over their heads to Flora, still seated behind her desk, 'Are you ready?'

'Ready for what?' Winifred demanded rudely.

'Ah! We have business to discuss, Miss Ticehurst,' he said teasingly, tapping the side of his nose.

'Hmph!' she muttered, giving him a furious glance and sweeping both herself and Elsie out of the bookshop door.

Within half an hour Flora had exchanged her desk for a chair at her kitchen table and was halfway through the giant sausage roll provided by Jack when she said, 'OK. I can't wait a minute longer. Tell me what you've discovered.'

Jack moved his empty plate to one side – his own roll had disappeared mysteriously quickly – and took up his mug of tea. 'I've news of Sir Frederick Neville.'

Instantly, she dropped the remainder of the sausage roll onto her plate. 'But so have I! How odd... but you go first.'

'I've found out why he's so desperate for money.'

Flora put her elbows on the table. 'Piers Neville has run up even more debts? Tyler is extorting money by menaces? Lovejoy is suing Sir Frederick for breach of contract?'

'Stop, stop! The answer is far more innocent and actually rather touching.'

She stared at him. 'Sir Frederick – touching?'

'I know. Who'd have thought it. But it seems he really did

love his wife, loves his wife, in fact, despite all those unpleasant rumours.'

'Elsie Flowers was repeating one of them this morning.'

Jack rocked back in his chair. 'It seems that Elsie and many others in the village have got it wrong. Lady Neville did have a breakdown after her son was killed in the war, that's true. Apparently, she'd always been a fragile creature but losing her only child sent her over the edge. But Sir Frederick didn't smother her in her bed as Elsie would no doubt suggest. He found her a place in a nursing-come-convalescent home, I suppose you'd call it. Capri Lawns. It's near Fulking.'

'Capri Lawns?' Her mouth had fallen open.

Jack grinned. 'My reaction precisely and, believe me, it was definitely a Capri Lawns.'

'You've been there!' She couldn't help sounding accusing.

'It's where I was yesterday when you telephoned, or on my way back. I offered to drive Mrs Teague and a very reluctant Charlie to the home to see an old employer of Mrs T's. Yes, I know, doing my knight-errant stuff again. But it paid off handsomely. Charlie's mum confided on the way that the home was very posh and very expensive – that was pretty obvious as soon as we turned into the drive – and that she'd heard a while ago that Lady Neville was an inmate.'

'And was she?' Flora felt her heart skip a little. Sir Frederick couldn't be accused of wife murder, at least.

He nodded. 'She's been there some fourteen years. Fourteen years for her husband to pay very high fees to keep her happy. That's what I meant about touching.'

'I may have misjudged him a little,' she conceded, 'but not entirely. People are complex. He might love his wife but still be capable of murder. Has he run out of money to pay? Is that why he's so desperate to sell the farm?'

'Pretty much. The fees have risen every year and are rising again, but the situation turns out to be worse than that. Capri

Lawns is not doing too well financially. Not enough wealthy people to keep it going, I guess. It may have to be sold.'

Flora thought for a moment. 'Do you think Sir Fred wants to buy it?'

Jack got up and took his china to the sink. 'It would be one certain way of ensuring his wife stays in a place where she's found peace.'

'From what you've said of this home, I'd imagine it would cost more than selling Birds Acre Farm would ever bring in.'

'That was my calculation, too,' he said, slopping his cup and plate through the soapy water. 'Which means he'll have to plunder other assets to make up the difference. And that means it will be more important than ever that he increases the regular income he can depend on.'

'The hotel and the Nevilles' rake-off once it's built – or commission as Piers so genteelly put it?'

'Exactly.'

'But if Sir Frederick knows the kind of man Tyler is – and it's evident from our meeting on Wednesday that he does – he must also know, or at least suspect, that if he sells to Tyler, there'll be no hotel.'

Jack hung up the tea towel he'd been using and took his seat at the table again. 'Maybe he's upped the price and is asking Tyler for a great deal more money than we think. That could be dangerous but if Tyler is still a villain, which seems generally accepted, and wants the farm for whatever nefarious purpose he has in mind, he could be willing to pay up.'

'He's not that willing. He's vanished.'

'He can come back when he's settled his account with Love-joy, whatever it is, and when the police are no longer poking around.'

Flora silently ate the rest of her sausage roll while Jack watched her appreciatively. 'So, what was your news of the great man?' he asked finally.

'You've stolen my thunder,' she complained. 'I have no news now.'

'Somehow, I don't think so. What happened yesterday?'

'I closed the shop and went to Worthing, to the Connaught Theatre, to track Prue Norland down.'

'Enterprising.'

'I thought so, but now I'm not sure,' she said sadly.

'Why speak to Prue?'

'I thought she might know what kind of threat Piers is holding over his uncle. If he'd told Prue what he'd seen at the farm, we'd have our murderer.'

'Did he?'

'No. She doesn't even think the threat has anything to do with Percy's death. She feels it's something from way past.'

Jack looked disappointed. 'That was all you learned?'

'Piers Neville is a beast.'

'She said that?'

'No, she's far too loyal. But she did admit that he'd slapped her. He's a violent man, but we knew that already.'

'And Sir Frederick?' Jack prompted.

'Prue is scared of him. She thinks he's more frightening than his nephew! But you've thrown that one up in the air.'

'Not necessarily. Sir Frederick's efforts to secure his wife's future by selling to a criminal means he'll stop at nothing to get what he wants.'

'That's more or less what Prue said.'

'There you are then. It has to be one of those two, or both of them together.'

'Or Lovejoy or Tyler. We can't discount either of them. There's no evidence to say they were at the farm that afternoon, but there's none to say they weren't. And don't forget Colin Palmer. He *was* there and I reckon, even though he looks a fop, he's quite capable of killing for money. He's a weasel.'

Jack groaned. 'Too much! Too much!'

24

After two restless nights in which she'd chased dozens of suspects in and out of the Birds Acre barns – they'd proliferated in number as she'd dreamt – Flora was only vaguely aware on Monday morning of the uncomfortable ride she was having on her way to the All's Well. It wasn't until her body jarred over a particularly bad bump in the high street, that she became conscious that something wasn't right.

'What's up today?' she whispered to Betty, bending over the handlebars.

It was as she did that there was a loud bang, a whooshing of air, and she found herself skidding across the road directly into the path of an oncoming bus, the first service of the day to Brighton. The driver slammed hard on his brakes, as Flora tumbled over the handlebars and landed inches from the vehicle's front wheels. From where she lay splayed across the tarmac, the double-decker bus looked a mountain ready to topple and crush her flat.

In seconds, the driver was by her side and Mr Houseman, too. He had rushed out of his greengrocery to help. Between them, they managed to scoop her from the road and, holding an arm each, haul her back onto her feet.

'Are you all right, luv?' the driver asked anxiously. 'You veered right across my path.'

'Yes,' she stammered, though every inch of her body hurt. 'Nothing broken, I think. And thank you for being so quick on the brakes.'

The driver grimaced. 'Gave me a right turn, you did.'

'Let me help you into your shop.' Mr Houseman held tight to her. 'If you can walk the few steps, that is.'

She gave him a grateful smile. 'I can, but Betty...'

The driver looked puzzled, then realised she meant her bicycle. 'I'll move it onto the pavement,' he said, 'then I'd best be off. I've folks here needing to get to work.'

Flora became aware of a swathe of faces at the bus windows, noses pressed to the glass. Feeling embarrassed, she tugged at her cotton skirt and, leaning on Mr Houseman's arm, limped to the front door of the All's Well, her stockings torn and two large bruises taking shape below her knees.

'Give us your key,' the greengrocer said, 'and I'll open up and make you some tea. That's if Violet's kitchenette' – he smiled at the word – 'is still in operation.'

He meant the cupboard that her aunt had insisted on calling a kitchen. It was a joke that had spread beyond the book-shop, enjoyed by most of the village.

'It is and thank you. But Betty...'

'Don't you worry about the old bike. I'll carry it into the courtyard once I've got you sat down.' Betty would not like that description, she thought.

She was sipping a vaguely drinkable cup of tea when Mr Houseman walked back into the shop after stowing Betty safely away in her shelter.

'It was your front tyre,' he began. 'A massive puncture.'

Flora frowned. 'That's strange. Michael only changed the

tyre two weeks ago. I must have hit a sharp stone. A flint, perhaps.'

He shook his head. 'Don't look like a flint to me, my dear. Looks like the tyre was slit. A small one that must have expanded as you rode. It's a knife job, if you ask me.' She stared at him. A knife, a deliberate sabotage? 'Don't say, you've upset someone!' He was passing it off as a joke, but she could see he was concerned. And why wouldn't he be? The thought was terrifying.

She'd been incensed when Jack had posed much the same question – who have you upset? Now, though, it was simple defeat she felt. Flora had upset quite a few people in her life, she knew, and would probably go on to upset a few more but, after Jack's prompting, she had thought back over the previous weeks and there was no one with whom she'd had any serious disagreement.

'Not that I can think of,' she answered him brightly. 'It must have been a flint I rode over.'

Mr Houseman shook his head once more, his expression suggesting that if that's what she wanted to believe, she'd have to, but he didn't. Aloud he said, 'As long as you're OK, I'll get back to the shop. Some lovely spring cabbage just in and it'll want unpacking. If you need help, just pick up the phone. I'm only across the road.'

'Thank you, Mr Houseman, but I'll be fine.'

If not fine, she was very glad that the rest of the morning brought few customers. For most of the time, she was able to sit at her desk, sorting paperwork and catching up on telephone calls. One was to Michael Worthington who promised to drop by on his way to work the next day and collect the bicycle. It might be a while before she returned, he warned, since he'd have to order yet another new tyre. Betty was proving expensive.

By lunchtime, Flora had recovered sufficiently to be free of a limp and, wanting to speak urgently to Jack, decided to try the walk to Overlay House during the hour the All's Well closed. Telephoning was not a good idea. Dilys, the postmistress, was quite capable of listening in to conversations and more than happy to spread any gossip she learned.

'What's happened?' Jack asked, as soon as he opened the door.

She tried to keep her smile from wavering, but she was never able to deceive him. He always knew when something was amiss, an unerring instinct that told him when she was in trouble.

'I had a small accident,' she began, and immediately found herself hugged tightly.

Only after several minutes did he let her go. 'Come and sit down,' he said.

In the sitting room, she made unerringly for the uncomfortable sofa he still hadn't replaced. It was familiar and familiar was what she needed.

'Brandy?' he asked, halfway to the small corner cabinet.

'Definitely not.'

'In that case, it will have to be strong tea.'

'I've done the strong tea. Mr Houseman made it for me.'

'Tell me then. What's happened?'

She did, and for a while he was silent, his eyes fixed sternly on the mantelpiece. What was he seeing there? she wondered.

'It was deliberate.'

'It could have been a sharp flint,' she said hopefully.

'Houseman said it was a knife slit. He'd know the difference from a puncture caused by stones. It was deliberate and another attack on you.'

He walked across to the sofa and knelt beside her. 'I won't ask the question again, Flora, but there has to be someone in this village who, rightly or wrongly, believes very badly of you.'

'There's no one,' she said despairingly. 'I've had a few minor disagreements here and there the last few weeks – the new woman in the bakery forgot to keep my loaf this Saturday, Mrs Waterford from Larkspur was annoyed she was sent the wrong book and it's true I'm not exactly Winifred Ticehurst's favourite person, her and her wretched petition, but none of them would behave that extremely. There's no one I can possibly think of. And... I am alive still.'

'Only just,' he said quietly. 'If the bus driver hadn't seen you in time, this morning could have turned out very differently. Who the hell is doing this?' he asked the room at large, getting to his feet.

It was a question Flora couldn't answer. Piers Neville? His uncle? Dennis Tyler? Aloud she said, 'Sir Frederick would hardly bother to tamper with Betty. To him, I'm a minnow, unimportant. And, from what you say, he's not the man we thought him. But, in any case, Jack, I can't believe any of our suspects are involved. It's the personal nature of the attacks that makes no sense – none of the people on our list know me well enough to choose how best to hurt me. Damaging Betty is just the latest assault on everything I love.'

'I don't think I'd discount either of the Nevilles entirely. Sir Frederick was definitely rattled by the grilling we gave him. The obsequious Palmer, too. Betty could be an obvious target if they wanted to get back at us.'

'It's not us, though, is it? It's me, once again.'

He sat down on the sofa, fidgeting to get comfortable. 'These cushions are lumpy, aren't they?' he said, surprise in his voice.

'How many times—'

'Never mind the sofa.'

'You never do.' Flora was recovering her spirits a little.

'Let's concentrate on what's happened to you. We've an escalating scale here.' Jack sat, his hands clasped together, as he went through a roll call of malice. 'First the shop, then the garden, then your house, and now Betty, which in effect means you.'

'It puts paid to your argument, doesn't it? That I'm being warned more gently than if you were the target. There's not much gentle about being mowed down by a double decker bus.'

'Well, you weren't exactly mowed down. It *was* lucky the driver had good brakes.'

'Thank you, Jack. It's always good to look on the bright side.'

'Sorry, sweetheart. I know it must have hurt. And it's worrying. Very worrying. I'm wondering now, what next?'

'There'll be a next, for sure. What *I'm* wondering is just how far this person will go.'

He turned towards her, gently stroking her hair. 'We need to get to them before they decide. We need to find them, Flora.'

25

The blackbird's fluted song went unheard by Flora as she walked to work later that week. Passing hedgerows ablaze with newly opened dog rose, she barely gave them a glance. The attacks against her had become commonplace and she no longer reacted with the despair she'd felt when they had first started. Instead, her heart was leaden. She'd come finally to recognise a bitter truth: that not only had she gained an enemy within the village but one who knew her well enough to pinpoint the most efficient way of causing her pain.

Accepting that such malevolence existed was one thing but working out what this person was trying to achieve was quite another. And who they were, yet another. The destruction of her books and the disabling of Betty suggested a plan to force her from the All's Well. The attacks on her home? To persuade her to move, maybe to leave the village for good? But why? And it wouldn't work, whatever the intention. Replacement books had been ordered, Michael would repair her bicycle. And the rowan tree? Perhaps she could plant a new one. But her aunt's photograph – that was lost for ever.

Mechanically, she got through the morning hours: opening

post, dusting shelves, rearranging a window display, and even serving three or four customers, a smile pasted firmly to her face. Glancing at the Victorian station clock, she was surprised to see it was nearly one. She felt not the slightest bit hungry but knew she should eat. She was joined in battle, one without a name or a known adversary but still a battle, and to fight she would need to keep strong, keep resilient. Time, maybe, to pay Kate a visit.

Locking the bookshop door, she walked quickly up the high street to the Nook, buttoning her jacket as she went. Yesterday's sunshine had disappeared, and the May sky was blanketed by a grey rug of cloud. It was a day to suit Flora's spirits.

Katie's smile, though, as she walked into the café, lifted her heart a little. She'd barely seen her friend these last few weeks – a quick visit to the Nook for a pie or a slice of fruit cake or flask of soup had been all she'd managed. Their usual Friday evening meal was in abeyance, hijacked first to celebrate Kate's engagement, then cancelled in favour of the meeting at the village hall and, last week, postponed when Flora had returned late from Worthing. There'd been no mention of one planned for this evening, either from Alice or Kate. The thought that the three of them might never return to their old custom added to Flora's gloom. Everything seemed at odds, the calm rhythm of her life hopelessly disrupted.

'Hello, stranger,' Kate greeted her. 'Sorry I haven't been over for a chat. I'd liked to have come across to the shop, but it's been so busy here and, with Ivy unwell and Alice far too busy at the Priory to lend much help, it's been a bit crazy. I've had to limit the menu quite severely.'

Flora could see how busy it was, even with a reduced menu. Nearly every table in the small café was filled with customers at various stages of their lunch, and Kate appeared to be the only one serving. She felt guilty. She hadn't known that Ivy was unwell, not that she could have offered Kate much support, but her friend had evidently been struggling.

'Tony's not able to help?'

'He would if he could but he's much too busy at the Priory. And he's been trying to help me with the wedding as well. I'd forgotten how much there is to organise. The church to book, the flowers to choose, the wedding breakfast. And then there are the dresses.' She paused for a moment, before rushing to say, 'I hope you'll be my maid of honour, Flora.'

'You have one of those the second time round?' she asked, then realised it might not sound the most sensitive thing to say.

'Yes, even the second time,' Kate said mildly. 'Tony's mother has been a brick. She's organising a holiday for us in Dorset immediately after the wedding. Somewhere quiet and by the sea.'

Flora managed a nod, hoping it looked as though she was pleased, but veered swiftly away from weddings and maids of honour to ask, 'Will Ivy be coming back soon?'

'Well, her appendix is well and truly out! But the doctors are telling her she needs at least six weeks' rest before she can work again and then only very part-time. I don't want to let Ivy down, but I'm thinking I'll have to find another assistant soon.'

'You wouldn't be letting her down. You'd be helping her. Any idea where you'll look?'

Abbeymead wasn't exactly a buzzing hub of enterprise. Young people searching for a catering job were far more likely to migrate to Brighton. Or even Worthing.

'Maggie Unwin seemed interested when I mentioned the possibility. Ever since that affair with Dr Randall, she's been uncomfortable working at the surgery. And when it closed for a few months and she worked here, she did very well.'

'I'll cross fingers for you that she agrees. Actually, Kate, I came over for a sandwich, but I can see how busy you are. I can do without.'

'That you can't,' her friend said stoutly. 'A sandwich is a minute's work. In fact, I've just made a batch of cheese and tomato. Would one of those do?'

'It would do beautifully.'

Kate disappeared into the kitchen beyond while Flora dug into her handbag for her purse, unaware the café bell had rung behind her. She was surprised when Minnie Howden joined her at the counter.

'Good afternoon, Miss Steele.'

Minnie's hair, she noticed, had been newly cut and shampooed and the wool jacket she wore was unusually stylish. The housekeeper looked a great deal less ravaged than when Flora had last seen her.

'Good afternoon, Miss How—' she began, coming to a stop when she noticed the left arm of Minnie's jacket hanging loose. 'Have you hurt your arm?'

'Goodness, yes.' Minnie sounded flustered. 'A fall. So very silly of me.'

'You've broken it?'

Minnie nodded rather helplessly. 'I tripped,' she said simply.

'But how? Where?'

'Outside my cottage. It *was* silly, Miss Steele. I heard a noise coming from the back garden and went to investigate. I should have taken a torch – you know how dark night-time is in the village – but I couldn't find one immediately and I was worried about the noise. In the end, it was probably only a badger snuffling around and nothing to worry about.'

'But how did you come to fall?' It might have been dark, but this was the housekeeper's own garden, one she'd walked in for years.

'I tripped over some wood. A piece of railway sleeper it looked to be when I saw it in the morning.'

'What was a railway sleeper doing in your back garden?'

'I've no idea.' Minnie smiled sadly. 'I don't recall anyone leaving it there, but I have a terrible memory these days.'

Was she being overly suspicious, Flora wondered, or did this set an alarm bell ringing? A noise in the night, a possible intruder, an obstacle appearing out of nowhere and rendering the garden path dangerous. Could it be that Minnie had become a target, too? But why on earth threaten Percy's former housekeeper? Was there something she knew about that fateful afternoon, but hadn't realised she knew?

'It will be good when you're living close to your brother,' Kate said, emerging from the kitchen with Flora's sandwich, wrapped in greaseproof paper. 'He can be your memory!'

'You're leaving Abbeymead?' Flora felt completely at sea. Where had she been these last few weeks?

'I've sold the schoolhouse,' Minnie said proudly. 'Subject to probate, of course. And for a lot of money,' she added in a whisper. 'A friend of Dilys's sister heard the schoolhouse might be for sale and when he came to visit, he loved it. He wants to buy my cottage, too. I'll be very sad to leave, but I decided I didn't want to stay living there, not with someone else in Mr Percy's house. It didn't seem right.'

Flora dredged her memory. 'Your brother lives in Surrey, doesn't he?'

The older woman nodded enthusiastically. At least she'd got something right. Flora thought. 'He does. A charming little village just outside Guildford. And he's found me a cottage, which is perfect. Only a few yards up the road from him.' Minnie's face was suddenly radiant. 'I'm starting a new life, Miss Steele.'

'How lovely,' Kate said.

'How lovely,' Flora echoed, wishing she could say the same. She could do with a new life as much as Minnie – right now, the old one was looking decidedly unattractive.

. . .

The remainder of the working day passed peacefully enough and, for a while, Flora could forget the unpleasantness dogging her. By the time Alice puffed into her shop just before closing time, she'd begun to feel a good deal happier. She might have known, however, that those few hours of calm would prove false.

'They've found another body!' Alice said without preamble, her voice almost a squeak. She clutched onto Flora's desk while she regained her breath. The news had evidently necessitated a swift trot, too important for a stroll to the bookshop.

Flora stared at her, hardly understanding.

'A body,' Alice repeated, her chest heaving. 'Another one!'

'Where?' She wasn't at all sure she was hearing correctly.

Alice began a frantic nodding, still barely able to speak. 'Out at the Lexington. A body in one of them bunkers, his head bashed in. I dunno who 'tis,' Alice managed in a more normal voice. 'We'll have to wait and see. It'll be round the village soon enough.'

They didn't have long to wait. Within a few minutes of Alice's arrival, Jack walked through the door, minus his jacket – he must have left home in a hurry, Flora thought.

'Have you heard?' he asked, looking directly at her.

'Another murder? Yes, we heard.' She paused. 'Is it Sir Frederick?' A body found on the golf course – he had to be the most likely victim.

Jack nodded while Alice took a breath deep enough to rattle her chest. 'I've just had a call from Ridley,' he said. 'His team is at the Lexington now, but Tring – the first officer at the site – identified the body straight away, despite the injuries the chap's suffered.'

'Sir Frederick Neville!' Alice muttered. 'I dunno what this village is comin' to. One death after t'other.' She turned to look at them both. 'It's ever since you two started this sleuthin' nonsense.' It was said more in sorrow than anger. 'You've brought trouble with you.'

Flora could have reminded her that trouble had come first, in the shape of a dead man in this very bookshop two years ago. It was only then that she'd begun on the 'sleuthing nonsense', as Alice termed it. She said nothing, however, and Jack, maintaining a similar silence, made no attempt at defence.

'Can I give you a lift, Alice?' he asked. 'I've the Austin outside and you're cluttered up with baskets.'

'These old things,' she said toeing one of the straw panniers she'd dumped at her feet. 'Weigh next to nothin'. No trouble for me. You take your young lady home and look after her. Both of you – look after yourselves!' Her finger wagged accusingly.

'There's something I didn't mention,' Jack said, as the door closed behind their friend. 'It was Colin Palmer who found the body.'

'Palmer? What was he doing at the golf club?'

'According to the account Palmer gave the inspector, he went to the Lexington to meet Sir Frederick. They were to discuss their next move, now that Lovejoy and Tyler have slipped from sight.'

Flora bent down to lock the small safe beneath her desk. 'But why meet there? Why not at Bramber Hall or even Palmer's office?' she said, her voice muffled.

'Palmer insists it was at Sir Frederick's request.'

'It sounds odd, don't you think?'

'I do, and the timing is odder still. The pathologist's best guess at the moment is that Sir Frederick died before breakfast. A trifle early for a business meeting.'

Flora collected her jacket from the kitchenette but, when she returned, she was frowning.

'Did the inspector discover why they chose to meet on a golf course at that time of the day?'

'All the agent would say was that Neville liked to go to the club early to practise his swings and, if his client wanted a meeting, that's very often where Palmer had to go.'

'*Had* Sir Frederick been practising?' To Flora, it seemed important. If Neville had been concentrating hard on how best to improve his technique, he would probably have been unaware of an assailant closing in on him.

Jack shook his head. 'No idea. We'll know more later perhaps. Alan has promised to call me when he has an update on the time of death. That timing might turn out to be crucial. But whenever it was, I reckon it's destroyed any idea of Sir Frederick being our murderer.'

'Sir Fred is now a victim, true, but one thing doesn't necessarily cancel the other.' Flora had had time to think about it since Alice dropped her bombshell. 'It's possible that he could have killed and, in turn, been killed. More importantly, the other part of the guilty duo is still alive and now a free man. Where was Piers Neville at the time of the killing? Has the inspector enquired?'

'He will, I'm sure. And discover the whereabouts of all the other players. According to Ridley, Lovejoy has left hospital though he's not clear if the man is still in Abbeymead. He's not at the Cross Keys, that's for sure. As for Tyler, apart from sighting him at the village hall, he's become the magician's rabbit – a vanishing species.'

'I think the inspector should concentrate on Piers. With Sir Frederick dead, it's Piers who inherits the estate. He'll be able to do whatever he wants with any of the Neville properties, including Birds Acre. He's already attacked Lovejoy as an obstacle to his getting the farm. Why not go for his uncle, too, since blackmail doesn't seem to have worked?'

Jack fidgeted for a while with his hat, turning it in his hands and smacking it lightly against his knee. 'OK,' he said at last. 'Piers has tried blackmail but failed. His uncle still intends to sell. Therefore, his uncle has to go, giving the boy free rein to do whatever he wishes. It's one scenario.'

'A good one.'

'There are others, though. Lovejoy and Tyler – could either of them have known Neville would be practising at the club at a time when so few people were around? Or did they lure the man there on the pretext of restarting negotiations?'

'If they wanted to restart negotiations, it would be better for Sir Frederick to be alive.'

'Not so fast, clever Flora. It might in fact be better for them if Sir Fred was no more, and they were negotiating with the new heir.'

'Why? They must know that Piers is dead set on having the farm for himself.'

'He was, but that was in the past, at a time when he needed the hotel to provide him with a top job. Now he doesn't need one – instead, he can glory in the status he's inherited. No, what he really needs is ready cash. The estate still costs oodles to run, whoever's in charge, and there could well be death duties to pay. *And* Lady Neville's bills.'

'If he intends to pay them.' Flora gave a derisive snort, while hoping her scepticism was ill-founded.

'There could be a clause in Neville's will that ensures his heir has to. Piers may be forced to sell Birds Acre and possibly other properties to cover the debts that will be left.'

'But he doesn't have to sell to Tyler. He knows what kind of man he's dealing with, and he'd look elsewhere for a buyer. I'm sure Sir Frederick hadn't got round to signing any agreement.'

'Sir Fred seems to have been stalling,' Jack agreed. 'Tyler might have suspected he was planning to backtrack and decided that Piers would prove easier to threaten. Either he or Lovejoy or both could be behind Sir Frederick's death.'

'You're presuming that Tyler still want Birds Acre.'

'His gang is on the run, according to Ridley, so where better to run to?'

'And Lovejoy, wherever he is, may still be involved?'

'I reckon he and Tyler are still working together. It was Piers Neville who attacked Lovejoy, not his boss.'

'It was Tyler who chased him out of the village hall,' she reminded him.

'True, but we don't know why. It might have been a simple hiccup. Lovejoy not reporting back as he should. Not being forceful enough with the Nevilles. Something minor that leaves the arrangement between them intact.'

'Let's hope the inspector can make a better job of disentangling events than we're doing,' was all she said, picking up her handbag from under the desk. 'Are you driving me home?'

'Your carriage awaits, but how is Michael getting on with Betty?'

'She won't be back for several days. He's run out of spare tyres.'

'She won't be a happy bicycle,' he said, picking up the small package of books from the desk. 'Are these to go with you? Hey, what's this? Another letter from France?'

He pointed to the telltale blue of the thin airmail she'd received last week but so far had refused to open.

'I imagine so. I haven't read it,' she said shortly.

Jack made no response, silently leading the way to the car waiting at the kerbside, a silence that lasted for the drive back to Flora's cottage. Levering himself from the driver's seat, he carried her box of books to the front doorstep, Flora following, then walked back to the gate and waved goodbye. Not a word had been spoken since his discovery of the letter.

Fitting her key to the front door lock, Flora was near to tears. What else could go wrong?

26

Jack couldn't understand why he'd responded to this second letter from Flora's one-time boyfriend in the way he had. He hadn't read it and he didn't want to, but Richard Frant seemed rather too interested in pressing information on Flora that she'd no wish for. Where the Steeles were buried had become a murky question for Jack from the moment he'd been unable to locate their graves in Highgate Cemetery, but he'd purposely kept silent on the subject.

It was the fact that Frant had written twice that sparked his irritation, Jack supposed. What was the man up to? Was there something going on about which he knew nothing? Had Flora responded to his first letter, despite saying she wouldn't? Despite making it plain that she rejected any suggestion her parents' last resting place was somewhere in the South of France?

He was rescued from spending too long in moody reflection when Alan Ridley phoned him the next day. Wresting his mind back to the case he and Flora were supposed to be working on, he tried to sound enthusiastic.

'Thought you'd like to know, Jack,' the inspector said. 'The pathologist puts Frederick Neville's death at no later than eight yesterday morning and probably a lot earlier.'

'He must have arranged to meet Colin Palmer at an extraordinary hour.'

'Palmer or someone else,' Ridley said drily. 'Or he decided to practise his swing at daybreak and his assailant found him conveniently alone.'

'Colin Palmer still maintains there *was* a meeting?'

'He does, though there's no evidence to prove it. It was arranged over the telephone and can't be checked.'

'Did he say any more of why Sir Frederick wanted to see him and why at that time?'

'They were meeting early before the business of the day got under way. That's all my constable got out of him. Mind you, when he was being questioned, the man was visibly shaking and looked like he might throw up any moment.'

'He gave your chap no indication of what this talk was about?' That in itself felt suspicious.

'He was asked, but he was hazy to say the least. I'll send Norris round to his office early next week – let the bloke get over his shock first – then speak to him again.'

He would prefer to get to Palmer first, Jack thought, before the man had had time to concoct a story to fit the facts. Really, he should involve Flora in any questioning, but she'd be busy in the shop, he told himself, and would find it difficult to close the All's Well. In truth, he was unsure how to be with her, feeling slightly stupid that his behaviour had been so churlish. It was only a letter, for goodness' sake. Flora was allowed to receive letters from whomever she wanted and, if a former boyfriend got in touch, who was he to object? There was no hard and fast agreement between them. They weren't even engaged, let alone married, yet he'd behaved like a jealous husband. Embarrassment joined the stupidity. A day or so's absence from each other would clear the air, he decided.

. . .

This third Saturday of the month saw the May Day celebrations at last take place on the village green, two weeks later than normal. High winds each of the previous weekends had caused disruption and even felled the all-important maypole, now hastily re-erected so that the children who had been practising their dance for weeks were not disappointed.

Flora was glad to close the shop at lunchtime and walk along the high street to the green. Celebrating May Day, even in a small way, was a distraction from the despondency she'd been unable to shake off ever since Jack had glimpsed that second letter from France. There was little danger she would meet him today: she couldn't see him enjoying maypole dancing or being too interested in the various stalls set up to mark the afternoon's festivities. Alice, though, was sure to have booked a few hours away from the Priory kitchen and it was possible that Kate, too, had found temporary help in the café. It would be a comfort to see her friends.

She spotted Alice as soon as she neared the green. Her friend was busily unpacking two enormous baskets at a cake stall that was already brimming with baked goods from nearly every kitchen in Abbeymead. The village had excelled itself, probably because proceeds from this year's May Day celebrations were to go to the local school whose assembly hall roof had been leaking for the past two winters. It was rumoured that earlier this term the caretaker had run out of space to put his buckets. The Victorian schoolhouse, it would seem, had proved more robust in withstanding the Sussex weather.

In the distance, the maypole stood proud, its red, white and blue ribbons fluttering free in a soft breeze that had been blowing most of the day. The children were not yet in evidence, but Flora had heard on the grapevine that Victorian costumes were to be worn for this big occasion.

She tapped Alice on the shoulder. 'How many cakes have you cooked?' she asked, eyeing the now empty panniers.

'Hello, my love.' Alice turned quickly to greet her. 'Not that many when you think about it – an angel food cake, a banana chiffon, a couple of batches of strawberry shortcakes and another two of plain old jam tarts. I reckoned as Miss Dunmore could always do with more. She'll need 'em to keep the stall going once the first tranche is sold.'

The vicar's housekeeper, who'd volunteered for the cake selling, looked grateful and murmured her agreement.

'I'm afraid I've come empty handed,' Flora apologised.

'Perhaps you can buy a cake instead,' Amy Dunmore suggested gently.

'I will, I promise. Certainly before I leave.'

'It's a grand tradition, isn't it?' Alice said, as they walked across the grass. 'Mebbe a bit pagan, I'm not sure Vicar's too keen, but there... people have been doin' it for hundreds of years.' She nodded towards the maypole. 'Makes no difference how much time comes and goes, May Day always means the start of summer. Even if it's pourin' with rain.'

Flora looked anxiously at the sky and was reassured; what clouds there were, were riding high and moving at speed. The array of wooden trestles set up at intervals around the perimeter of the green could be sure of staying dry. Alongside the cake stall was an even larger one bursting with fruit and vegetables and, next to it, a table bearing an unsteady mountain of bread rolls and fruit scones. There was a stall for children's toys and another selling second-hand clothes. A fortune teller had set up her booth at the far end and, opposite her, an artist was offering to draw people's likeness.

'The clothes stall seems as popular as the cakes.' Flora pointed to the tumbled mounds of men's, women's and children's clothing, a chaotic mix of colour and style.

'It does, too, and Mr Preece's pie stall is doin' well. He's a queue already.' Alice nodded towards the small booth that crouched beneath a blue-and-white-striped awning. 'I'm not surprised. I like a good pie and mash myself.'

A fair number of people were already eating, either a late lunch or an early tea, sitting on upturned barrels or using them as makeshift tables. The smell of cooked meat floated in the air and, mixed with the sticky sweetness of the candyfloss machine nearby, made Flora feel slightly nauseous.

'Come on, let's find a perch,' Alice said. 'The children will be dancin' soon.'

They were lucky enough to find an empty bench a little way from the maypole but close enough to see the performance. Within a few minutes of settling themselves, the music struck up, a man playing an accordion accompanied by two young girls on fiddles – his daughters perhaps? The first bars of music were a signal for people to put down their knives and forks, stop buying the blouse they fancied, or hastily pay for the cake they'd selected, and troop across to the maypole.

'Look at those little loves,' Alice cooed, as the line of small children, the girls in long dresses and button boots, the boys in knickerbockers and collarless jackets, trooped into view.

The music paused for a moment, to allow the children to take their places in boy, girl, boy, formation, then at the first new note, the dancers moved forward to collect their ribbons. Stepping to the music and weaving around each other, they began to wind their ribbons into a multicoloured pattern that crept steadily down the pole.

'They're doing it very well,' Flora observed admiringly. 'I know when I was a child, I got myself into a terrible tangle.'

'They've been practisin' for weeks – that Miss Bancroft told me all about it, t'other day at the mobile library. The teachers haven't had a day of peace all term. *Can we practise now, miss* is all the kids have been sayin'. You can see why. Out in the open air, jumpin' around to music. Even the boys like it.'

The dancers had completed their pattern and were now reversing their steps to undo the ribbons. 'That's to represent the lengthening of the days as summer approaches,' Flora said knowledgeably.

'How d'you know that?'

'It was something Jack told me when I mentioned how the village celebrates May Day.'

'It would be him, but why isn't the lad with you? He should be here.'

'Jack is busy,' was all Flora would say.

Alice looked slightly askance. It was clear she thought it odd that in what spare time they had, they chose to spend it apart. Fortunately for Flora, she was saved from further explanation by the eruption of loud voices behind them.

People's heads turned and she and Alice swivelled as one. It was Winifred Ticehurst, clutching tight to a sheaf of papers.

'More petitions,' Flora groaned.

'But what's she haranguing that boy for?'

That boy was Piers Neville and, as they watched, the argument between the two became louder and a good deal angrier.

'They're goin' fair hammer and tongs. What on earth is it about, d'you think?'

'She seems to be trying to dump her petitions on him,' Flora said, frowning. 'Poor Miss Ticehurst. Petitions aren't going to be much use now there's a different owner of the farm.'

Alice looked uncertain. 'The lad will have inherited, I suppose?'

'I imagine there's no question. I doubt Sir Frederick had much freedom in how he left his estate. Entailments, or so on,' she said vaguely, not really knowing but sure such things must be involved.

'It's a terrible business what happened to his uncle. Nobody was talkin' about anythin' else at the Priory yesterday. Winifred should leave the lad alone. It'll be a painful time for him.'

Flora subdued her immediate thought that Piers was an unlikely mourner. 'Miss Ticehurst could never have got to her appointment with Sir Frederick,' she observed. 'She'll want to persuade his nephew against selling Birds Acre, and she probably thinks it's a good idea to strike now.'

'Well, mebbe she'll be lucky,' Alice said thoughtfully. 'Winifred Ticehurst knows what she wants, and the boy looks a bit of a softy.'

'You could be wrong there.'

'Well, I for one hope not. I hope she's gets her way. Piers Neville should look for another tenant – it's what most of the village want. You never know, she might win him over. She knows the lad well.'

'Really?' That was news to Flora.

'There, they've finished.' The children were taking their bows and curtseys and the maypole's coloured ribbons were once more floating free. 'Used to teach him as a boy.'

Flora frowned, interrupting her clapping. 'Piers Neville went to the village school?' It seemed highly unusual.

'Nothin' like that. Well, the nobs don't, do they? No, she taught him tennis in the holidays when he was back from his boardin' school. I did hear that she was a pretty good player once. Played for the best club in Sussex in her youth.'

That was something she should store away to tell Jack. But even as she thought it, Flora felt a hollow open inside. Suddenly, she needed to talk about the gap in her life, a gap that had appeared from nowhere.

'I had another letter from Richard Frant,' she said.

'That man! Not about your parents again.'

'Sort of. He's insisting that he saw their graves in France.' She'd opened the letter last night, but then pushed it away, hiding it in a cupboard she rarely used.

'He's a persistent blighter. Was that all?' her friend asked suspiciously.

Flora kicked at a tuft of grass. 'No, not all. He asked me to go to France.'

'Does Jack know?' was her friend's immediate question.

'He knows about the letter but not about going to France.'

'Ah.' Alice's face took on a knowing look. She's settled on the reason Jack isn't here this afternoon, Flora thought. 'And are you goin'?'

'I don't know, Alice.' Flora kicked at another tuft. 'Something tells me I should, but it's complicated.'

'Isn't life always?' her friend said placidly. 'But best be quick and make up your mind. The longer you leave it, the more complicated it'll be.'

27

Jack had spent an unprofitable Sunday. There had been little gardening to do, apart from a swift mow of the front lawn and, when later he'd sat down at his typewriter, the paper had remained stubbornly blank, its untouched white a constant reproach.

He was more than glad to see Monday dawn and, as soon as he'd had breakfast, shrugged on his jacket and walked into the village, intent on seeing Colin Palmer. Travelling on foot was far less conspicuous than driving the red Austin and inconspicuous was what he wanted to be. He'd made no attempt to book an appointment with Palmer. Surprise would be best, he'd reckoned, even though the man could well be on a visit to one of the several estates for which he worked.

Jack was lucky. He caught him in the outer office, just as Palmer was about to grab his hat and a smart-looking blazer from the coat rack.

'Mr Palmer, good morning.' Jack tried a smile. 'Can I beg a few minutes of your time? I won't keep you long.'

'Actually, I don't have time this morning, Mr Carrington. If you could make an appointment.' He waved a hand towards the bespectacled lady sitting behind an ancient typewriter. She hadn't been there when he and Flora had called, Jack remembered. Was she an innovation, a recently acquired shield to deter uninvited callers?

'I realise what a busy chap you must be.' Jack was still smiling. 'And I won't keep you more than a couple of minutes. It's a small thing I wanted to check with you.'

Palmer looked slightly relieved. 'In that case, Miss Harrison will almost certainly be able to help you.' His hand did more waving at the assistant, her face severe and unbending.

'I think it would be best if I talk to you,' Jack said firmly. 'Shall we?' And before Palmer could raise any further objection, he had walked to the door of the inner office and looked likely to enter without invitation.

Palmer bustled forward, his expression none too pleased. 'You'd better come in,' he said grudgingly, pushing past Jack and making sure he was seated in his own managerial chair before gesturing to his unwelcome visitor to take a seat.

'Well, what is it?' His tone was ungracious.

'Sir Frederick,' Jack announced, directing an amiable glance at the man's scowl. 'But first, allow me to offer my condolences. A terrible thing to happen.'

'Yes, terrible,' Palmer muttered.

'And in such a place, too.'

When his reluctant host looked bemused, Jack said kindly, 'The poor man was killed playing golf, wasn't he? Not normally an activity that leads to death.'

He was met by silence.

'Sir Frederick was a long-term member of the Lexington club, I imagine.'

Palmer simply nodded.

'Was it his habit to practise so early in the morning?'

'I believe so.'

'How many people would know that?'

'I've no idea.' Palmer picked up a ruler and tapped it impatiently along the desktop. 'What is this about, precisely?'

'Sir Frederick,' Jack answered blandly.

'Mr Carrington, I am a busy man—' he began.

'Me, too, Mr Palmer. So, let's cut to what I want to know. Why did you go to the Lexington at such an unusual time? Barely an hour after daybreak.'

'I was asked to meet Sir Frederick there, though what business it is of yours, I fail to see.'

'I've been charged with helping,' Jack said, making sure he kept his answer fuzzy. 'Sir Frederick's death has been an enormous shock to Abbeymead and beyond, and people have questions. But tell me, why would Sir Frederick wish to see you on a golf course?'

'He didn't. I was to meet him in the clubhouse, but it wasn't open when I arrived, and I walked around to the fairway. I found him at the final bunker.' He gave a shudder – manufactured? Jack wondered. 'Submerged in sand.'

'Sir Frederick must have known the clubhouse wasn't open so early. Why arrange to meet you there?'

'I believe there are days when it does open early.'

'But not this day. Did he telephone you to make the appointment?' The more questions Jack asked, the odder it seemed.

'It was his housekeeper who telephoned.'

'Did she mention why he wanted to see you?'

'Just that there were things to discuss.'

'At six in the morning?'

'Sir Frederick is a busy man.'

'So much busyness.' Jack sighed. 'The discussion must have been urgent.'

'It was.' Palmer bit down on his lip, as though stopping himself from saying no more than was necessary.

'Did it by any chance concern Sidney Lovejoy's offer to buy Birds Acre Farm?'

The man inclined his head an inch, and Jack took it as a yes. 'But the offer had lapsed, surely? Mr Lovejoy had been attacked and ended in hospital; the man employing him, Dennis Tyler, had disappeared, back to his criminal friends in London if the police are guessing correctly.'

Palmer said nothing.

'Well, are they guessing correctly?'

'I've no idea,' he said angrily. 'Lovejoy's offer was an excellent one and Sir Frederick was keen to revive it. We were to discuss how best to do so, now circumstances had changed.'

'Because Sir Frederick badly needed the money? Even criminal money.'

'It would have been fine,' Palmer suddenly burst out, 'if that wretched nephew of his had kept out of it. Lovejoy wouldn't have been attacked and the sale would have gone ahead without any trouble.'

'Piers Neville knew there would be no hotel, didn't he? That's why he attacked Lovejoy to put a stop to any negotiation, but you were desperate to carry on. After all, you'd earn an excellent commission at a time, I hear, that your business isn't doing too well. You were as desperate as Sir Frederick for the sale to go ahead. Perhaps more so,' he speculated.

He saw Palmer start. It had been an inspired guess, based on the inspector's remark that the police might look into Palmer's finances as well as those of the Nevilles.

'Maybe there was more at stake than a simple commission,' Jack continued inexorably. 'A bribe paid by Dennis Tyler perhaps? You ensure his purchase goes through, and he gifts you a little additional help.'

'That's nonsense.' Palmer almost choked the words out.

'Is it? It's likely, you see, that Percy Milburn was lured to the farm's cellar to meet his death. Someone did that luring. I wonder, was it you? And Sir Frederick – had he begun to waver, decide that maybe his nephew was right and that he shouldn't sell to Tyler? Was he lured to the golf club and persuaded to continue with the sale and, when persuasion didn't work, despatched in a similarly brutal fashion?'

Palmer leaped up from his desk, knocking his chair to one side. 'How dare you suggest I was involved in either of these men's deaths?'

'It's just a tad suspicious, wouldn't you say, that you were at two meetings, both of which resulted in murder. You were at Birds Acre Farm when Percy Milburn was killed and yesterday at the Lexington when Sir Frederick met his end.'

'I found him,' Palmer croaked. 'That's all. I walked out on the fairway and found him.'

'Quite a find,' Jack said. 'But I won't keep you any longer. You're a busy man.'

28

Flora had spent Sunday itching to tell Jack of the argument she'd witnessed the previous day, and the suggestion of a possible link between Miss Ticehurst and Piers Neville. A small thing, she knew, but it could prove crucial to deciphering the full picture. It was a thin blue airmail that was standing in the way. Part of Flora rebelled at the idea that Jack should have a say in whom she talked to, either by letter or in person, but another part of her understood. He had been so badly hurt by his one-time fiancée, Helen Milsom, that even the slightest hint of betrayal was enough to send him scuttling for his shell.

Unsure of how best to tackle the impasse, Flora was still debating the problem the next morning. At around eleven she decided it was comfort food she needed. Katie's Nook would be quiet, the early morning rush over and Kate's lunchtime customers not yet on the horizon. There would be time to talk to her friend over an iced bun. Alice had been characteristically blunt: decide what you want to do, she'd told Flora, and do it. Kate, she knew, would adopt a gentler approach.

She had paid for her bun and was beginning to launch into her sad story when Jack walked through the café door. Flora saw him almost imperceptibly draw back when he caught sight of her at the counter, but then he fixed a smile on his face and greeted them both. Kate, looking from one to the other, was clearly aware that something wasn't quite right.

'I was hoping you'd have a spare cheese and onion pasty,' Jack said, in a voice that was a little too hearty.

'I might be able to find you one. Alice cooked an extra tray Saturday morning and I know we didn't sell out completely. Why don't you have a cup of tea while I have a look through the refrigerator?' She gestured to a waiting table. 'You, too, Flora. I'll bring you both a pot.'

Kate had judged the situation perfectly, Flora thought, but wondered if she could do the same. She would need to say the right thing in the right way. Jack had taken a seat opposite her and, looking into his grey eyes, darker than ever this morning, she saw the hurt, and it was easier than she'd imagined.

'I'm sorry about the letter,' she said impulsively.

There was a minimal shrug. 'There's no reason for you to be. It's your business.'

'No.' She reached out and took his hand. 'It's our business, Jack. I didn't reply to Richard, you know. I didn't ask him to write again.'

Jack left his hand lying in hers. 'He seems an insistent chap.'

'He does, and I wish he weren't. He's stirred up all kinds of feelings I'd rather not think of, but he seems so convinced that it's made me feel I should check the truth for myself.'

'And will you?'

'He's asked me to go to France,' she confessed. Jack said nothing, looking fixedly at the sugar bowl. 'But I'm not going. I think things are best left as they are.'

'You want to know about your parents,' he said quietly, 'and it's right that you do. You should go.'

'And if it's a wild goose chase?'

'Then you've chased and can forget it. When is he suggesting you visit?'

'Any time I choose. He'll find me a hotel room in Paris, then drive me down to Provence. But I'm not happy about it, and not just because I might discover something I'd rather not know. I'll feel uncomfortable meeting him again, and what do I do about the All's Well? I can't just up and leave for what could be at least a week. I've no Sally this time to run the shop for me. And then there's the investigation we're on. I'd be abandoning that. Abandoning Percy. I know it doesn't look like it, but deep down I feel we're groping our way to the truth.'

'Me, too,' he said, 'and I'd better confess – I've been galloping ahead. I went to see Colin Palmer this morning. There's something decidedly dodgy about his business. He may just be a greedy man after the biggest commission, but I sense something more serious is going on.'

'You think his agency might be folding?'

'It's a possibility. Palmer needs money, I'm sure, and he was at the site of both killings. What if he'd made some kind of deal with Tyler in order to save his business?'

'How would that work?'

'It's only a thought. But if Tyler was at the farm – and the jury is still out on that, I know – could he have bribed Palmer to lure Percy down to that cellar? He says Percy never turned up for the meeting, but that's only his word.'

Flora thought about it. 'The broken staircase, though? If he was luring Percy to the cellar, he wouldn't have smashed up the steps.'

'He could have done it afterwards. It gives credence to his claim that he didn't think Milburn would have gone to the cellar once the chap saw the damaged stairs.'

'OK, Tyler pays him to persuade Percy into visiting a place where he can kill him easily. The obstacle Tyler faces in buying the farm is disposed of. But Sir Frederick? Why is he dead?'

'Say that Tyler still wants the farm despite all the hoo-hah, but Sir Frederick is about to go back on his word. He'd have to die, too.'

'And Palmer – what role does he play?'

'Possibly much the same. He's taken Tyler's shilling and finds himself forced into earning his money again. So... he arranges a meeting with Sir Frederick that he's no intention of making and leaves Tyler to do his worst.'

'There's one big flaw in that. If Palmer arranged the meeting, intending Sir Frederick to be killed, why was he stupid enough to be the one who found the dead man?'

'Is it that stupid, though? If he's the one to find his employer, it supports his contention he was meeting him as arranged and, in a way, deflects suspicion. Why would he hang around if he'd played a part in the killing?'

'Here you are.' Kate arrived with a tray of tea and a brown paper bag. 'Tea for two and you're in luck, Jack, a couple of cheese and onion pasties.'

'Wonderful! That's lunch sorted.'

'Too many questions,' he said, when Kate had returned to the kitchen. Picking up a spoon, he stirred the pot of tea and poured cups for them both. 'So, any nuggets from you?'

'Winifred Ticehurst, though I'd hardly describe her as a nugget. She was at the May Day celebrations and trying to press Piers Neville into taking the stack of petitions she's gathered. I suppose it would have to be her next step – he is Sir Frederick's heir, after all – and the petitions would have gone to his uncle if he were still alive. But Piers wasn't having any of it. He pushed the papers away, quite roughly, and whatever conversation they'd been having descended into a monumental row.'

'Does the argument get us anywhere?'

'Not obviously, but Alice tells me that Winifred taught Piers as a young boy – tennis – so they have some kind of relationship. Alice reckons that could well sway his decision in

Winifred's favour and push him into finding a new tenant for the farm. It didn't look much like it, though.'

Jack shook his head. 'He won't get a tenant. He's going to need cash for the estate, just as Sir Frederick did. The question is will he hand Birds Acre to Dennis Tyler for a mighty sum or keep to his hotel scheme and hope that in the long term he'll make more money?'

Flora put down her empty cup. 'If he does the latter... how will Dennis Tyler react? Shrug his shoulders and give up, or make Piers the next on his list?'

Jack passed a hand through the flop of hair that never sat straight and tried to flatten it. 'Let's hope not. Three dead bodies would be a record.'

Getting to his feet, he piled the used china back on the tray and walked it to the counter. 'Thanks, Kate,' he called out to their hostess, then turned to Flora. 'I'll come back to the shop with you. If you've no customers, we can keep talking. Maybe decide what to do next.'

Flora felt a lightness in her heart. They were working together once more.

'It's difficult to see what but we need to do something. There are two men dead already.'

'Ideas?'

'I think we should go back to the farm,' she said with certainty, walking beside him.

'Is it worth it, though? The police will have gone over the place with a fine-tooth comb.'

'I know they've searched, but they can miss stuff. There are two barns and several outbuildings as well as the farmhouse to cover. Inspector Ridley is short-staffed, and they would have been under pressure to complete the search as quickly as they could. Anyway,' she added, 'apart from the golf course, it's the only site that might still hold clues.'

Jack looked doubtful, and she bent herself to persuade. 'The murderer must have hidden somewhere in the farm while he waited for Percy to arrive. He might just have left something behind that the police didn't notice.'

'I guess we haven't much to lose—' He broke off.

'What is it?'

'That was Lovejoy ahead, I'm pretty sure. Taking the turning to Church Spinney. Come on, let's nab him. He's not bolted for London after all and, if he's still hanging around the village, it means that in all probability Tyler isn't too far away either.'

Flora had to trot to keep up with Jack's long stride but was rewarded, when turning into the lane that led to Church Spinney, she saw a pair of checked trousers and a black felt beret disappearing into the trees.

Jack increased his pace, Flora following as quickly as she could, and was in time to hear him say, 'Mr Lovejoy! What a pleasant surprise!'

Lovejoy might have stopped, but his body was poised to leave, the corduroy jacket hunched at the shoulders ready for flight.

'Mr Carrington, isn't it?' the man said doubtfully.

'It is. And very glad to see you. I must say I didn't expect you'd still be here.'

'And Miss...?' Lovejoy queried, not responding to Jack's comment.

'Steele,' Flora helped him. 'I hope you're fully recovered.'

'No problem,' he said blandly. 'Superficial injuries.'

That wasn't what she'd heard but she let it pass. 'You're not returning to London after all?'

'Soon, very soon. But business has to come first, don't you know.'

'Business as in buying Birds Acre Farm,' Jack put in.

'That's right, squire.'

'You're still representing Mr Tyler then? He's still hoping to purchase?'

The suggestion of a smile flitted across the man's face for a moment, then vanished. 'That's right,' he repeated.

'I'm surprised you're still working for him,' Flora said cheerfully. 'I saw you at the village hall. You were being chased by Mr Tyler at the time, and he didn't look at all happy.'

The smile that was more like a grimace returned. 'Water under the bridge. A slight misunderstanding. I've assured Mr Tyler the farm will be his very soon, and he's been happy to accept my assurance.'

'And if you aren't successful,' Jack asked, 'are you likely to be chased again?'

'Or put into hospital again?' Flora added.

Sidney Lovejoy wagged a finger at them. 'Don't you believe it. Dennis and me are firm.'

'Which is as well, seeing you owe him a good deal of money.'

Lovejoy stiffened, his figure more hunched than ever. 'How d'you know that?'

'We know quite a bit. But not where Mr Tyler is right now.'

'He's around,' was all Lovejoy said. 'But so am I and it's me that will be doing the business.'

Jack shook his head, a sad look on his face. 'I doubt it. Not now Piers Neville owns the farm. You must have heard his uncle is dead? Murdered.'

'Yeah, shame about that. But Piers will come good.'

'He's a man desperate to keep the farm for himself. He's hardly going to agree to sell.'

'We'll see.' Lovejoy rubbed his hands together. 'Everyone has a price.'

'You may be mistaken. Piers Neville really wants that hotel. He has his heart set on it.'

Lovejoy's eyes were hard, his eccentric figure suddenly

more chilling. 'More ways than one to pay a price, folks. Gotta be off now but nice talking to you.'

'Was that a threat?' Flora asked, as the man loped away between the trees.

'It sounded very much like it, but then I've always thought Piers would prove more vulnerable than Sir Frederick.'

'Do we just sit and wait for Piers to be attacked?'

Jack looked quizzical. 'You still think going to the farm will help?'

'It's a hope.'

'Not much of one, but OK, we'll go tomorrow after you close. I'll pick you up around five.'

~

When Jack returned to Overlay House, he telephoned Alan Ridley.

'Alan, I thought it best you know that we're intending to pay Birds Acre a visit tomorrow evening. We won't be getting in the way of anything the police are doing, will we?'

'Not a chance. We finished there weeks ago.'

'And there's no objection to us going?' He'd expected Ridley to pour cold water on the scheme, maybe actively prevent it.

Instead, there was only a small puff of breath down the phone before the inspector said, 'You might as well. There's darn all else. We're still looking at the Nevilles' financial records and just started on Colin Palmer's, too, but it takes an age. I'm not even sure it will yield anything useful.'

'And Tyler? Any news of him?'

'He doesn't seem to have made it back to his old haunts yet.'

He must still be here, Jack thought, which tied in with their conversation with Lovejoy.

'Interesting information from London, though,' the inspector continued. 'The Met carried out another string of raids recently – my opposite number was on the blower this morning. They've been gradually prising the worst of the baddies from their hideouts. I reckon it confirms why Tyler is so keen to buy Birds Acre Farm. An out-of-the-way place, but within easy travelling distance of London. What could be better?'

Jack silently agreed. It sounded exactly why Tyler was still bent on getting the farm. 'I'll let you know if we find anything there.' He could visualise the inspector shaking his head as he said the words.

'We went over that place inch by inch, Jack. There really is nothing left to find, but if you fancy a little evening jaunt with your girlfriend, who am I to stop you? I might come by myself after I finish up in Brighton. Always happy to eat humble pie if you turn something up.'

29

At five o'clock the next evening, Flora looked out of the bookshop's latticed window and saw Jack's red Austin parked outside. Her sense of relief was palpable. Not that she'd imagined he'd fail to turn up as promised; it was more the solace of feeling anchored, of solid ground beneath her feet, of knowing the two of them were once more in harmony – well, almost. This evening they would be a team again hoping, no matter how unlikely, to bring this murder investigation to a successful end.

'Where should we start first?' Jack asked, as they drove up Fern Hill to take the road out of the village that ran beyond the Priory and the golf club.

'The house, perhaps? I know the police will have searched, but it's the obvious hiding place for whoever was bent on murder that afternoon.'

'And we include the cellar?'

A creeping sensation ran down Flora's spine. It was a whole month ago that they'd found poor Percy Milburn, a month ago that she'd glimpsed that dreadful sight, and once seen she'd not been able to unsee it. It was something that would never leave her.

'I suppose we must.'

Jack nodded and said nothing more. A mile past the Lexington Golf Club, they turned off the road onto the rough track that led to the farm, bumping their way over jagged stones and around potholes.

'It looks more deserted than ever,' he said, coming to a stop outside the farmhouse.

Flora glanced around. Weeds sprouted aggressively from between the cobblestones, dead roses hung sad and uncut on the farmhouse walls, and grimy windows looked out at them from beneath a coat of dirt.

'It would break the Martins' heart to see the farm looking like this. They were so hard-working, so dedicated and... they loved Birds Acre.'

'I'll try the front door,' he said, clambering from the car. Minutes later, he called back to her, 'It's not locked. At least I'm spared a window scramble.'

Flora made haste to join him. 'Don't you think it's strange that it's not locked?'

'It looks,' he said, running a hand down the side of the door, 'as though it's been busted open. Youngsters maybe?'

'Or someone looking for shelter for the night?'

'Whoever it was, Piers Neville needs to get that door fixed or there won't be much left to inherit. Right,' Jack said, taking charge, 'kitchen first, I guess.'

'Cupboards first,' she added.

For a second time, they went through every cupboard the kitchen possessed, along with the larder and the Aga – this time searching more seriously. They were no longer looking for Percy, but for anything that might lead them to his killer.

From the kitchen, they moved on to the sitting room and, afterwards, the narrow room that ran along the rear of the farmhouse used by Robert Martin as his study. Every room was as bare as they'd last seen it and took no more than a few minutes to search despite Jack reaching up to curtain poles and picture rails and Flora diligently inspecting the skirting.

Venturing next to the cellar, they found the staircase had been mended and the large space swept clean, with not a single barrel in sight. 'Nothing.' He grimaced. 'But then what did we expect? If there had been any material worth analysing, the police would have bagged it.'

'We've still the bedrooms.' As always, Flora was reluctant to face defeat, though in her heart she recognised this was a last-ditch attempt – to find something, anything, that would lead them to their killer.

But the bedrooms proved similarly disappointing, and what small hope she'd nurtured trickled away. Feeling utterly depressed, she was ready to forget the outbuildings, having seen the barns abandoned and desolate as they'd driven in. A neighbouring farmer must have taken what straw was left, with or without permission, and the emptiness was complete.

Jack was determined, though. They'd come to search the farm and search they would. But it was a mechanical walk they took around the interior of each outbuilding, truffling through spikes of old straw, glancing up at rafters, poking the gaps between the rotten boarding.

'Nothing,' Jack said again. He thrust his hands into his pockets. 'What do we do now?'

There was something in his tone that challenged Flora: she'd been the one to insist they come here, he seemed to be implying, and it was up to her to pull a rabbit out of the hat.

'What do we do? Give up, I expect,' she said quietly. But then, on impulse, 'There used to be a log store at the rear of the house. We can look there – the police might have ignored it.'

'And find wood?'

'You never know what we might find.'

The garden to the rear of the house had also deteriorated since their previous visit. The grassy expanse of lawn had lain

uncut for months and was now verging on wilderness.
Flowerbeds, only just distinguishable, were overrun with weeds
and the ornamental pond that had looked so pretty was choked
with algae.

Turning sadly away, Flora pointed to a flagged pathway that
ran beneath the rear windows of the farmhouse. 'It's this way, I
think. I remember a small clearing with a wooden shed.'

She'd remembered correctly. The wood store was there, just
as she recalled, but when they reached it, it was to find the door
padlocked.

Jack frowned. 'The front door is wide open, but the wood
store is padlocked. Odd. But there's no getting into that shed
and I'm not dislocating my shoulder in the attempt.'

Despite her frustration, Flora recognised he was right. The
effort needed to break in would hardly be worth the pain. A few
steps back along the path, though, and they both stopped dead,
one behind the other. A muffled thud had reached them. A
thud that had come from the wood store.

Jack lifted a warning finger and they stayed motionless and
listening. Another thud, this time louder.

'You were right to come,' he murmured. 'Someone is locked
in there – and very definitely trying to get out.'

'How are we—' she began.

'Not with my shoulder, for sure. The padlock doesn't look
too heavy duty, this should do the trick.' He'd picked up a large
stone from the narrow flowerbed at the side of the path – once
Mrs Martin's attempt at a rockery.

It took several blows at the lock before it sprang open and
fell with a clunk to the ground. In a swift movement, Jack held
out his arm to prevent Flora from dashing ahead.

'Me first,' he said and flung wide the door. 'Good grief!' he
muttered.

Flora joined him, crowding the doorway and peering into

the gloom. Hunched into one corner of the shed, the ghostly outline of a figure was just visible.

She took a step forward. 'Piers Neville!'

'Something nasty in the woodshed after all!' Jack sounded almost amused. 'Your hunch was right, oh clever one. How do you do it?'

Piers had been bound hand and foot and with a gag tied tightly around his mouth. 'That's the first thing to go,' Jack told him, beginning to unknot the rough piece of cloth that was half choking the young man. 'As for the rope round your ankles and wrists, we'll have to go back to the farmhouse and look for a knife. Hopefully, Mrs Martin might have left one in her kitchen drawer.'

Piers made an agitated face at him. 'It's OK. The gag is almost untied,' Jack reassured him. 'Just keep still.' But the boy's eyes were desperate, his head wagging to and fro.

'Something's not right, Jack.' Flora was alarmed. It was clear that Piers was trying to communicate something to them.

'Of course, it's not right—' Jack started to say, when a figure sprang suddenly from behind the open door.

Flora had only a glimpse of a whirling arm and some kind of tool – a mattock? – being swung wildly at Jack. She rushed forward, trying to grab the frenzied arm. Oh, for another hat pin! But then stopped for an instant, disbelief turning to astonishment. It should be Sidney Lovejoy at the end of that mattock, or Dennis Tyler or maybe even Colin Palmer.

But no, it was Winifred Ticehurst.

Shaking herself out of her stupor, Flora dived for the woman's legs while Jack spun around, twisting himself out of range and attempting to wrest the implement from his assailant's hand. The mattock swung crazily in the air and was about to descend, where Flora wasn't sure, when Inspector Ridley and Constable Tring appeared in the doorway.

'Well, that's a turn-up for the books,' the inspector remarked. 'Tring, do your stuff.'

'Better give it to me, Miss Ticehurst,' the constable said stolidly. 'You could do a bit of damage with that.'

Winifred's furious gaze travelled around the circle of people, looking as though she would launch herself into another attack but, with a loud exhalation of breath, she threw the mattock to the ground and subsided into a huddle.

'Handcuffs, Tring,' Ridley barked.

'Oh, right.' With some difficulty, the policeman rifled through his large uniform pockets and brought forth a pair of handcuffs. 'If you'll turn around, Miss Ticehurst, hands behind your back,' he said politely, 'I'll have these on in a tick.'

'I'm glad I brought him along,' the inspector said. 'He does it with style, wouldn't you say?'

Turning to his constable, he handed over a set of car keys. 'Get this lady into the car and I'll be with you in a minute.'

When Constable Tring had disappeared along the pathway with his prisoner, the inspector smiled broadly. 'Good job, Jack. Good thinking. And you, too, Miss Steele.'

'Searching the wood store was Flora's idea,' Jack said quickly.

Ridley nodded as though he expected nothing less and turned to go.

'What about me?' a reedy voice asked. Jack had managed to dislodge the gag sufficiently for Piers Neville to find his tongue.

'I'll want to talk to you later, Mr Neville – or is it Sir Piers now? – but meanwhile, can you sort him out?' Ridley looked enquiringly at Jack.

After they'd dropped an extremely ruffled Sir Piers at Bramber Hall, Jack drove on to Flora's cottage and, without waiting for an invitation, followed her inside. The troublesome letter appeared forgotten, and she felt happier than she had for days.

Unbidden, she made tea, fetching down from the top shelf a tin of biscuits she'd been wading through since Christmas. Jack could help her eat them.

'Winifred Ticehurst,' he said, sitting down at the scrubbed wood table. 'Another killer we didn't figure out.'

Flora's expression was bleak. 'It's worried me all the way home. We've been even more at sea this time than when the curate was killed. Are we getting worse at investigating, do you think?' She laid out cups and saucers on the kitchen table and warmed the pot.

'Perhaps our heart hasn't been in this one.'

'Mine has,' she said sternly. 'Percy was a good friend.'

'But after Percy died? Nothing seemed to gel, did it?'

'I don't think it was that so much. It was more that all the people involved were so unlikeable, it was hard to know where to focus – Lovejoy, Tyler, Sir Frederick, even Piers.'

'Particularly Piers.' Jack grinned. 'You'd think he might be a teensy bit grateful at having been spared death by mattock, but all he did on the way back to the Hall was complain. Interesting that Prue Norland turned up as we arrived.'

'She'd come to collect a scarf she'd left behind and I don't think she'll be going back – it felt like a final farewell.'

'Probably wise. Piers might improve, but he has a long way to go.'

Flora poured tea for them both and pushed the biscuit tin towards him. 'I wonder if he'll get his hotel?' she said, taking a first sip. 'After this last drama, I can't see Tyler hanging around much longer.'

'If Piers does build his hotel, it will probably be a disaster.' Absently, Jack helped himself to a chocolate biscuit and took a bite. 'How long have you had these? Are they stale?'

'No, of course not,' she said stoutly. 'Well, perhaps a little. I need you to help me finish them.'

There was a pause while they drank tea and dunked biscuits. At length, Jack said in a quiet voice, 'Have you thought any more about France?'

'I'm not going – I told you.'

'Not because of me, I hope.'

She shook her head. 'Not because of you,' she repeated. 'I'm happy with you, Jack, and I've no feelings for Richard. He trashed them when he left me high and dry to cope with my poor aunt.'

'He may be hoping to rekindle them.'

'I don't know what he's hoping. And I care even less. If I went to France' – she emphasised the 'if' – 'it would be to discover why Richard is so convinced my parents are buried in a Provençal churchyard. It would be to discover at last what happened to them and maybe put my mind to rest.'

'And if it didn't give you peace of mind?'

She tugged her hand through waves that had tangled badly, unscrambling them as best she could. 'That's the problem. That's what worries me.'

Jack said no more but poured them both a second cup of tea.

30

Constable Tring paid them both a visit the following day, Jack at Overlay House and Flora in her bookshop. Laboriously, he noted down in his pocket book a full account of their trip to Birds Acre Farm and its outcome.

'That should please the inspector,' he said, flicking closed the last of the scrawled pages. 'Nice and thorough.' It should be, Flora reflected, she'd been talking for at least half an hour. 'It'll need typing up, though,' Tring continued. 'Mr Carrington's statement, too. Inspector Ridley will let you know when you're to sign.' With a satisfied grunt, he tucked the notebook into his uniform pocket and replaced his helmet.

∼

'It means a trip to Brighton,' Jack said, when they talked on the telephone a few days later. Ridley had contacted him that morning to say their statements were ready and waiting in his office. 'Why don't we make an afternoon of it?'

'Are you fancying another visit to the pier?' Unseen, Flora pulled a face.

Remembering what had happened the last time they'd walked on the Palace Pier, Jack said a definite no. 'If the weather's kind, we could take a walk along the seafront instead. Whet our appetite for a fish and chip supper.'

He was keen to make the trip enjoyable, a way perhaps of making up for his earlier peevishness. Flora seemed happy enough, but he was unsure of how she truly felt. He'd reacted foolishly about the letter, displayed a stupid jealousy over nothing, and it nagged at him that he might have damaged what felt a none too secure relationship.

The weather *was* kind – a bright, clear day with little wind and the occasional peep of sunshine. Brighton was looking at its best this afternoon, its white Regency grandeur sparkling against an unusually blue sea.

'Signing the statements shouldn't take too long,' he assured her, as he parked the Austin outside the neo-classical façade of Brighton Town Hall.

Together they circled round to the rear of the building, its once honey-coloured stone faded to an indeterminate grey, making for the basement entrance that housed Brighton police.

At the reception desk, he gave the sergeant on duty their names and waited, Flora gazing around her with interest. This was her first visit here, he realised.

'Jack and Miss Steele!' Alan Ridley bowled along the corridor to greet them. 'Good to see you both. Come into my office. And Sergeant, could you rustle up some tea?'

The small box of a room, little more than a store cupboard, was as crowded as when Jack had last seen it. Paper, piled thick and high, still covered every available surface, seeming to drain the air of any freshness.

'Take a seat. I've cleared two chairs especially for you!' The inspector rootled through the mounds of files that filled his desktop. 'There's not a lot for you to do. I've your statements right here.' He withdrew two sheets of paper, typed front and back, from the least battered of the files. 'Give them a scan and, as long as you're happy, sign on the dotted line.'

In silence, they read through their individual statements, interrupted only by the sergeant bringing in a tin tray with three mugs of what Jack presumed was tea. Evil-looking tea.

'You know, I should say thank you,' Ridley said when they'd signed and returned the documents to him. 'You led us to the killer. An extraordinary killer at that. Have a cuppa – you must be parched.'

'If we're into thanks, we're grateful you turned up when you did.' Jack took a cautious first sip.

'You always seem to manage that.' There was a hint of suspicion in Flora's voice.

'Sometimes – don't mock – I get these hunches,' the inspector said. They looked at each other, not sure whether to laugh or groan. Traditionally, Flora was the queen of hunches.

'Presumably, Miss Ticehurst *is* the killer you're after?' Jack asked.

'Do you doubt it?' Ridley looked amused.

'It seems so unlikely. An ex-teacher. A harmless middle-aged woman.'

'Not that harmless, as it turns out. Winifred is a woman with a passion. A sort of Messiah complex, I think you'd call it. She was the chosen one, she'd decided. She was the one to save the village and rescue Abbeymead from desecration.'

'A decidedly dangerous passion,' Jack mused.

'I'd say. She wasn't content with setting up a preservation society, gathering petitions and generally haranguing people, she had to take action. Unfortunately so, for both Mr Milburn and Sir Frederick.'

'Has she confessed to their murders?'

'We couldn't stop her. She had to give us every small detail – we've pages of it. She saw preserving the village as her life's work and felt – still feels – wholly justified in removing anything or anybody she considered were obstacles. Even that poor housekeeper of Milburn's suffered.'

'It was Winifred Ticehurst who planted a railway sleeper in Minnie's back garden. I knew it!' Flora exclaimed.

'Spot on, Miss Steele. That was Miss Howden's penance for daring to sell the schoolhouse instead of turning it into a museum.'

'At least she didn't kill her,' Jack remarked.

'Not important enough is my guess. And the deed was done. The house sold. All that was left for Winifred was to mete out what punishment she could.'

'A railway sleeper, even a part of it, would be extremely heavy,' Flora said thoughtfully.

'Miss Ticehurst is a solid lady – physically very strong. She was able to do what most women her age would have found beyond them.'

Flora put down her teacup, the liquid barely touched, Jack noticed. 'Like Percy...' she faltered, 'he was... drowned. That would have required enormous strength.'

'True, but Mr Milburn was a fairly slight chap, as I remember, and Miss Ticehurst was a one-time PE teacher. That gave her quite an advantage. And don't forget, the poor man was unconscious. He would have been a dead weight, but he couldn't have put up a struggle.'

Jack put his own cup down, still half empty, his mouth withered by the tannin. 'How did Ticehurst plan that murder?'

'She got wind that Milburn was meeting Sir Frederick and his agent at the farm and, with a twisted logic, reckoned that if she got rid of Milburn, the farm wouldn't be sold and therefore wouldn't be turned into the hostel she hated. That afternoon, she arrived at the farm earlier than anyone else. Arrived on foot, leaving no trace she'd ever been there. She knew Mrs Martin always held a spare key in one of the barns and she was lucky. The lady had forgotten about it when she moved out and it was still just where Miss Ticehurst remembered. If she hadn't found the key, she planned to jump Milburn whenever the opportunity offered. Anyway, once inside the farmhouse, she booby-trapped the staircase – if she could heave a grown man into a barrel, destroying the stairs down to the cellar would have been child's play – and waited.'

'But how could she be sure Percy would go to the cellar?' Flora objected.

'The short answer is that she couldn't. She needed to use persuasion. Mr Milburn was expecting to meet Sir Frederick and his agent and was bemused to see Miss Ticehurst when she popped out of the woodwork. It put him at a disadvantage straight away. Then, apparently, she apologised for the way she'd spoken to him earlier – when she was arranging the meeting at the village hall. Or I should say, she pretended to apologise.'

'And the cellar?' Flora pursued.

'The woman is crafty, I'll give her that, asking Mr Milburn to explain how exactly his plans would work. Naturally, he was only too keen to tell her, hoping to get a general go-ahead from the village at the meeting that evening. When she made suggestions of how he might use the cellar, he was keen to check whether they'd work. She'd already scouted out the barrels and it couldn't have been too difficult to creep up on him, push him down the stairs, then drag him unconscious across the cellar floor and tip him into one. She hadn't expected the cider, though, and when she heard the agent coming, she had to refit the lid quickly and escape. It meant she was too hasty and messed up the pressure valve, which is why you had a lid hurled in your direction, Miss Steele.'

Flora and Jack sat dumb, astonished by the tale. 'And then...' Flora murmured, finding her voice at last.

'Then the woman hid out in the house until the agent and

Sir Frederick gave up waiting for a missing Milburn and left the farm.'

'And if Percy had refused to go down to the cellar?' Jack asked.

'She'd thought of that, too. Armed herself with a rounders' bat. A relic of her past, I guess.'

'Was it a rounders' bat she used on Sir Frederick?'

'No, that was a golf club. Fitting, really. By then, she was getting desperate and took a huge risk. There were only a few people around at that time of day – the club bar was closed – but the course was open for practice. Anyone could have seen her. She told us that she'd been watching Neville's movements for weeks. She knew his schedule, knew the morning he routinely went to the club early, and saw that he always practised alone.'

'I give you that Percy was a fairly slight man,' Jack commented, 'but Sir Frederick certainly wasn't. Yet she managed to overpower him.'

'Attacked him from behind. Waited for the right moment. He must have been bending to retrieve the ball from the bunker when she crept up on him and caught him smack on the back of his head. Then, when he was face down in the sand, followed it up with a few more blows. Like I say, she was one desperate woman. In interview, she kept saying that she hadn't wanted to kill anyone, but they just wouldn't listen to her.'

'Sir Frederick died because he wouldn't listen?' Flora sounded appalled.

'She'd hoped he would drop the idea of selling once Mr Milburn died, but he didn't. Just the opposite. Percy Milburn's death freed Sir Frederick to negotiate with Sidney Lovejoy and obtain a higher price. When Lovejoy was attacked – by then, she'd discovered what the man was doing in Abbeymead – she'd been about to kill *him*, except someone else got there first.'

'She must have hoped she'd hear no more of the sale.'

The inspector nodded. 'With Lovejoy in hospital, she was certain Sir Frederick would forget the whole deal. But, again, he didn't. He seemed to be waiting for Lovejoy to recover before resuming negotiations. She had to kill Sir Frederick, she said, because, if the man was dead, he wouldn't be able to sell. There's some logic to that, I suppose.'

'Except that Piers Neville would inherit. She still wouldn't get what she wanted,' Flora put in.

'Miss Ticehurst isn't stupid. She realised that. She was in a bit of a bind, you could say, but thought she'd be able to persuade Piers in a way she'd never manage with his uncle. She'd known the lad as a boy and felt she had some influence on him. Our Piers, however, wasn't to be persuaded and, when she discovered that he was still intent on turning the farm into a building site, this time for a damn great hotel, she saw red.'

'That must have been the argument I witnessed at the May Day dance. But how did she lure him to the farm?'

'She pretended to be Colin Palmer's secretary. If Neville had had any wits about him, he'd have remembered that Miss Harrison only works part-time, and not on a Tuesday. We've been digging into Palmer's accounts, and it looks like he's in deep trouble. A full-time secretary was an expense he couldn't afford. Anyway, Miss Ticehurst convinced Piers, or I should say Sir Piers, that Palmer wanted to meet him at Birds Acre. There'd been developments, she told him, which the agent wanted to talk over on site. Piers was as bemused as Mr Milburn had been when he found her at the farm but followed her round to the back of the house after she assured him that Mr Palmer would soon be with them.'

'Didn't he think it odd that she appeared to be working with Colin Palmer?' Jack asked.

'I don't think young Piers has too much upstairs, to be frank. She spun him some yarn about wanting to come to an agreement with him after the quarrel you mentioned, Miss Steele.

Convinced him that she'd had second thoughts about the hotel and had ideas she wanted to share. Neville wanted a quiet life and if it calmed the old biddy down – they were his words not mine – he was willing to spare her a few minutes. When they got to the wood store, she suggested as an idea that he could turn it into one of those sauna things.'

Jack and Flora looked puzzled.

'I know, nor me. It's a Scandinavian habit, I believe. Tice-hurst said she'd read an article in the *National Geographic* and fixed on it as something that might persuade Piers into the shed – he'd bragged to her that *his* hotel would boast the latest in luxury. She'd already scouted the farm thoroughly, of course, and decided the shed was where she'd keep him prisoner.'

'Prisoner? So, she didn't intend to kill him?'

'God knows what she really intended. She was astute enough, just about, to realise that continuing to kill wasn't going to work. If Piers died, someone else would inherit the farm and she'd be faced with the same problem. She seems to have come up with the crazy notion that she could keep him locked in the shed and starve him into signing an agreement. Any agreement extracted under duress wouldn't have been legal, but by then she was halfway to a complete breakdown.'

'I can see that she could push Piers into the shed from behind and padlock the door on him,' Flora said slowly, 'but he was bound and gagged. How on earth did she manage that?'

'Chloroform,' Ridley announced, a grin on his face.

'What!'

'Well, a kind of chloroform, if not the pure thing. Miss Tice-hurst is nothing if not resourceful. She mixed a measure of household bleach with acetone, she told me, then soaked a pad in the liquid ready to knock him out. It didn't quite work the way she'd hoped. Neville is a skinny bloke but he's tall and she misfired. Still, he breathed in sufficient fumes to make him stagger and before he knew it, he was being trussed up like the

Sunday joint. Winifred whipped out her rope and gag, and Bob's your uncle.'

'That's some story, Alan!' Jack leaned back against the hard ridges of the wooden chair, the best the police station could offer.

'She's quite bonkers, of course. Not mad by any official definition, but bonkers, nevertheless. Consumed by the goal she'd set herself. It meant she lost all sense of normality.'

'All sense of morality, too,' Jack commented.

Ridley folded his hands. 'She still reckons she only did what she had to. If these people hadn't behaved the way they had, they'd be here today.'

'She's utterly warped.' Flora sounded troubled.

'Totally,' the inspector agreed cheerfully. 'And the more warped she became, the more devious her strategies. It's no wonder none of us cottoned on to her. Particularly when a known criminal was in the mix.'

'It's ironic that Dennis Tyler turns out to be innocent.'

'Not only innocent but frustrated by the killings. They drew unwanted attention to Birds Acre, a farm he had every intention of buying on the quiet.'

'The farm was to be used for criminal purposes? That's definite?'

'As definite as we can make out, Jack. Tyler, when we caught up with him, admitted nothing, and Lovejoy has gone to ground. I imagine he'll be coerced into finding another hideaway soon enough – he must still owe Tyler money – but he'll be lucky to find anything as perfect as Birds Acre. Deep in the countryside, remote but not too remote from Tyler's base in London, with a cellar, barns and outbuildings. What more could he want?'

The inspector looked from one to the other of them. 'Well, folks, if you've finished your tea...'

It was evident he wanted to get back to work, the stacks of

files on his desk suggesting at least another year's hard labour. Picking up her handbag ready to leave, Flora hesitated.

'Miss Ticehurst obviously did a lot of talking.'

'Hours of it.'

'Did she mention me at all?'

Ridley frowned. 'You in particular?'

'Yes,' she said and waited.

'Let me think.' The inspector ran his fingers along the side of the desk. 'She did say something a bit odd, now I recall.'

Flora leaned eagerly towards him. 'What was it?'

'She said she thought you were dangerous.'

'Dangerous?'

'Yes, strange, isn't it? Too curious, I think she meant. Too willing to get involved in what didn't concern you.'

'And Jack wasn't?' she asked indignantly. 'Jack wasn't dangerous?'

'She didn't seem to know much about Mr Carrington. Knew he was a writer, but it seems she only reads the classics, so the crime bit passed her by.' The inspector paused. 'She knew you, though. Known you from childhood, she said. But she liked your aunt. Respected her. That's something, I suppose.'

'It was Winifred who targeted me,' Flora said decidedly, as they walked along East Street, making for the seafront. 'It has to have been her, even though she hasn't confessed.'

'It was certainly Winifred,' he agreed. 'Maybe she feels shame at what she did and that's why she's kept silent.'

Flora's smile was wry. 'It seems unlikely. And I still don't really know why she attacked me.'

'I imagine that by destroying the things you love, she hoped to upset you so much that you'd stop being curious. Stop investigating.'

'Perhaps. She might even have hoped to drive me from the bookshop and out of the village altogether.'

'Or she thought she'd keep you so busy sorting out the problems she caused you, that you wouldn't have time for sleuthing.'

Reaching the end of East Street, they crossed the wide expanse of King's Road to walk along the promenade.

'A calm day.'

Jack stopped to look out over the sea. In the silence between passing cars, the susurration of tiny waves as they hit the pebbled beach came floating towards them on the air. Suddenly, a beam of sunlight broke through the cloud and traced a brilliant path across the water's glass-like surface.

Flora leaned against the white-painted railings and followed Jack's gaze. 'Winifred knew Aunt Violet and liked her. Maybe that's why she didn't hurt me physically, why she chose a different punishment. A kind of emotional torture.'

'It's possible,' he agreed, 'if she wanted to stop you investigating, but not destroy you.'

'Unlike poor Percy.'

He turned towards her, running his finger gently down her cheek. 'He'll have justice now. Think of that.'

She nodded. 'I'm trying to,' she said sadly, then brightened. 'Fish and chips might help.'

He offered her his arm. 'I think it might. Let's go. The Regency restaurant, I think.'

31

Their afternoon in Brighton had been a happy one. The easy relationship that for months she and Jack had shared had been renewed. If there were topics they were wary of, things they chose not to talk about – their future together and marriage in particular – did it matter? Jack appeared content to leave any discussion to one side and enjoy the present and that suited Flora admirably. It was a wedding that was actually happening that made her worry, though she tried whenever possible to shuffle from her mind the fact that very soon Kate would be marrying again. She was still convinced it was a bad mistake, no matter how amiable a chap Tony Farraday was.

The wedding Flora didn't want to think about returned with a vengeance when mid-week she called at Katie's Nook for a lunchtime sandwich. Walking through the café door, she was surprised to see Prue Norland waiting at the counter.

'Flora!' The girl bounced forward, hugging her enthusiastically. 'How lovely to see you. I've just been boring Kate on how lucky I've been. Now I can bore you!'

'I'm sure you won't.' Flora smiled. 'How lucky?'

'Very,' the girl replied dreamily. 'The show I'm in – the

Christie murder, you remember? – is going on tour, and I'm going with it! Colchester is our first stop, but after that we have masses of dates ahead. Three months of solid work.'

'That's wonderful.' Flora was genuinely pleased. It looked as though Prue had got the break she deserved.

'Isn't it? The only sad thing is that I shall miss Kate's wedding. She's very kindly invited me, and I would love to have come.'

Flora glanced at Kate, her eyebrows slightly raised.

'We have a date now,' Kate confirmed, a trifle nervously. 'The last Saturday in August.'

'Which is when I shall be... let's see... probably somewhere in Wales!' Prue announced.

Flora wished that she, too, could have been somewhere in Wales, but she marshalled herself into making the right noises, endorsing Katie's evident pleasure that the wedding was now firmly on the Abbeymead calendar.

'Will you still be around this Sunday, Prue?' Kate asked.

The girl nodded. 'I don't leave until next week. Why?'

'I'm hoping to decide on my dress for the day. I've had patterns and swatches of material from the dressmaker – she's keen to make a start. And I'd love some advice. We could maybe have lunch first and then take a look.'

Flora listened to these plans in silence until Kate turned to her, saying wistfully, 'I'm still expecting you'll be my maid of honour, Flora. We need to decide on your dress, too.'

Prue looked uncertainly from one to the other. 'Lots of decisions then,' she said brightly.

There had been no escaping the lunch at Kate's. They were to make a party of it, Alice announced, and had promised to cook a feast for the occasion. It wasn't every day a dear friend got married, she reminded Flora, her tone somewhat baleful, while

Flora cast desperately around for an excuse, any excuse, as to why she couldn't make the date.

She hadn't succeeded but, arriving at the wisteria-covered front door of Katie's cottage and breathing in the tantalising aroma escaping from the kitchen, she felt a little better. It would be the beef casserole and braised onions that Alice did so well. And there would be dumplings, too, she knew.

It was Alice who answered the door, wiping her hands on her apron, her cheeks burnished red from the oven. 'All under control,' she said happily. 'Lunch in thirty minutes. Meantime, we've a nice of bottle of elderflower to get through.'

She took Flora's jacket and hung it over the wooden banister. 'That Prue is a nice girl, isn't she?' she said in a low voice. 'I've really taken to the lass. She could do a lot better for herself than Piers Neville, I'm sure.'

'She is doing better,' Flora responded, amused by Alice's championship of her new protégée. 'She's abandoning Piers and going on tour with her theatre company for three months.'

'I'm glad to hear it.' Then, as Flora went to walk into Kate's small sitting room, Alice put out a detaining arm, saying, 'I'm glad you've agreed to be Katie's maid of honour. I was worried that you... well, you know.'

Flora reflected that she'd had little choice in the matter, but she wasn't about to cause division on such an important day as this. Digging deep, she found her best smile.

Lunch was every bit as tasty as she'd expected and made even better by Prue's tales of the theatre and the various, mostly eccentric, actors with whom she'd worked. She was an amusing storyteller and, before Flora realised, they had emptied the large casserole of beef and dumplings along with dishes of peas and carrots, followed by a hefty slice each of marmalade pudding and custard.

Kate was pouring tea for them all when Flora asked their guest, 'Does Piers know yet that you're going on tour?'

Prue's face shadowed. 'He does. I went to see him as soon as I knew. He's moved from the Brighton flat, you know, and is living at Bramber Hall now.'

'I gathered that when we dropped him off after his horrid experience at the farm.'

'He called at my lodgings yesterday and told me all about it. Thank goodness you and Jack chose that afternoon to visit Birds Acre.'

Alice gave an audible tut. Along with the rest of Abbeymead, she'd heard all about it, too, and strongly disapproved of such goings-on.

'The last few weeks have been a tremendous shock for him,' Prue went on. 'He didn't get on well with his uncle, but Sir Frederick was the only real family Piers had, the only link he had to his father. Sir Frederick's death has hit him hard when I don't think he expected it,' she said frankly. 'And then to be imprisoned by that madwoman, Ticehurst! Piers truly believed she was going to kill him.' There was a pause before she said sorrowfully, 'It's been a dreadfully unsettling time.'

'How does he feel about you going away?'

'He seems to have accepted it. Even congratulated me! I think it's helped that I've been living in Worthing, and hardly seen him these last few weeks. We hadn't been getting on too well for some time and the truth is we both needed a break. My career matters to me, I want to give it all my attention, and Piers needs time to do some thinking. In a way, I feel he's glad to be on his own for a while. This whole horrible business – how close he came to following his uncle – is only just sinking in.'

'What's he goin' to do about Birds Acre?' Alice asked the question that everyone was asking themselves. 'Is he goin' to sell, or what?'

'It's still undecided, but I'm almost certain he's abandoned the idea of a hotel. It was always too grand a plan, and I think Piers has realised he hasn't the energy to manage such a huge

project, raising the finance and so on – especially right now.'
Her beautiful eyes were sad. 'He seems to have become a shell
of himself,' she finished.

'So, there'll have to be a tenant.' It was Alice again, pushing
for information.

'The estate needs money, that's for sure, and I guess a
tenant paying the right rent would help. But there's also the
nursing home to consider. His uncle was clear in his will that
Lady Neville has to be taken care of and the fees are
considerable.'

Flora stirred her tea slowly, thinking it might be the right
moment to fill one of the gaps in the case they'd tried to build.
'We thought, Jack and I, that Sir Frederick might have a plan to
buy Capri Lawns.'

'Piers couldn't do that,' Prue said with surety. 'The estate
has nowhere near enough money. But he has mentioned that
he's been talking to a group of businessmen who seem interested in investing in the home. Piers could take a small stake, so
that he had some say in how the place was run.'

'Really? He sounds a changed man.' The remark was hardly
diplomatic, but the Piers Neville that Flora knew was, in her
view, an unlikely champion for a nursing home.

'I believe he is changed,' Prue said. 'He wants to do the right
thing, and I hope for Lady Neville's sake that it works out.'

'Shall we look at the patterns the dressmaker has suggested?' Kate's question lightened the slight gloom that had
descended on the circle. 'Flora, I thought you might look good
in this.'

The pattern Kate handed her was of a knee-length dress,
sleeveless with a sweetheart neckline. The skirt was wonderfully full, billowing forth from a fitted waist.

'And maybe this material would work.' A swatch of fine
eau-de-nil chiffon landed in Flora's lap.

As she looked at the pattern and allowed the material to

trickle through her fingers, she knew with certainty that this would be a dress she would love. Her imagination took fire, and in her mind's eye she was following Kate down the aisle in a cloud of pale green chiffon. Cream satin shoes, she thought. Ivory pearls as a headdress. And a simple bouquet of freesias and cream roses. Maybe, after all, the wedding wouldn't be as uncomfortable as she feared.

'I think it's beautiful,' she said.

Kate smiled, Prue smiled, and Alice fairly beamed.

32

Jack had chosen the picnic food carefully. A hamper filled with cheese and tomato sandwiches, miniature sausage rolls, devilled eggs made by Kate and – the height of sophistication – a salmon roulade, was sure to please, and pleasing was what he intended. At the last minute, he'd packed a bottle of wine rather than the ubiquitous flask of tea, thinking the trip a kind of celebration.

Checking the hamper was in place on the back seat, he locked the Austin's door and turned to walk the few yards to the All's Well. It was Wednesday and half-day closing, and he was looking forward to an afternoon spent with Flora. An afternoon when he hoped the familiar ease with each other that over the months they'd learned to value would return in full.

As he neared the bookshop, he saw Alice walking towards him, an overflowing basket testimony to her morning's shopping.

'You off somewhere nice?' she asked, blocking the pavement as she stopped to talk.

'That's the plan. It's a beautiful day and I thought a trip to the river would make best use of it.'

She bent her head, peering through the car window. 'A picnic by the look of it.'

'A special picnic,' he said, smiling. 'A hamper stuffed with food, and blankets in the boot.'

Alice fixed him with what Jack always thought of as her 'look', half-severe, half-hopeful. 'That's good,' she announced. 'Katie and I have been worried about you two. Not just because you keep getting involved in what doesn't concern you, though you do, but because we don't like to see the pair of you at odds.'

'We're fine,' he said breezily. 'More or less.'

'Hmm,' she muttered. 'You need to sort it out.' And when Jack looked puzzled, she nodded towards the shop window. 'With that girl.'

He followed her glance and through the lattice could see Flora tidying her desk before she went for her jacket.

'I don't like it that there's gossip,' Alice went on, depositing the heavy basket at her feet. 'And there will be. More and more of it, the longer you don't sort things out.'

'By that, you mean getting married?'

'Well, you're as good as already, aren't you?'

'I wouldn't say so.' Ruffled, Jack moved towards the All's Well's door. He turned to say goodbye and saw Alice raise a pair of doubtful eyebrows.

'It's what the village thinks,' she said.

'The village will have to think it, I'm afraid, and be content with just one wedding this year.'

'I know the lass is headstrong...'

'You don't say. I hadn't noticed.'

'Go on with you.' Alice reached out and tapped him on the arm. 'I know she can lead you a merry dance, but sometimes she doesn't know what's good for her.'

'And I am?'

'You are, and you need to make her see that.'

Jack sighed. 'I've tried, believe me, Alice.'

She let go of his arm. 'You're an honourable man, I'll give you that. But Flora... she's not as clever as she sometimes thinks.'

He saw the girl he loved waving at him, a wide smile on her face, and felt an immediate need to defend her. 'Flora is wedded to her freedom, which for her means staying single. Independent. Any mention of marriage brings her out in hives.'

'Mebbe, but there'll come a time when it won't. Make sure you're there when it happens!'

The riverbank where they spread their blankets was the very same place in which, not so long ago, they'd endured a terrifying ordeal.

'I wasn't sure whether we should come here,' Jack confessed. 'But I knew if we parked in Mr Lenister's farmyard, there'd only be a short walk to the river.'

'It's a perfect place,' she said easily, taking pleasure in the crisp, cold aroma of fresh water. 'Whatever happened in the past is over. Well and truly.'

Beneath a cloudless sky, the waters today ran softly, a clear greeny-blue between high banks that were already rich with vegetation.

'Another rowing boat,' she remarked, seeing a bright yellow vessel anchored to the wooden post where the river bent sharply. 'Alas, poor *Mabel*.' She was remembering their ill-fated trip in Diggory Moore's small red boat.

'Poor *Mabel*,' he agreed, opening the hamper and spreading their feast across one of the blankets.

For a while, they ate in silence, happy to lose themselves in the quiet of the landscape. The gurgle of water on the stony riverbed and the twittering of sparrows from bushes on the opposite bank were the only sounds that reached them.

Looking regretfully at the last devilled egg – she'd already eaten too much – it was Flora who spoke first. 'Do you think

Sidney Lovejoy is still hiding in the village? Or gone back to London?'

'Neither, I think. Alan Ridley is probably right. Sidney is Tyler's stooge and he'll be on the move again, goodness knows where, but busy scouting for another hideaway. With all the noise that's gone on, Abbeymead is very much a dead duck.'

'And Tyler himself?'

Jack packed the few remaining morsels of food back into the hamper. 'In London, I guess – and why not? The police can't touch him. He's done nothing wrong. Trying to buy a property isn't a criminal offence and there's nothing to prove he was planning to turn it into a nest of crooks.'

She gave a small sigh. 'No, it's Winifred that's in custody.'

'Not for too long, I would think. It's an open and shut case. She's confessed and, as far as I can see, there's not one mitigating circumstance. The fact that she's a woman changes nothing; Miss Ticehurst is destined to suffer the fate of all murderers.'

Despite the warmth of the May sun, Flora was shrivelled by the horror of it. In some strange way, she felt a responsibility for what had happened. She hadn't understood Winifred sufficiently. Hadn't properly tried. If she had, if she'd picked up on clues a little earlier, taken on board how truly angry Winifred was – the woman had made no attempt to conceal it – committed herself to the idea that the killer was the same person attacking her, the story might have had a less catastrophic ending. A clever barrister could have argued that Winifred's murder of Percy had been a moment of uncharacteristic madness, brought on by the stress she'd put herself under. But with the guilt of a second killing and a kidnapping, there was no hope she could be saved from the very worst punishment.

'Do you think we're losing our touch, Jack?' she asked. 'We

didn't come close in this case, did we? And in the last investigation, we were caught out as well.'

He leaned back on his elbows, looking up at the blue dome of the sky. 'You think we should give up sleuthing?'

'I'm serious,' she said, seeing his lazy smile. 'I don't want to give it up, but I'm disappointed we didn't do better.'

He levered himself upright. 'But could anyone? Winifred Ticehurst was a one-off.'

'Aren't all murderers, though?'

He frowned. 'There's usually a strong motive,' he said. 'A reason for killing that you can fix on and pursue. Sir Frederick and money, Piers Neville and the hotel he was desperate to build, even Colin Palmer and the business he's trying to save. But Winifred – the preservation of Abbeymead?'

Flora sighed. 'I know. I find it almost impossible to understand. I keep asking myself why. Winifred wasn't personally threatened, nor anyone she cared for. If the farm had been sold, she would have continued to live in Abbeymead and share a house with Elsie. Her life would have gone on just the same. It makes no sense.'

'It's what Alan said, a passion that got out of hand. One that became distorted and unstoppable. She had to force people to agree with her, to bully them into taking action: the meetings, the petitions, Minnie Howden intimidated over the schoolhouse. A compulsion that took over her life – meaning she had to get rid of whatever or whoever was in her way.'

'I suppose with Winifred under lock and key, I can breathe more easily. No more destruction of everything I hold dear. That's a happy thought, at least. You wouldn't know, but Constable Tring came to the shop yesterday and returned my photograph of Aunt Violet. The police team found it when they searched Winifred's room – under her bed of all places. And I'll have Betty safely home again soon. Michael must be sick of seeing her in his workshop.'

'It's not just Betty that will be safe. It's your cottage, too, and your garden. Speaking of which, I'm about to collect a sapling for you. I found a grower just outside Littlehampton and I've booked Charlie to help me plant it this weekend.'

Flora thrust herself upright, her eyes wide. 'A rowan tree?'

'How did you guess?'

'You are the kindest man I've ever known, Jack.' She wrapped her arms around him and hugged him tight. 'And a man of excellent taste. That was the most delicious picnic.'

'I wanted to make it perfect,' he said simply.

'And you did.' Snuggling down on the blanket and lulled by the river's murmur, she closed her eyes against the warmth of the sun and was only vaguely aware of his moving beside her.

He bent over and dropped a kiss on her lips. 'We're OK again?'

'We're OK,' she said, kissing him back. 'More than OK. I never want things to change.'

That was the problem, Jack reflected ruefully, but Alice was a wise owl. He held her words close and believed they'd come true. There would come a time.

A LETTER FROM MERRYN

Dear Reader,

I want to say a huge thank you for choosing to read *Murder at Abbeymead Farm*. If you enjoyed the book and want to keep up to date with all my latest releases, just sign up at the following link. Your email address will never be shared, and you can unsubscribe at any time.

www.bookouture.com/merryn-allingham

The 1950s is a fascinating period, outwardly conformist but beneath the surface there's rebellion brewing, even in the rural heartlands of southern England! It's a beautiful part of the world and I hope Flora's and Jack's exploits have entertained you. If so, you can follow their fortunes in the next Flora Steele Mystery or discover their earlier adventures, beginning with *The Bookshop Murder*.

If you enjoyed *Murder at Abbeymead Farm*, I would love a short review. Getting feedback from readers is amazing and it helps new readers to discover one of my books for the first time. And do get in touch on my Facebook page, through Twitter, Goodreads or my website – I love to chat.

Thank you for reading,

Merryn x

KEEP IN TOUCH WITH MERRYN

www.merrynallingham.com

 facebook.com/MerrynWrites
twitter.com/merrynwrites